CHRISTOPHER BUSH
THE CASE OF THE SECOND CHANCE

CHRISTOPHER BUSH was born Charlie Christmas Bush in Norfolk in 1885. His father was a farm labourer and his mother a milliner. In the early years of his childhood he lived with his aunt and uncle in London before returning to Norfolk aged seven, later winning a scholarship to Thetford Grammar School.

As an adult, Bush worked as a schoolmaster for 27 years, pausing only to fight in World War One, until retiring aged 46 in 1931 to be a full-time novelist. His first novel featuring the eccentric Ludovic Travers was published in 1926, and was followed by 62 additional Travers mysteries. These are all to be republished by Dean Street Press.

Christopher Bush fought again in World War Two, and was elected a member of the prestigious Detection Club. He died in 1973.

CHRISTOPHER BUSH

THE CASE OF THE SECOND CHANCE

With an introduction
by Curtis Evans

DEAN STREET PRESS

Published by Dean Street Press 2019

Copyright © 1946 Christopher Bush

Introduction copyright © 2019 Curtis Evans

All Rights Reserved

The right of Christopher Bush to be identified as the Author of the Work has been asserted by his estate in accordance with the Copyright, Designs and Patents Act 1988.

First published in 1946 by MacDonald & Co.

Cover by DSP

ISBN 978 1 912574 97 1

www.deanstreetpress.co.uk

INTRODUCTION

LABOURING UNDER SUSPICION
CHRISTOPHER BUSH'S CRIME FICTION IN THE POSTWAR YEARS, 1946-1952

SEVEN YEARS after the end of the Second World War, Christopher Bush published, under his "Michael Home" pseudonym, *The Brackenford Story* (1952), a mainstream novel in which a onetime country house boots boy, having risen for some time now to the lofty position of butler, laments the passing of traditional English rural life in the new postwar order, as signified by the years in which the left-wing Labour party held sway in the United Kingdom (1945-51). The jacket description of the American edition of *The Brackenford Story* reads, in part:

> *The Brackenford Story* is the story of a changing England. William saw the political enemies of the Hall gradually successful, whittling away the privilege it stood for. He saw squire begin to sell his land, the taxes increase, the great Hall sold, the beautiful trees along the drive cut down. And then with a Second World War, nationalization, rationing, pre-fabricated houses and queuing. William recalled with gratitude the kindness of his masters and their sense of responsibility for others. He saw that the bad old days of Toryism were not so bad after all. And he never lost his sense of outrage at the loss of something he felt was worthy of preservation.

A few years earlier, in July 1949, Anthony Boucher, the postwar dean of American crime fiction reviewers and a highly socially conscious liberal (small "l"), wrote with genial bemusement of the conservatism of British crime writers like Christopher Bush, in his review of Bush's latest crime opus, *The Case of the Housekeeper's Hair* (1948), making topical mention of a certain anti-Utopian novel penned by a distinguished dying tubercular English writer, which had just been published in June. "However much George Orwell, in *Nineteen Eighty-Four*, may foresee the forcible suppression of 'crimethink' under 'Ingsoc,' English socialism in 1949 takes pleasure in exporting mystery novels which disapprove of the Government and everything about it," Boucher observed with wry irony. "Like most of his colleagues, Christopher Bush is tartly critical of the regime; and an understanding of his unreconstructed Tory attitude is necessary if you're to hope to understand the motivations of this novel."

In both the detective novels and mainstream fiction which Christopher Bush published between 1946 and 1952, Bush, like many other distinguished mystery writers of the Golden Age generation (including Agatha Christie, Dorothy L. Sayers, Georgette Heyer, John Dickson Carr, Edmund Crispin, E.R. Punshon, Henry Wade and John Street), indeed was critical of the Labor government and increasingly nostalgic about a past that grew ever more golden in blissful, if perhaps partially chimerical, remembrance. Yet keeping Bush's distinct anti-left bias in mind, fans of classic crime fiction will find between the covers of the author's crime novels from these years--*The Case of the Second Chance* (1946), *The Case of the Curious Client* (1947), *The Case of the Haven Hotel* (1948), *The Case of the Housekeeper's Hair* (1948), *The Case of the Seven Bells* (1949), *The Case of the Purloined Picture* (1949), *The Case of the Happy Warrior* (1950), *The Case of the Corner Cottage* (1951), *The Case of the Fourth Detective* (1951) and *The Case of the Happy Medium* (1952)--fascinating observation of postwar social malaise in the age of British imperial decay and domestic austerity, as well as details about the rise of rationing, restriction and regulation, the burgeoning black market and, withal, that ubiquitous flashily-dressed criminal figure from Forties and Fifties Britain: the spiv (dealer in illicit goods).

Puzzle-minded mystery readers also will find some corking good no-nonsense "fair play" mysteries. "Few writers can equal Christopher Bush in handling a complicated plot while giving the reader a fair chance to solve the riddle himself," avowed the American blurb to *The Case of the Corner Cottage*, while Anthony Boucher applauded Bush's belated return to the American fiction lists after the Second World War, declaring: "It's good to have Mr. Bush back after too long an absence . . . he presents the simon-pure jigsaw-puzzle detective story with unobtrusive competence." Concurrently in the United Kingdom, author Rupert Croft-Cooke, who himself wrote fine detective fiction as "Leo Bruce," pointedly praised Bush's "urbane and intelligent way of dealing with mystery which makes his work much more attractive than the stampeding sensationalism of some of his rivals."

In the pages which follow this introduction by all means attempt, dear readers, to match your keen wits against those of that ever-percipient gentleman sleuth, Ludovic Travers. Frequently in tandem with his old friend Superintendent George Wharton and with occasional input from his smart and sophisticated wife Bernice Haire, the former classical dancer, Ludo continues to hunt, in his capacity as a sort of special consultant to Scotland Yard (or "unofficial expert," as he puts it), more not-quite-canny-enough crooks. Additionally Ludo, a confirmed fan of American crime films like *The Blue Dahlia* (1946) and *Call Northside 777* (1948), comes to find himself in ownership of the Broad Street Detective Agency, perhaps the finest firm of private inquiry agents in London. In these old and new capacities in the postwar world Ludo confronts his greatest cornucopia of daring and dastardly crimes yet.

Curtis Evans

PART I

CHAPTER I
Busman's Holiday

THIS IS THE STORY of a second chance, and second chances, as we're often told, are pretty rare things. There is a saying, for instance, that the cards never forgive, and that once you mess up a good hand it'll be a precious long time before you hold another. Shakespeare tells us – and to quote from *Julius Caesar* is going to prove remarkably apposite in this story – that those who miss the high tide inevitably end up on the rocks or shallows.

But those preliminaries require a word or two in defence, not only of myself but far more urgently of George – Superintendent to you – Wharton. We never had what might be called a good hand. A promising one and deludingly so perhaps, but nothing like a stone certainty. Nor, to continue the metaphors, did we squander chances or let the high tide pass. We did as we have always done: played our cards in the best way that experience had taught us, and I still hold that it wasn't our fault that we didn't make game. Perhaps that was why the cards did forgive and long afterwards we got a second chance. And a strange second chance it was, for the very same hands were dealt again. But perhaps I'd better cut the prologues and explanations and get on with the story.

It was in October 1942, and I was home on leave. My wife was away, and on the first day, a Friday, I looked up my old friend George Wharton at the Yard. George and I had worked together for years on murder cases; I having been originally called in as what they call an expert on something or other, and thereafter being considered sufficiently useful to act as George's factotum. The meeting was quite a cheerful one and that night I stood him a dinner, and we both did ourselves well. I remember I tried to pull his leg about the grave loss he had suffered when the Army had called me up, and he was equally facetious about my masquerading as a real soldier. I know we parted like sworn brothers, and George said regretfully that there was never a Case on hand to enliven part of my fourteen days' leave. But we promised to meet again before that leave was up.

When I woke the next morning, and with the least bit of a hangover, I too was feeling regretful that there was nothing doing in the murder line, for I should have all the time in the world on my hands, and to work with George would have been the perfect way of spending fourteen days. To work with George is to run the gamut of the emotions, even if they are ersatz ones of his own making. Maybe we always got on so well because no two people could have been more different.

George is so much of a mixture that he ought even to include myself. He is six foot and with a back like a barn-end, but to disguise his height he can put on a pronounced stoop. His eyebrows are shaggy and his moustache is one vast overhang that conceals his flexible mouth. It, and the stoop, gives him a harassed look, and that is all by design, for those who come into contact with him for the first time are inclined to put him down as what used to be called an old fogey, and, to their ultimate disadvantage, underestimate him accordingly. That is only one of the hundred acts that George can put on. He can draw himself suddenly to his full height, and be the dignified, or even scarifying, embodiment of the law. In a matter of minutes he can cajole and wheedle, chuckle and crow, rage and threaten, gloat and despair, sneer and insinuate. But behind that impresario and his one-man troupe of tricks is a remarkably calculating brain, and, as I've said before, no mere mountebank could nowadays hold with distinction a place in the Big Four.

As for myself, I am six foot three and lean at that, and it has been said that my horn-rims make me look like a secretary bird. On the other hand an impressionable journalist once called my face patrician, by which I imagine he thought it somewhat of the hatchet type. As for my methods of crime detection – well, I haven't any. I just tag along at George's heels and when I see something obviously in need of explanation, then I do my best – and generally to George's infinite disgust – to furnish both explanation and theory. For that my only tools are a brain that has been called agile. I prefer to describe it as flibbertigibbet; sharpened on crosswords rather than chess. To stimulate that brain I have only a vast curiosity and impatience. In the matter of the first, my main hobby has been the study of my fellow men, and in the matter of the second, the unsolved and apparently inexplicable gnaw at me like an aching tooth and I get no rest till I can find a something that satisfies at least myself.

But to get back to that Saturday morning. As I said, I had time to spare on my hands, and when I'd read the papers and polished off the crosswords in *The Times* and *Telegraph*, it wasn't far from midday. So I told myself I'd take a stroll in the Park and then lunch at the club, and after that I might possibly do a cinema show. It was just as I was going out, overcoated and gloved against the really raw morning, that the telephone went.

'That you, Travers?' said George's voice, and rather urgently.

'In person,' I said flippantly.

'Can you be on the National Gallery corner, St Martin's end, in five minutes?'

'Certainly I can,' I said. 'Anything doing?'

'Maybe,' he said guardedly, and then as a kind of after-thought: 'Just slipping along to Hampstead. Charles Manfrey's dead.'

Inside three minutes I was waiting for George, and I was to have five minutes further in which to do some thinking. I regaled myself with the thought, for instance, that George wouldn't have mentioned death if that death hadn't been caused by murder. And if regaling seems a scandalous term to employ in connexion with death, I hasten to add that detection is a highly impersonal business. And, like a good many more, I'd never had any private use for Charles Manfrey.

The great days of the actor-manager have passed, but Manfrey was the nearest to what may be called a survival. But he was actor-producer rather than actor-manager, and he owned no theatre, nor was any particularly connected with his name. In age he was in the middle fifties, and for well over twenty years he had been among the heads of his profession. As an actor he was in the great tradition of Kean and Irving, and in the roles of Cassius and Iago he was held never to have been surpassed. Those characters give a clue to the man himself.

In my view, and I had come into close contact with him many times, there was always about him something waspish, malevolent, and even furtive. He could ape the bluff and hearty when in the company of those who might be called his equals, but he was quick to change, and a sudden sneer here or an innuendo there or even a spare gesture showed a man as fretted by strange jealousies as ever was Cassius and as subtle in his hates as Iago himself. Few men liked him and many loathed him, and most for what was thought to be a miserly strain, for though he would accept entertainment he rarely entertained, and in his smallish Hampstead house was something of a recluse. And he had, strangely enough, a bad reputation for women. His wife had left him after two years of marriage, and it was said that she had consistently refused to give him a divorce.

A car turned the corner and drew up at the kerb. A constable moved quickly across to move it on and then drew back with a salute. I nipped in at the back with George and the car shot on. George was huddled in his corner with his shoulders hunched and his ears well into the black velvet collar of his ancient overcoat. I don't know if his conscience was worrying him about his overnight debauch or if he hadn't quite thawed out, but he merely grunted as I wriggled into my corner.

'What's happened to Manfrey?' I ventured to ask.

'Don't know yet,' he told me gruffly. 'Bashed on the skull in his room, or so I gathered.'

I gave a Whartonian grunt and began thinking it over. George regarded the grunt with suspicion.

'Know anything about him?' he asked as he shot me a look.

I told him as much as I knew, and that's as much as I've mentioned already. I added a bit of scandal that had connected his name with a musical comedy actress and another now in revue.

'Pretty well off, wasn't he?' was all that he said.

'He's made a lot of money in the last ten years,' I told him. 'And he's still making it. *The Careless Man* is his show.'

'That's been on a couple of years, surely.'

'Just about,' I said. 'And he's got other irons in the fire. And he's got a new play shortly coming on.'

We were already past Camden Town and drawing up the long hill towards Hampstead. In a couple of minutes we were in that comparatively open residential part that lies near the Heath and then the driver suddenly turned into a side road. He turned as suddenly again and we were in a part of Hampstead quite unknown to me.

'Hallam Avenue,' George said, and began easing himself from his corner. 'A road runs parallel to it. Grove Lane.'

On the left was the Heath, or maybe some extension that I didn't know, and everywhere on the right were trees. We passed three or four embowered houses and then slowed down. Then we drew up before another house and I knew we were there, for on the gate was 'The Cote'.

The house, set well back from the road and shielded at each side by shrubberies and trees, looked like late Georgian. It was of medium size and might have had about five bedrooms, and those none too large. A gravelled way led to a garage built in the style of the house itself, and a wide path led from the centre gate to the front door with its rococo fanlight. As our car drew up, a plain-clothes man appeared from nowhere and waited till we neared. George waved a hand and through the front door we went.

We were in a fairly spacious hall, from which ran a flight of stairs. A cloakroom was on the right, and outside it hats and a waterproof and an overcoat were hanging on wall pegs. Narrow passageways led from each side of that hall and bang in front of us was another door and through it were coming faint sounds. George turned the handle and we went through.

That room was about twenty-five foot square, and had been the dining-room before Manfrey had changed it to a kind of lounge-office. On the far side were two windows and between them a french window through which I could see a crazy paving path that led to a gate that opened into Grove Lane. A quick glance round the room showed a flat-topped desk on the left with a filing cabinet alongside it, and a swivel chair. To the right were bookcases, a couple of genuine Heppelwhite chairs, and a Victorian side-table on which were miscellaneous papers and magazines.

There were several people in that room. Broad, the local Inspector, met us and introduced the Police-Surgeon, an elderly man named Cave. Photographs had been taken, Broad said, and the room was being finger-printed. Then at Wharton's unspoken question he waved a hand, and we had a look at the body.

Manfrey lay on his back and slightly away from the desk towards the french window. An electric fire had one of its burners on and two off, and it stood in the recess of what had been an ordinary fireplace and about six foot from the body.

Wharton gave a little shiver.

'This room's damn cold, isn't it? Why didn't he have more burners on?'

Broad shrugged his shoulders. Wharton looked down at the body again, and frowned perhaps at the little he could see. On the face was still that peevish, and yet what one might call that aloof, distinguished air that had marked it in life. It was the face of a man of breeding and yet there was about it a curious repulsiveness. The forehead, scant of hair, was too high, and the lips too sensually thick. And the lips were set grimly too, as if death had closed them with some final sneer or as if the brain at that last moment had lingered about some ancient jealousy or bitter grudge. It was the face of the dead Cassius turned upwards to the unseen sky on the lost field of Philippi.

'What killed him?' asked Wharton.

'A blow on the temple,' Cave said, and showed the livid mark. 'That's the primary cause, of course. There might be something else when we get him open.'

'Weapon?'

'This is the only likely thing,' Broad said, and pointed to a poker that lay on the desk. 'No prints on it, though.'

'What's a poker doing here?' Wharton wanted to know. 'You don't want a poker for an electric fire?'

Broad moved a few feet beyond the fire and pointed out a small shovel and a pair of tongs lying by the wall beneath a side table.

'He only used this fire in what you might call the between seasons. The housekeeper says that at any time now the electric fire would be taken away and this ordinary coal grate be used.'

'How long has he been dead?'

Cave looked at his watch and said it would be about an hour. Wharton pulled out his note-book and dictated to himself that the time of death was eleven-thirty approximately.

'I suppose the coldness of the room makes no difference?' he asked Cave.

'I don't think so,' Cave said. 'It's what you might call ordinary heat.'

'You ought to know,' Wharton told him, and in a tone that implied that heaven would have to help him if he'd made a mistake. Then he was stooping and feeling the dead man's jacket. It was one of those thin black alpaca coats one wears in the height of summer.

'Damn funny thing to wear this time of the year.' He grunted. 'And in a room as cold as this.'

'You never know, sir,' Broad told him. 'He might have had all three burners on some time this morning and have felt too hot.'

'That's no answer,' Wharton said testily. 'The two things cancel each other out. If he was too hot and put on a thin coat, that's no reason why he should keep the same coat on when he'd turned off two burners.'

He gave a quick look at me as if to let me know that the Old Gent – as he would deprecatingly allude to himself – was already in form. Then he made another note in his book, and I was thinking how incongruous that coat looked against the rest of the lounge suit, which was a warm-looking grey tweed. Then I almost whipped off my glasses – an instinctive trick of mine when at a sudden loss or on the edge of as sudden a discovery. There was something else that was mightily peculiar about that alpaca coat, even if I wasn't minded as yet to bring it to Wharton's attention. Maybe he'd see it for himself. And if he didn't, then he wouldn't like me to tell him in front of Broad that there was a something he'd overlooked.

'Who discovered the body?' was his next question.

'The cook-housekeeper,' Broad said. 'A Miss May Clarke. She'd been out shopping and she found it when she came in.'

'Anybody else in the house?'

'Yes, and no, sir,' Broad said. 'The secretary was here earlier. A Miss Violet Lancing. She left about five minutes or so before Miss Clarke discovered the body.'

Wharton sighed as if everything was as clear as mud. 'And where's the secretary now?'

'At her flat, sir. She'll be here in a few minutes. I got hold of her just before you came in.'

'Where's the flat?'

'Just along by Mornington Crescent. She shares it with another girl, so Miss Clarke told me.'

'Good,' said George commendingly. 'Any other news?'

'Several bits, sir. For one thing, when Miss Clarke tried to get in here she couldn't. That hall door was locked and so was that other one there. Both from the inside.'

'Where's that one lead to?'

'To the secretary's room. Little more than a cubby hole, sir.'

'I see. And what else?'

'Well, first of all, sir, we found this french window wasn't locked. Miss Clarke was bringing him a cup of coffee and some dry toast, the same as he always had round about half past eleven – when he was in – and when she couldn't get in any other way, she came round to the french window and tried it. That's when she saw the body.'

'Any prints on the handle besides hers?'

'None, sir. And hers aren't any too clear either. I reckon she smudged them. Must have been a bit upset when she caught sight of the body.'

'She saw it before she opened the door?'

Then Wharton had a look for himself and I followed suit. From the outside one could see the body quite clearly. And naturally, as I told George, she'd have a preliminary peep to see if Manfrey was there.

'That seems all in order,' Wharton told Broad. 'Anything else?'

'Yes, sir. Miss Clarke got back just before half past eleven. As she was putting her things away she heard the sound of quarrelling in this room. She was out in the hall at the time. One of the voices was Mr Manfrey's and the other she didn't recognize. But she says she's heard it somewhere, though she can't put a name to it.'

Wharton was quite cheerful at something into which to get his teeth.

'No panic,' he told Broad genially. 'I'll get all that from Miss Clarke at first hand. But the secretary. She'd gone by then?'

'No, sir. She was just going. She was in the kitchen when Miss Clarke told her there was the devil of a row going on here. Miss Lancing says, "Who is it, May?" and Miss Clarke says she doesn't know. Then Miss Lancing says she's going to fly, and she gets her things and off she goes.'

I think Wharton and I were both staring. What Broad was saying didn't make much sense. Wharton put the crux of it into his question.

'Why should she fly?'

'I can explain that, sir,' Broad said. 'She only came in on Saturday mornings to deal with the correspondence and she likes to get away well before eleven. When she said she was going to fly she meant two things, as far as I can gather. She wanted to get off before he could find her another job, and she didn't want to be mixed up with the row that was going on in here.'

'I get you,' Wharton said. 'What we don't know she can make clear when she comes.'

'Just one other thing, sir,' Broad said, and picked up an engagement book from the desk. It was open and he showed Wharton the page. I looked over his shoulder.

'Eleven-twenty – Henry Nevall,' said George, and looked round at me. 'He's an actor, isn't he?'

'That's right,' I said. 'He's appeared with Manfrey on more than one occasion.'

'And he was due here at eleven-twenty,' George said, and shook his head. 'Sounds too easy.'

Another shake of his head and he was whipping round on Broad.

'Done anything about it?'

'Yes, sir,' Broad told him placidly. 'I got hold of him at his flat in Gower Street and asked him to come here as soon as he could. He said he would.'

'You didn't tell him why?'

Broad ventured on a grin.

'Oh no, sir. I just said we'd expect him and then rang off.'

'Good work,' said Wharton. 'Looks as if we're going to have our hands full in a minute or two. Anywhere to park them when they get here?'

Broad said the sergeant was already in the hall. Nevall could wait there and Miss Lancing in the drawing-room.

'Right,' said George. 'Let's clear up the oddments and then I'll have a word with May Clarke.'

The oddments, as George had called them, didn't interest me. By the time they were over and the body had been carried out by the french window to the ambulance in Grove Lane, I had made a short tour of the room. There wasn't a great deal that I could gather – or at least I thought so then. On the walls were framed playbills both very old and reasonably modern. In the bookcases were a large number of volumes on matters theatrical, such as lives of actors and actresses, plays that ranged from the Elizabethan to the modern, books on costume and scenery and lighting, and the works of famous dramatic critics.

On the desk were various papers and I gently moved them about with my gloved hands. Manfrey, I gathered, was putting a company on the road with *The Careless Man* and those papers related principally to casting, and arrangements at various theatres on the proposed circuit. None of the proposed cast was known to me, so I moved on to the filing cabinet. That looked normal enough and far from interesting, so I made my way to the door in the far right-hand corner. The key was on my side and the door was unlocked.

The room, as Broad had said, was little more than a cubby-hole. There was a flat-topped desk on which was a typewriter covered with the usual black dust jacket, and there was also a standing rack filled with books of reference. There was a hanging corner-cupboard which was locked, and a board with three hooks on which to hang garments. A small electric fire was in the corner well under the cupboard. By it was another door which opened on a corridor, and from the smells I judged that it led to the kitchen. Quite a large window gave plenty of light and through it one could see the trees that fringed Grove Lane, and the path to the back gate and the untidy lawns each side of it.

My next visit was to that large cupboard that stood in the left corner of Manfrey's room nearest the desk. I don't know why, but I opened the bottom section first and my eyes fell on the most miscellaneous collection of odds and ends I think I've ever seen in so small a space. There were two shelves. On the top one were paper-bound books, more old newspapers, a ball of oddments of string, an empty paste bottle, one tennis shoe, a large Victorian paper-weight, and heaven knows what else, and when I raised the dust by poking some of the papers aside, there was an old-fashioned square attaché case and the other tennis shoe, and more oddments than I could list in five minutes. As for the second shelf, that was almost as bad: more books and papers, more this and more that, and plenty of dust. But the top half of that cupboard was by contrast uncannily clean. It was a kind of drinks cabinet with various bottles and decanters, and quite an assortment of glasses, together with a chamois leather duster.

When I closed the cupboard door I saw that Broad's men had gone. Wharton was saying that he'd see May Clarke at once. But no statement at the moment. Just an informal chat.

'Let her know that,' he told Broad from the door, and then he turned to me. 'Find anything that looked interesting?'

'I don't know that I did,' I said. 'Except that alpaca coat Manfrey was wearing.'

'Oh?' he said, with that sharp look of his. 'What was wrong with the coat?'

'Nothing particularly,' I told him. 'Except that it was still wrinkled from the way it had been folded. The creases were perfectly plain.'

'Meaning?'

'Don't know,' I said. 'Unless it was that he hadn't worn that coat for a long time until this morning, and then he took it out of the drawer where he'd kept it.'

'Damn funny day to take out an alpaca coat?'

'I know,' I said. 'That's just what I thought.'

He gave me another quick look, then made a note in his book. Before he had finished scribbling it, in came Broad with May Clarke.

CHAPTER II
The Finger Twister

THERE ARE TWO THINGS which I ought to make perfectly clear. From the very outset you may have gathered that the Case of Charles Manfrey was not going to be immediately solved, a fact which, if true, meant beginning a story on a note of anti-climax. But it needn't be so. A certain solution *was* found, but it remains your concern to agree or disagree with it. Provided that every fact gathered at every inquiry is put fairly and fully before you; if, in other words, you know as much as the police, then you have the chance of pitting your wits against theirs. And now, looking back on the Case, I think the challenge to you is scrupulously fair. If we were wrong, then you may see what we overlooked and you may place the right emphasis on what to us seemed unimportant, and by the time this short first part is finished, it may be you who are decorating your caps with feathers.

As to the information to be placed before you, that shall be only what is needed to solve the crime. You shall not be bored by long-winded inquiry or distracted by verbiage and tortuous side trails. And with that in mind we get back to the early Saturday afternoon and the entry of May Clarke.

She was a woman of about fifty; double-chinned and looking as if she had a heart of gold. From the very first she struck me as well up to her job as cook-housekeeper, and she spoke as a person of some education and in a pleasant throaty voice. Wharton, who loved handling women witnesses and boasted always that he could twist them round his little finger, looked for once to be on a very good thing. He didn't even take trouble to improve on his usual opening gambit.

'A bad business this, Miss Clarke, though you've nothing to reproach yourself with. In fact we're greatly indebted to you.'

He was placing a chair for her. She was saying nothing at the moment, but trying to sum us up perhaps, though she smiled at Wharton's praise. And Wharton noticed something that had struck me as curious – that she hadn't done any crying. I had expected red eyes, but there was never a sign of tears.

'Now, Miss Clarke,' said Wharton more briskly. 'There's a lot of things you can help us about. You've been here a good many years?'

'Eight years now, sir,' she said.

'Mr Manfrey was a good master?'

She hesitated a bit there.

'Well, sir, he had his good and bad points like all of us.'

'True enough,' said Wharton heavily. And then, with a touch of archness, 'What were his bad points?' He looked round at Broad and myself. 'Interesting to hear the human side of great men.'

'Well, I don't know that he had many bad points,' she said. 'A horrible temper, of course, when he was upset.'

'Really?' said Wharton, quite shocked. 'You had experience of it yourself?'

Only when she'd been at The Cote for a few months, she said, and then she'd done some straight talking. Over a silly thing too – being a few minutes late for something. A stickler for punctuality, Mr Manfrey was. And about a year ago he'd got into another of his fits of temper over much the same thing, but she'd talked to him straight. She wasn't standing for it, and if her ways didn't please him, then he had his remedy.

'That settled his hash?' asked Wharton.

'Well, he sulked for a day or two, sir, and ever since he was all right.'

'Good,' said Wharton. 'And now about this morning. When was the last time you actually saw Mr Manfrey alive?'

It was when she took up his breakfast, she said. He break-fasted at about nine when he wasn't actually acting, at which times he had no breakfast at all but slept till near noon.

'Did you see any of his clothes laid out? On a chair, for instance?'

'I might have done, sir, but I didn't really notice them.'

'And yesterday. What suit did Mr Manfrey wear?'

'His grey, sir.'

'With the grey coat?'

She stared, looked away, and then knew what Wharton was driving at.

'You mean he didn't put it on today?'

'That's it,' Wharton said. 'He had on the trousers and waist-coat but not the jacket. I suppose you couldn't tell us why?'

She hadn't the least idea. Wharton tried another angle.

'Suppose he sent that jacket to be cleaned. Imagine he'd spilt some ink on it, or something. Would he have taken it to the cleaners himself?'

'Oh no, sir,' she said, perfectly shocked. 'He'd have told me to do it. I've taken things to the cleaners heaps of times before.'

'I see. And what about the alpaca coat he was wearing? Have you seen that before?'

He'd worn it on every warm day throughout the summer, she said.

'But not recently?'

She thought for a moment or two and then said she hadn't noticed him wearing it since the warm spell we'd had in late September.

'You keep an eye on his clothes,' Wharton said. 'Where did he keep that alpaca coat when he wasn't wearing it?'

That she didn't know. Last year she'd found it in the cupboard and had taken it upstairs for the winter and spring. This year, she hadn't noticed it, though her idea was that he'd put it in the cupboard again.

'Well, we'll leave it,' Wharton told her. 'And now about this morning. I want you to take your time and not get at all flurried. We're simple, homely people like yourself. All we want is an account of everything that happened here from the time you took up breakfast till the moment you discovered the body.'

This is the gist of her story, with the relevant times. She heard Mr Manfrey come down at about ten o'clock, though she didn't see him. Miss Lancing had arrived soon after nine o'clock and had remarked that the post was fairly heavy, which meant that she mightn't get away till eleven instead of her usual ten thirty on a Saturday morning. Then about ten minutes to eleven May slipped Miss Lancing a cup of tea in her little room. Miss Lancing said if May waited a few minutes she would go with her as she wanted to buy something in Hampstead, but May said she was late and would have to get on with the shopping.

Off May went then, and it was just short of half past eleven when she got back. A moment or two later Miss Lancing got back too, but meanwhile May had heard from the hall the sound of a violent quarrel going on in Mr Manfrey's room. The voices were very angry in sound. One of them was Mr Manfrey's and the other she had heard somewhere but couldn't say just where. She had mentioned the matter to Miss Lancing, and there Wharton tried to get the exact words that had passed between them.

> V.L. 'Wonder who it is this time? Whoever it is, I'm going to fly. If he wants me, May, say I'm gone.'
>
> M.C. 'You get your things, Miss, and nip out. And mind you don't slam the door. I'll hurry up with his coffee or else he'll be on to *me*.'

That was the last May saw of the secretary, but a moment or two later she slipped along to the hall to listen, and there was absolute silence from Mr Manfrey's room. A very short time after that she took the tray with its coffee and toast to the door, tapped at the door and then tried the handle, but the door was locked. She listened and there wasn't a sound. Mr Manfrey must have gone out for a moment, she thought, so she slipped round to the secretary's room, intending to go through that way and leave the tray on Mr Manfrey's desk. But that door was locked too. Very puzzled she went through the side door of the kitchen, and, as she saw no sign of a soul, went to the french window to see if Mr Manfrey had returned. Then she saw the body. For a minute or two she was in a panic. Then she tried the french window and found it unlocked. Using the telephone on Mr Manfrey's desk she rang the police.

'A very clear statement,' was Wharton's summing up. 'The sort of witness we dream about. And that's all we're going to trouble you with at the moment, Miss Clarke. Later we shall ask you to make a formal statement, and if it's as good as this one, then it'll be good indeed. But just one other thing. I'd like to have a look at your kitchen. Didn't I gather that you can't see this back path from your window?'

Wharton and I went with her: as soon as we saw the kitchen lay-out, everything was plain enough. That kitchen was fairly light and airy but it faced east and with its one large window staring at nothing but the shrubbery. And that was awkward sometimes, as May said. Tradesmen came in by that back path from Grove Lane to the kitchen door, and instead of being able to know who they were long before they arrived, she had to wait till they got to the door.

When we came back through the hall, Broad whispered that Miss Lancing was waiting.

'Bring her in at once,' Wharton told him, and just as he spoke, there was a ring at the front door. That would almost certainly be Henry Nevall, but we didn't wait to see. But in a moment or two Broad was coming in. Mr Nevall had a matinée that afternoon and would have to leave again almost at once, so would Wharton see him first. Wharton grudgingly consented.

Nevall – he liked the accent on the last syllable – was a fine figure of a man. There is quite a good story he would tell about himself, how that in the height of the pageant craze he had been waiting for a train at a certain large junction, when he saw a woman regarding him at considerable length. He didn't know her, but she was a certain eccentric if famous pageant mistress. At any rate, after her inspection was over she suddenly pounced on him, and with the astonishing remark: 'I've got you now. Pontius Pilate!'

I don't know of a play in which Pontius Pilate occurs, but I do know that Nevall was as fine a Brutus as I have ever seen. He and Manfrey were Brutus and Cassius respectively in that historic show at the Coliseum and thereby hangs a tale, or rather a piece of scandal. Manfrey definitely tried to hog that show. Stole the limelight, I think the term is, but it was said that ever since that time – which was 1939 – the two hadn't been even on nodding terms.

What made Nevall so good a Brutus was possibly the fact that in private life he struck one as more of a philosopher or dreamer than a man of action. But, unlike Manfrey, he had a private reputation that stood very high. And whereas Manfrey was a grass widower, Nevall was the genuine thing, for his wife had died just before the war. Personally I found Nevall very uninteresting off the stage. There was something vague and nebulous about him, though maybe it was only a natural diffidence with which I couldn't somehow bring myself to be in sympathy.

'You don't know why we've asked you to come here this morning, Mr Nevall?' was Wharton's opening.

'I haven't the least idea,' Nevall told him. 'I only gathered it was something to do with the police.' He coughed nervously. 'I hope Manfrey hasn't got himself into any trouble.'

'Trouble?' said Wharton quickly. 'You anticipated trouble?'

'Not at all,' Nevall told him. 'All the same, a man like Manfrey is always . . . what shall I say? – where trouble is.'

'You mean?'

'Well, his perfectly ungovernable temper.' He held up a hand as if to stop some imaginary traffic. 'But I'd rather not talk about that. Perhaps you'd be so good as to tell me what it is you wish to see me about.'

Wharton told him, and never did a man look more surprised and even shocked.

'Well, there we are,' Wharton said. 'He's dead, and somebody killed him. That's why we wanted to see you. To find out, for instance, if he was alive when you left him this morning.'

'When I left him!'

Wharton looked just as surprised.

'You saw him this morning, didn't you?'

'What you're driving at I don't know,' Nevall said, and spread his palms in dismay. 'It's well over a month since I spoke to Manfrey, except over the telephone.' Then he thought of something. 'But what makes you think I saw him this morning?'

'Just this,' Wharton said, and showed him the engagement book.

Nevall had a look, frowned and then gave a dry smile. 'That's easily explained. Manfrey rang me earlier in the week and asked me to see him today. He suggested eleven-thirty. Later the same day I said I couldn't see him till Sunday.'

'I see,' said Wharton smoothly. 'He made the entry and forgot to erase it, or to alter it to the Sunday.'

'That's the only solution that fits in,' Nevall said, and then thought of something else. 'But wait a moment. It's written down as eleven-twenty. I can definitely swear that the original appointment was for seven-thirty.'

'Yes,' said Wharton and pursed his lips. 'But wasn't he a bit of a faddist in the matter of punctuality? Mightn't this entry have been a kind of warning to himself that though you wouldn't be coming till half past eleven, he had to be ready for you, or something like that?'

'Maybe,' said Nevall with a shrug of the shoulders. 'But all I would state, and most emphatically, Superintendent, is that it's six months since I set foot in this house.'

Wharton made a great show of agreement. He was sorry Nevall had been troubled and there was no need to detain him longer. And then came the postscript. Mr Nevall would however recognize that no loose ends had to be lying around. A short statement would have to be made some time in the near future, and, just by way of reinforcement, an account of Mr Nevall's whereabouts that morning. Then there hastily followed the usual jocular reminder that innocent men had no fear of inquiry, and the assurance that such statements – once checked – would guarantee no further questioning by the police.

Nevall made no bones about stating his whereabouts that morning. He had slept till about ten o'clock and then had dressed. Next he cooked his own breakfast and then he'd read a couple of newspapers till about midday. Then he slipped out to his tobacconist – only a few doors away – and then he'd gone back to the flat. He was thinking of going out for lunch at his club when he had been rung by the police.

'We're very grateful to you,' Wharton said. 'We shall have to check up with your tobacconist and that'll be the end of the matter as far as you're concerned. But just one last thing before you go. I suppose you don't know anyone who could have killed Manfrey? Someone with an honest-to-God motive?'

Nevall's smile was definitely ironic.

'I daresay I could give you a list as long as my arm – if I cared to. Anybody in my profession could do the same.'

'Not a nice person, was he?'

'Concerning the dead nothing but good,' said Nevall dryly. 'I'd rather you got your information elsewhere. Plenty of people will tell you, for instance, that Manfrey and I haven't been on good terms for quite a long time.'

'Ah well,' said Wharton with a grimace and a sigh. 'But would you care to tell us why he wanted to see you this morning?'

'It was I who wanted to see him,' Nevall said. 'When he rang me earlier this week it was in reply to my insistence that I should see him personally. What I'm saying is in confidence?'

'Most decidedly,' Wharton assured him.

'Well, I'm playing in *The Careless Man*, as you may or may not know. People think that play is Manfrey's property, but it isn't – quite. I have a part share, which he tried several times to acquire and in none too straight a fashion. Then lately I was suspicious about – well, we'll say the allocation of profits. That's what I wanted to see him face to face about. And I didn't want to see him today for a very good reason. Certain inquiries which I'm making won't be – or wouldn't have been – complete till tomorrow morning. That's why I put him off.'

'Clear as daylight,' said Wharton and held out his hand. And it was he who accompanied Nevall to the front door.

When he came back I had something to point out to him, but he was in too much of a hurry to listen.

'This engagement book,' he said to Broad. 'Get his prints off it and see if they tally with any you've got already. Do it straight-away before I see that secretary.'

Broad brought in his sergeant and another man. I drew George over to the french window.

'This is what I wanted you to see,' I told him. 'This crazy paving path runs down to the Grove Lane gate. But do you see the other end? The path branches off to our right against the gate and the second path runs along the shrubbery to the kitchen door.'

George had a look, than grunted.

'Well, what of it?'

'Only this,' I said. 'May Clarke said she came round specially to this french window to see if Manfrey was in. But she'd come in just before that from her shopping, and then Manfrey *was* in, and so was the man he was quarrelling with. If there'd been only the one path straight from the gate and past this window, then she must have heard Manfrey from outside. But she didn't come by the main path. She took the other path straight to the kitchen.'

'Fairly obvious, isn't it?' George said off-handedly.

'Maybe,' I said. 'But anybody else could have come to this room by the main path, and May Clarke couldn't have seen him from the kitchen. Whoever killed Manfrey left by this french window. If May had been in, she couldn't have seen him. As he could have walked on the grass, she wouldn't have heard any footsteps.'

'I still don't see what you're driving at,' George told me impatiently. And then Broad was reporting that no prints found in the room bore any likeness to Nevall's. George looked disappointed.

'Take down these instructions,' he said. 'As soon as we've seen that secretary, you can get on the move. Ready? One. Get full details of Nevall's flat. Could he have left it unobserved, for instance. And underline that word *full*. Two. Check up with the tobacconist. Try to get times. Three. Get a photograph of Nevall. A newspaper morgue will probably have one. Make a few copies and then try the local Tube Station to see if anyone saw him round about a quarter past eleven this morning.'

He peered over the top of his antiquated spectacles.

'Got all that? Right. Then let's see that secretary.'

I had seen a few handsome women in my time, but rarely one like Violet Lancing. I suppose nowadays one would call her a girl, since she was unmarried and only about twenty-three, but that's rather beside the point. The real trouble is that I'm no hand at communicating my impressions. In my younger days, perhaps, I might have achieved quite a purple patch of description and have waxed lyrical, as the good old cliché has it, over Violet Lancing.

She looked about five foot eight, which is nicely above the normal height for a woman, and she had a figure as svelte and suave as velvet. Her hair was jet black and her complexion had that lovely Irish quality of warmth and redness. The whole face was enormously attractive, almost mesmerizingly so, and yet there was just one thing wrong, or so it struck me. The lips were just a bit too thin and calculating. And maybe I *was* wrong, and what I had taken for hardness was no more than a perfect poise. When she came in, with just a suspicion of a smile at the two of us, it was impossible not to be struck by her perfect self-possession.

Wharton placed a chair for her and began his usual blether about having bothered her and torn her from an afternoon of holiday.

'I wasn't doing anything in particular,' she said, and quite naturally. 'I did wonder a bit why you should want to see me.'

'You've no idea why we sent for you?'

'Not the least idea,' she said, and smiled. Then the smile went, and she gave a quick instinctive look round the room. 'Unless anything's happened to Mr Manfrey?'

Her voice, by the way, had nothing particularly attractive about it. It was pleasant, pitched a bit too high perhaps, but without accent and generally what one might call educated. So lovely a girl, I thought disappointingly, should have had a voice of more warmth and depth. But Wharton was cutting in, and bluntly.

'Mr Manfrey is dead,' he told her. 'He was killed in this room at about half past eleven this morning.'

She stared, lips parted, then for a moment or two her body went limp.

'It's a shock to you?'

She smiled faintly and shook her head.

'It is. A terrible shock.'

'You're feeling all right?' The tone was most solicitous. 'I'm all right,' she said, and the same wan smile came again. 'You did say he was killed?'

'Yes. He was killed.'

'I can't believe it,' she said. 'It's silly of me I know, but . . . well, this is the first time I've known anything like this.'

'It's a bad business,' Wharton told her. 'That's why we want you to help us. Not a formal statement – that will come later. Just anything that will help. Everything you yourself have done here today, for instance. And, of course, everything in the most implicit confidence.'

This was her story, with the exact timings. She came on a Saturday morning only to deal with any correspondence, and once that was finished with, she was free, and naturally she always tried to get away at the earliest moment. She was entitled to that because during the week she often worked late hours without extra remuneration. Her salary, by the way, was five pounds a week.

That morning she had arrived just after nine o'clock. When Manfrey came down soon after ten, she had everything ready for him, and she took down his instructions. All she would have to do then was to' write answering letters and put them on his desk, and she had that done by a quarter to eleven. Then he gave her another job – to type out the part of Mary Bligh in *The Careless Man*. She didn't have to take that in to him, but to put it in a drawer where he'd get it himself. Just before eleven o'clock May Clarke popped in quietly with a cup of tea. Then at eleven o'clock Victor Yarnell arrived.

George glared round at Broad and me as if to demand why he had not been told of that before. I could see from Broad's face that Yarnell's call was as much news to him as it was to Wharton.

'Who's Victor Yarnell?'

She looked surprised.

'He's the actor. He's in film work at the moment. I was simply thrilled when Mr Manfrey rang through and asked me to see him out.'

'Wait a minute,' said Wharton with a look of humorous despair. 'We're getting on a bit too fast. This Victor Yarnell arrived at eleven o'clock. Who let him in?'

She said Mr Manfrey let him in. May was out and there was nobody else in the house but herself, and Mr Manfrey never expected her to answer doors. During the week there was a woman who came in every day to help May.

'But Mr Manfrey rang for you to see this Victor Yarnell out.'

'That's right,' she said. 'That wasn't so unusual.'

She explained. If the front door bell rang, the caller might be anybody, even men selling something. But once a caller was for Mr Manfrey, that made things different. It was really part of her duties then to see the caller out, though that only meant being in the hall when he left Mr Manfrey's room.

'I get you,' Wharton said. 'And you heard Mr Yarnell talking to Mr Manfrey?'

'Oh yes,' she said, and smiled quite excitedly. 'I was ever so thrilled.'

The reason for the thrill was quite an interesting one. Violet had begun life as an orphan brought up by an aunt. She had started her working life as a trained secretary-typist, and then the aunt had died and had left her quite a small sum of money –

the main sum had been invested in the aunt's annuity – and the lease of the Mornington Crescent flat, and its furniture. Violet, who'd always hankered after a stage career, then tried breaking into film work, and she got odd jobs as an extra at Imperial Studios, Gerrard's Cross. That was where she first saw Victor Yarnell, though naturally there was a great gulf fixed. He was a principal and she an insignificant extra, and she had never spoken to him in her life. Then later, through a friend, she heard about Manfrey's need of a new secretary, and she got the job. Film work had been disappointing in its prospects. There were short cuts, she told us frankly, but she hadn't been prepared to take them. And she was hoping that Manfrey would ultimately be induced to try her out in some minor part in one of his plays.

But to get on with that Saturday morning. Violet had a sudden idea. She was in any case going to the shops because she had seen a cap and scarf she wanted to buy.

'I'm wearing them now,' she told us with a smile.

'Doesn't look like a cap to me.' Wharton told her humorously.

'It's really a pull-on turban,' she told us.

'Whatever it is, it suits you.'

'You really think so?'

Wharton assured her that he did, and then gently prodded her back to the story.

Her scheme was to be ready to go out when Yarnell left. It worked, and she had the pleasure of walking with him to the shops, for he was going home by Underground. During the walk she told him about herself and where she had seen him. He was perfectly delightful about it all and even accompanied her jokingly into the shop – Marie-Louise was the name – where she bought the cap and scarf. That didn't take long, for she'd tried on the cap the day before and it was being held for her. Then as they passed the Yellow Tulip, Mr Yarnell suggested she should have coffee with him. Most reluctantly she had to refuse, for that might have meant best part of a quarter of an hour in the tea-shop, and she had an engagement at twelve o'clock in Camden Town.

As it was she fairly flew back to the house, letting herself quietly in with her own key. It was then about half past eleven.

'The front door, of course,' Wharton said. 'So you must have heard something happening in this room.'

'I did,' she said. 'It was like two people having an argument. "Hallo," I said to myself, "he's ticking off May about something," and that's all I thought. You see I was in a hurry to get away. Then as I went the back way to my room I actually heard May in the kitchen. Before I could tell her I'd heard something, she told me that Mr Manfrey was having a fine old row with someone in his room. All I said was that if that was so, then I was going to fly. I didn't want him to know I was in my room or he might have rung for me for something, and then I mightn't have got away for heaven knows how long. So I slipped back to my room, put the cap and scarf into my case and – well, that's all I know.'

'A very excellent witness,' said George with the usual look round at Broad and myself. 'But when you went to your room to get your case, Miss Lancing, was the quarrel still going on?'

'It wasn't. I thought perhaps May had made some mistake, and then I did hear a sound in the room, and that's why I simply flew.'

'What sort of a sound?'

'As if Mr Manfrey was moving about.' She ventured on another smile. 'That's why I hurried away.'

'Just one question I'd like to ask, sir,' broke in Broad. 'Did Mr Yarnell go into the Yellow Tulip?'

'Oh yes,' she told him.

'And you arranged no further meeting?' I asked, and as flippantly as I could make it.

The lips tightened. She was definitely not amused.

'I'm afraid you didn't understand,' she told me evenly. 'I wasn't thinking about anything like an affair with Mr Yarnell. That would have been just too ridiculous.'

I duly shrivelled. Broad came to the rescue.

'Just a kind of hero worship,' suggested Broad.

'If you like to put it that way – yes,' she told him sweetly.

'Well, everything's clear as far as I'm concerned,' announced Wharton, and gave a look round. 'Perhaps we'd better have a word with this Mr Yarnell. You don't happen to know his number, Miss Lancing?'

'I haven't the faintest idea.'

Broad went to look it up. Wharton produced the engagement book, and in the process knocked off the desk a very elaborate paper knife. It was a wicked-looking thing with quite a sharp edge. I know, for it was I who picked it up and put it back.

'This entry about a Mr Nevall,' Wharton said. 'Did you know anything about it?'

She looked most surprised.

'And Mr Manfrey didn't mention to you that he was coming?'

'I don't think I've heard Mr Manfrey ever mention his name,' she said. 'Besides, he never mentioned callers to me, unless I had to get something ready for them.'

Broad had the number of Yarnell's telephone and Wharton at once rang. I ventured to pass Miss Lancing my cigarette case and she was graciously pleased to take a cigarette, and to give me a delightful smile after I'd held the lighter. Wharton's voice broke in. He told Yarnell frankly that he'd probably been the last to see Mr Manfrey alive, and, from other things he let fall, it was plain that the news of Manfrey's death had come to Yarnell as very much of a shock.

'At two-thirty then,' Wharton said at last. 'Sorry to trouble you like this, Mr Yarnell. Merely a matter of form, but these things just have to be done.'

That was that. Wharton said there didn't seem anything else for which we should want Miss Lancing, and then he found another question.

'What jacket was Mr Manfrey wearing when you first saw him this morning?'

'His black alpaca one,' she told him, rather surprised.

'A curious thing to wear on a morning like this?' he suggested.

'I don't know,' she said. 'He was an awful faddist about temperature and all that. He'd put all the burners on and then keep switching them about.' She smiled. 'You know. Like people are with electric ovens. You get a certain heat and then switch off.'

'I know,' Wharton said, and if he did know, then he was quicker on the uptake than I was. 'But what about yesterday? What jacket did he wear then?'

'The jacket of the suit,' she said.

'And what time did you leave last night?'

'At about six o'clock,' she said, and then thought of something. 'I told him it was ever so stuffy in here. Perhaps he changed into the thin coat then.'

And that was all, and as soon as Wharton announced the fact, Violet Lancing got to her feet with a smile of relief.

'We have your telephone number,' Wharton told her, 'so if you're wanted for an official statement, we can get you tomorrow.'

Something had struck her, and not too pleasantly.

'What's worrying you?' asked Wharton.

'If I make a statement you won't put in all that nonsense I told you about Mr Yarnell?'

Wharton had to laugh, she had looked so scared.

'Never a word about that, my dear young lady. Nothing but a few facts. It'll all be over quicker than going to the dentist. And guaranteed painless.'

She gave him the most charming of smiles, compared with which mine and Broad's were only courteously valedictory.

George rushed forward to open the door and it was he who showed her out. Broad caught my eye and I'm pretty positive that he winked.

CHAPTER III
No Tears for Manfrey

WHARTON RANG the Yard and advised that the Press should be simply informed that Charles Manfrey had died suddenly at his Hampstead house. Then he told Broad that the house was to be kept free of reporters and photographers. And there was one other order before Broad left – to check up at the Yellow Tulip to see at what time exactly Yarnell had entered and how long he had stayed.

'What'd you think of the Lancing woman?' he asked me.

'What the BBC comics are accustomed to call a nice piece of homework,' I told him flippantly. It pays to be flippant with George. It draws him out and stops opinions and suggestions from being too one-sided.

'A very smart girl, I'll grant you,' George said. 'Seemed a good reliable witness, don't you think?'

I said most people were good witnesses who had nothing to conceal. I also added that, in my opinion, if she'd had anything to conceal she'd have been perfectly capable of doing so.

'She's a competent woman. No doubt about that,' George said with a nod of approval to himself. 'What they call a woman of the world.'

He pursed his lips in a moment or two of meditation, then fired a sudden question.

'What do you know about this chap Yarnell?'

George has said that I have a colossal social experience. He exaggerates even if he means that I know a colossal number of people. But, as I've already said, I like people. All sorts interest me, and always have. I like to know the whys and wherefores of things and what makes the wheels go round. At the two clubs to which I belong one meets scores of people and listens to talk and scandal, and so a man who's lived in town as many years as I have can't very well help having a pretty extensive knowledge of a certain social stratum. And you will have gathered from George's method of putting his question that he'd have been quite upset if I'd had to reply that about Yarnell I knew little or nothing.

'I know as much as you,' I said. 'You've seen *Green Altar*?'

'Can't say I have. Been too busy lately.'

'Quite a pleasant little social comedy at the Stoic,' I told him. 'I saw it the last time I was home on leave. It's off now, by the way. The blitz killed it. Yarnell had the part of Humphrey Glare. A very good part and he gave a very good performance.'

'That all you know?'

'My God, George, you expect me to be a walking encyclopedia,' I told him, amused if exasperated. 'What else do you expect me to know?'

'No need to fly off the handle,' he told me reprovingly. 'All I thought was that you might know something about his film work.'

'I don't know a thing,' I said. 'I do know Imperial Association Films, to give them their full name. At least I know Benny Markstein, which is the same thing.'

'Well, there's no need to jump hurdles till we get to them,' he told me. 'Anything else you did notice this morning?'

'As a matter of fact I did think of something,' I said, and showed him that engagement book. 'This entry "Henry Nevall". Isn't it rather unusual?'

'How do you mean?'

'Well, why the full name? Why not the initials only, or just "Nevall"?'

'Hm!' went George, and began turning the back pages. There he found various entries, some as initials only, some as surnames, and one or two in full.

'I'll bet if you checked up on those entries,' I said, 'you'd find that all those with initials only or surnames are people he knew pretty well.'

'Suppose that is so,' he said. 'Where's it get us? It's his writing, isn't it? Compare this "Henry Nevall" with this "Ann Gloster" for instance. And if he wrote the "Henry Nevall", then what are you trying to prove?'

'Nothing now,' I admitted ruefully. 'But it just struck me as an odd sort of entry about a man Manfrey knew.'

George looked at his watch.

'A quarter to two. I don't know about you, but I'm most devilishly hungry.'

I suggested we should interview May Clarke. She had had her own meal, she said, and she hadn't had anything to prepare for Mr Manfrey for he had intended to lunch out. Easy enough to make us some sandwiches, she said, and a bit of cheese to follow, and a pot of tea.

'Mind if we sit here while you get it for us?' Wharton said. 'Funny, isn't it, how everybody loves a kitchen? Even men. And a spotless kitchen this is, and I'll say so to your face.'

We were made pretty comfortable after that and George even had a cushion for his chair. George went on with his blarney and I wasn't listening till suddenly he came to that matter of the alpaca coat. That was when we were ready to begin our meal.

'I spoke to Miss Lancing about that grey coat which goes with Mr Manfrey's suit,' he said, 'and she told me he hadn't said anything about having it cleaned. I wonder if you'd mind having a look upstairs, Miss Clarke, and seeing if you can find it. You know where all his things are.'

Off she went to have a look. George said it'd bound to be up there somewhere. He'd had a look in the cupboard and the desk drawers and it wasn't there. Then we settled to our meal, and we'd just finished eating and were smoking our pipes over our second cups of tea when May came down again.

'I can't understand it,' she said. 'There's never a sign of it anywhere.'

'Funny,' said George. 'There isn't any place you've overlooked?'

'I know this house like I know the palm of my hand,' she told him. 'You have a look for yourself, sir.' She sniffed at George's pungent tobacco. 'If you do find it, sir, I'll buy you an ounce of tobacco out of my own pocket.'

'Your word's good enough for me,' George told her. 'Not that I wouldn't mind asking you to have one more good look later, so as to make absolutely sure.' He put on his antiquated spectacles again and gave her an arch look over their tops. 'If you do find it, I'll stand you fifty cigarettes.'

'Who told you I smoked, sir?'

'This room did,' George said. 'And that ash-tray.'

She gave a chuckle at that and I wondered why she didn't dig George in the ribs. Like two bugs in a rug, they were.

'Just one thing more,' George said, and as if by some miracle he'd remembered it. 'That row that was going on in Mr Manfrey's room. Did you hear any actual words?'

She tried to look indignant. 'You surely didn't think I was the sort to go listening at key-holes, sir?'

'I certainly should have listened,' George said, and then went unblushingly on. 'Mr Travers here was saying the same thing. Two people having a violent row and not listen? You couldn't have stopped me.'

'I expect Miss Clarke caught a word or two,' I put in helpfully.

'A word or two is about all, sir,' she told me. 'And them I couldn't help hearing. The way they were going for each other was enough to frighten anybody. Not that I hadn't heard Mr Manfrey in his tantrums before.'

'What were the words you actually heard?' Wharton wanted to know.

'Well, sir, I heard some words I couldn't make out and then whoever it was called Mr Manfrey a rascally scoundrel. I heard that plain as you hear me now. Then there was some more I couldn't hear and then this other man says, "I didn't do it." Then Mr Manfrey bellows at him, "You did", and this other one he hollers back that he didn't. And he calls Mr Manfrey a fool. And that's all I heard, sir. And enough too, if you ask me.'

George had no more questions to ask, and she said she'd have that other look upstairs, even if it was a waste of time. And she'd hunt downstairs too. George left me to slip a tip under the plate, and then we adjourned to Manfrey's room to spend the five minutes before Yarnell was due. George made some notes in his book and I jotted down, before I should forget them, the words May Clarke said she had heard in the course of that quarrel in Manfrey's room.

Broad came in then. He'd personally made inquiries at the Yellow Tulip and everything was in order. Yarnell had entered the tea-shop just before half past eleven. He had ordered coffee and biscuits and had stayed there for about a quarter of an hour.

'That settles him then,' George says. 'Not that he mightn't be able to give us some useful information.' He looked at his watch. 'The damn fellow's five minutes late already. Why people can't be on time beats me.'

He was still muttering and grumbling when May knocked at the door. She had looked in every conceivable spot, she said, and there was never a sign of that jacket. Then Broad had to have new instructions. Every cleaner in the area was to be questioned, and, if nothing arose from that, then Manfrey's tailor was to be rung up. Wharton had the name which he'd taken from a tab on the back of the trousers. If the tailor knew nothing, then local tailors should be tried.

'I suppose he couldn't have given the jacket away,' ventured Broad.

'Given it away?' glared George. 'Who to?'

'Well, somebody might have come begging this way.'

'I don't think Manfrey would have given much away,' I said. 'And even the most warm-hearted of us would have thought twice about spoiling a perfectly good suit.'

George muttered something about perishing Good Samaritans, whatever that might mean, and then there was a ring at the front door. It was Victor Yarnell, and nearly a quarter of an hour late.

Yarnell was a good-looking fellow of about thirty-five, with what is known as a well-cut face and only a slightly weak chin to spoil it. One of his ears had a slight nick in it, though that was hardly noticeable, for his longish wavy hair hung artistically over it. What definitely was noticeable was his nervousness of manner, though that was probably due to an awareness of being late. Wharton graciously accepted his apologies, and added his own apologies for spoiling an afternoon.

'Everything strictly confidential and everything free and easy,' George went on. 'All we really want from you, Mr Yarnell, is the statement that you left Mr Manfrey alive and in good health this morning. What did you come to see him about, by the way? Strictly between ourselves.'

'It was really a kind of errand of mercy,' Yarnell said. His voice, by the way, was the most attractive thing about him, for he wasn't the sort to whom one immediately takes a liking. It was not, in fact, till he'd got over his initial nervousness and could venture on a smile that he looked a far more likeable person.

There was an actor Roger Farnham, he said, who had had some very bad luck, and who had also been a bit of a fool. Yarnell knew about that *Careless Man* company that was going on the road and he wondered if Farnham could be fitted in. Much as he disliked coming to see Manfrey, he thought he ought to do what he could. As he had only made up his mind at the last moment, so to speak, he had chanced his luck about finding Manfrey in.

'Did you have any luck?' Wharton wanted to know.

Yarnell smiled ruefully.

'Manfrey wouldn't hear a word. He said his company was virtually complete.' The smile became even more rueful. 'He was almost abusive about it, and about my not making an appointment. That was why I wasn't in this room more than five minutes or so.'

Then something suddenly struck him.

'You told me he was dead!'

'That's right,' said George, and waited.

'Yes, but why should you – I mean the police – be here? He didn't die . . . naturally?'

'Twenty minutes after you last saw him he was murdered,' Wharton told him bluntly.

'My God, no!'

'Unhappily, yes,' Wharton said piously. 'Murdered he was, and that's that. But he was alive when you left him?'

'Very much alive,' Yarnell said, and shook his head bewilderedly. 'He pushed the bell for his secretary and waved his hand for me to get out, just as if I was dirt.'

'Well, that seems clear enough,' Wharton said, and then turned speciously to Broad and me. 'What about the official records? Do you think we ought to ask Mr Yarnell to tell us what happened to him after eleven thirty?'

I said it might be as well, and Yarnell made no bones about giving us a full account, and that account was in absolute agreement with the one we'd had from Violet Lancing, though told from a different angle. He described her for instance, as 'quite a nice' girl, and apparently he was wholly unaware of her hero worship.

'Well, that seems to be all the official business,' George said. 'But just as a matter of routine you might give us the address of that Roger Farnham. I know it's apparently unnecessary, but you know what the bureaucrats are. Everything's got to be nicely docketed and tied up with red tape.' That drew a smile from Yarnell and I passed him my cigarette case. As I held the lighter for him, I brought things round to a more personal note. What were the flats like in Marylebone Road, for instance.

He said his wife didn't like living in town at all, though he himself was used to it. If only one could be sure of continuous work with Imperial Associated, then one could think of a little place in Buckinghamshire.

'But you have a contract?' I said.

It wasn't that, as he told me. One bomb on the studios and there'd be the devil to pay. And what use a house in Buckinghamshire if the studios had to get makeshift premises scores or hundreds of miles away?

Everything was now very free and easy, and Yarnell had lost all his nervousness. Wharton asked what chance there'd be some day of having a look over the studios, and Yarnell said any day.

'By the way,' insinuated George, 'what were your personal views on Manfrey? Not too nice a character, so we've gathered.'

'I don't think you'll find many who'd give him a good name,' Yarnell said frankly. 'Mind you, he was a fine actor. A very fine actor, in fact. Almost a great one.' He shook his head. 'A pity really that he should have been such an awful outsider in private life. There wasn't a single thing he shied at provided it looked like working out to his own advantage.'

That seemed about all. Wharton asked if Yarnell could slip along in the morning – say at eleven o'clock – and sign a formal statement, and added jocularly that there could be a taxi at Government expense.

'Well, what did you make of him?' Wharton asked us when he came back from seeing him off at the front door.

'He seemed a very decent sort of chap,' said Broad.

I said much the same thing, but George was wondering why he'd been so damnably nervous. I said anybody would be nervous after hearing that someone was dead to whom he had been talking only a short time before. And then being requested to come and see the police.

'This case isn't going to be so easy as it looks,' George said, 'and I'll tell you why. Most witnesses we can see through. If we can't, then we can make a pretty shrewd summing up from their general manner. But we're dealing with actors. People used to acting and playing parts. They're not likely to make any slips.'

'A pretty sound observation,' I said. 'If there's anything concealed it'll be tough work digging it out.'

'Well, no use panicking about that,' George said. 'Another day or two and things might be more clear. I suppose either of you hasn't any ideas already?'

'Well, sir,' said Broad, 'if Mr Yarnell was telling the truth, then anybody might have murdered Manfrey. From ten minutes past eleven till half past there wasn't a soul but Manfrey in the house. Everybody agrees that Manfrey had plenty of enemies and any one of them might have called and been admitted. Then there was a row and this caller cracked him over the skull with the poker, and then he nipped out down that path.'

'Maybe you're right,' George said. 'But that means more work for you. Pity this house is so secluded. Still, you'd better inquire everywhere. Somebody might have seen someone coming out at Grove Lane at half past eleven. Inquire of the tradesmen too. Their delivery vans. And the milkmen.'

He added that that was all routine, but it was striking me that Broad and his men looked like having a hectic time for a day or two.

'But that jacket's a queer business,' George was going on. 'It hasn't anything to do with the case – or it needn't have – and yet I don't like it.'

That brought another idea. The district pawnshops should be tried. Somebody might have stolen the jacket – though heaven knew who. May Clarke was suggested and at once discarded, if only because she looked honest as the day.

'That reminds me,' George said. 'She was scared of being in the house all alone. I told her you'd have someone here night and day – especially at night.'

Still more work for Broad, and there was no wonder that he said he'd be on the move, and doubtless in case anything else should occur to Wharton. When he had gone, George said there was nothing else to keep me. At half past nine the next morning he'd take the official statements, and if anything arose in the meanwhile he'd let me know.

'Something tells me we ought to learn a little more about Yarnell,' I said.

'What do you mean?'

'Damned if I know,' I said. 'Maybe it's only a hunch.'

'Mightn't do any harm,' George said, if a bit grudgingly. 'How are you going to do it?'

'I might try to get hold of Benny Markstein,' I said. 'Only a matter of using the telephone.'

George considerately went off on some business of his own in the kitchen I think – and left me to it. First I got Imperial Associated at Gerrards Cross, and it took me ten minutes to learn that Benny wasn't there. Then I tried Benny's house, near Denham, and there he was.

'You likely to be in town this weekend, Benny?' I said.

'Never a hope, Mr Travers,' he told me. 'Did you want to see me about something?'

I said I did, even if it wasn't highly important.

'Come along here,' he said. 'Come this afternoon. Come to tea. The wife's gone out to see her father and the kids are at school.'

I took a quick look at my watch and then said I'd be delighted.

I always did like Benny Markstein, and I think I shall go on liking him for a good time yet. He had plenty of money but he didn't spread it or himself around. In matters of business I'd trust him further than I could see him, and his artistic judgement was beyond question. Benny had his flops like other directors and producers, but even his flops brought a good word from the critics, if only to the effect that it didn't do to let ideals run clean out of sight of the box-office.

'What have you been doing with yourself, Mr Travers?' he asked me. 'It seems a long time since I saw you.'

We talked about that, and the old times, and then settled down to tea. It was only when the maid cleared away that I told him Manfrey was dead. And since Benny was the soul of discretion, I told him that he had been murdered, though he mightn't read that in the papers.

'You don't know who did it?'

I said we hadn't the faintest idea, but apparently Manfrey had a good many enemies. And out of that remark, and maybe out of the very peace of that room and its friendly intimacy, came a tremendous stroke of luck. Mind you, I might have arrived at the same result in a direct way, for I had intended to bring the conversation round to Yarnell, but that might have meant telling even Benny just a bit too much. And he might have prefaced what he told me by the strict injunction that everything was highly confidential, and what use would that have been?

'Well, I oughtn't to say it,' said Benny in his quiet way, 'but he's had it coming to him for a good while now. Here,' he said, and leaned forward, 'I'll tell you something, just to show the kind of man he was. Do you know Victor Yarnell?'

I had to start filling my pipe before I could say I'd heard of him, and wasn't he the man who was playing in *Green Altar*?

'*Green Altar*,' said Benny. 'That's just it. Strictly between ourselves, we're negotiating for the film rights of that play. Manfrey had acquired the play as a speculation after it was blitzed off. In fact, we'd as good as bought it.' He shrugged his shoulders resignedly. 'Now we'll have to deal with the executors. But about Manfrey. He'd taken a dislike to this Victor Yarnell. Didn't like his acting, or something, and what does he do but make an express stipulation that if we handled the play, Yarnell shouldn't have his old part, or any other part. What do you think of that?'

'I saw Yarnell in the part,' I said, 'and I thought he gave an absolutely first-class performance. What the devil was Manfrey up to?'

'Pure jealousy,' he said. 'Won't admit there're any young actors worth the name.' He leaned forward again. 'But there was another reason. Yarnell is a very distant relation of his wife. You know about the wife? Well, that was enough to damn him from the start.'

'Well, if I was Yarnell, I'd have been perfectly furious,' I said. 'Did Yarnell know about the stipulation?'

'I had to tell him,' Benny said sorrowfully. 'He's a nice boy is Victor, and I hated hurting his feelings. Only yesterday it was. He took it rather well, though. He's a nice boy, as I said.' He smiled. 'Seems a boy to me. All the difference, Mr Travers, between sixty-five and thirty-five.'

'You've said it, Benny,' I told him.

As for the rest of the time I spent with Benny that afternoon, it doesn't matter. But as soon as I was back in town I tried to locate George, and without success. Then later I got him at the Yard. He'd been busy, and there oughtn't to have been any need to have reminded me. There had been Manfrey's solicitors to get into touch with, and other business contacts to make, and a dozen other things it had never been my lot to think of. So I nipped along to the Yard and saw George there. He wasn't as excited as I'd hoped, and finally I came round to his point of view, which, in his own words, was this.

'Motives don't matter at the moment. What does matter is that he's got a perfect alibi. Bust the alibi and then we can talk about motives.' He nodded himself a pat on the back. 'All the same, that's no reason why we shouldn't give him a fresh overhaul tomorrow morning.'

CHAPTER IV
The Test

I WAS in no hurry to get to Hampstead that morning, even for another sight of Violet Lancing, but I did do some thinking about her when at last I was on my way, and there was one thing which I could not help wondering. There may be something pharisaical about a claim that I am not lasciviously minded. Rabelaisian, yes, if only on occasions, and, thank heaven, I've other vices enough and to spare. And yet in our game it is necessary to be many-minded and to impute to other people the vices which do not happen to encompass one's particular self. That's why I wondered why the lovely Violet had told us so frankly that she hadn't been prepared to take short cuts in her profession.

For she didn't strike me as a woman absolutely devoid of sexual experience. Far from it. She was, as Wharton had not too aptly put it, a woman of the world. That she was a go-getter was shown by her equally frank admission that she had left the screen and become Manfrey's secretary with the view to a back-door entry to the stage. And she must have known Manfrey's reputation in the matter of women. And no one was going to convince me that Manfrey wouldn't ask the usual price for any favours bestowed.

And in that context there was another of Violet's admissions – that she had long since fallen for Victor Yarnell – I can think of no terser expression for it – and that that morning she had deliberately made a pass at him. Was she then not calculating after all? Was she so naive as to imagine that men, men who were flesh and blood and apprehensive as *Julius Caesar* has it, men like Manfrey and Yarnell, would be all agog to grant her free favours? I didn't somehow think so, and that's what made me wonder.

But I forgot all about Violet Lancing when I got out of the station at Hampstead, for I was thinking I would like to go to The Cote by the way that May Clarke had taken after her shopping. It was easy enough to find, and when I reached the gate in

Grove Lane I had a look back at the fairly long straight stretch by which I'd come. I also realized that both the Avenue and the Lane were a kind of deep salient jutting into the Heath. Grove Lane, in other words, ran parallel to the Heath and was separated from it by a straggling fringe of trees.

As for the gate, from which the crazy paving path led to the french window of Manfrey's room and from which a fork branched to the side door of the kitchen, it was set in that Victorian monstrosity, a laurel shrubbery, and those laurels made a dense screen. Then I wondered if there was any communication between Lane and Avenue, and about twenty yards further along I came to it, even if it was only a widish path, bordered by iron railings. And how does all that matter, you may ask? It matters a good deal, that much I can tell you now, though I didn't appreciate the fact at the time. All I was doing was to familiarize myself with the surroundings of The Cote, and that was a routine job and as important in any case as the studying of *terrain* may be to a general in the field.

I peeped into Manfrey's room and then entered. Violet Lancing was just leaving and Broad told me that there had been no variants in her statement. The statements were being taken, by the way, in her room, which made for more intimacy.

George came back from seeing her out and he seemed in quite a good humour. At least he wished me a facetious good-afternoon, and looked at Broad to see if he was appreciating the joke.

'And how was the fair Violet?' I asked.

'In very good form,' he told me, and then, with a sideways nod of the head: 'That woman certainly knows how to dress.'

I pricked my ears.

'Wonder what her income is?'

George shot me a look, and then told me, not too reprovingly, that I had a nasty mind. Then the telephone bell went. And to telescope, as it were, what happened, I'll give you the conversation that followed. Wharton and Nevall were the speakers.

N. Is that Superintendent Wharton?

W. Speaking.

N. Good morning, Superintendent. This is Henry Nevall.

W. Good morning, Mr Nevall. What can I do for you?

N. I've been thinking about that request of yours that I should make some sort of official statement. Doesn't that strike you now as being absolutely unnecessary?

W. Maybe it is, sir, but my instructions always are to get every bit of evidence that has any bearing whatever.

N. Yes, but listen. Anything I could tell you is purely negative. I'm just one of the millions of people who *didn't* see Manfrey yesterday morning.

W. Well, if you feel like that about it, sir, we can let it stand over. But mind you, sir, I can't guarantee what will be the attitude of my superiors. After all, you *are* connected with the case. Your name *was* on that engagement book page. The medical evidence might need support in proving, we'll say, that he had something on his mind and forgot to cancel the engagement or alter the date.

N. Surely, Superintendent, that's straining at a gnat!

W. Maybe, sir, and maybe not. Still, we'll let it stand over, as I said. But I take it you'll be prepared to pass on any information or ideas that happen to crop up?

N. Delighted to.

W. That's all right then, sir. Goodbye.

'Well, what do you think of that,' Wharton asked us. 'What's his idea?'

'Looks to me as if he's being his own counsel and keeping himself out of the witness box,' Broad said.

'I don't know,' I said. 'If I think of myself as a private citizen like Nevall, I know I should be damned annoyed if I had to come here and state officially that I didn't see Manfrey yesterday morning.'

'Even if you and Manfrey weren't on good terms?' asked George.

'Even if you're making Nevall a likely suspect, that doesn't alter my point of view,' I said. 'Find anything pertinent about his movements yesterday morning, or anything contradictory, and then the complexion of the whole thing changes.'

George pursed his lips and gave a long contemplative frown.

'Well,' he said, 'we haven't found anything contradictory – as yet. But we do know he could leave that flat of his without being under observation – if he took only reasonable care.'

'What sort of a flat is it?'

'A very nice place indeed, sir,' Broad told me. 'It's above a little typewriting agency which is closed on Saturday mornings, and you can come out at a side door into Gower Street or go down a fire escape and through Morley Court and into Tottenham Court Road.'

'And what about that visit to the tobacconist?'

'All in order,' he said. 'Nevall hadn't on an overcoat. Only a hat. Just as if he'd slipped out specially. About midday, it was.'

'As an alibi it isn't worth a damn,' Wharton said contemptuously. 'Suppose he was here yesterday morning. That quarrel ceased at about half past eleven, which was when Manfrey was hit on the head. And it was that blow on the temple that killed him, by the way. And it's a hundred to one the poker did it.

'All right, then. Nevall slipped out to Grove Lane. If he walked fast he could be at the station in five minutes, and he needn't have taken the lift. He could have been as near Gower Street as dammit inside a quarter of an hour. He could have gone indoors the back way and then have come out the front way to the tobacconist. Alibi, my foot! And another thing. He was an actor, wasn't he? As soon as he left here he could have disguised his personality – facial expression, if you like. He could have made himself look quite different from any studio portrait we've been hawking round.'

'There's something in that, George,' I said, even if I didn't think there was as much as he thought. Then the front door bell rang, and a glance at my watch told me it would be Yarnell.

*　*　*

He seemed just as nervous, or should I say diffident, as he had on the previous day. Wharton, with a facer all ready for him, was as genial and solicitous as I've ever known him.

'Just as simple, sir, as going into a cookshop, as they used to say in my young days. You're here to help us and we're here to help you. You merely say what happened in those ten minutes yesterday morning, the clerk will type it and then you'll read it through and sign.'

But Yarnell didn't make a move towards that other room. He held his ground and was fidgeting rather nervously. Wharton gave him a look.

'Anything the matter, sir?'

'Well, no,' Yarnell told him. 'I was just wondering something.'

Wharton waited, eyes narrowing in expectation.

'What I was wondering was whether it'd make any difference if I modified the statement I made yesterday morning.'

'None whatever,' said George, metaphorically licking his lips. 'What alteration did you wish to make?'

'Well, it's this,' Yarnell said, and now he was getting to the point he seemed much more at ease. 'When I said I came to see Mr Manfrey about Roger Farnham, that wasn't strictly true. I did come to see him about Farnham, but that was only a blind. I really wanted to see him about something else.'

Wharton let out a breath of disappointment.

'And what was that, sir?'

'Well, I'll tell you what happened. I played in *Green Altar* till it came off this year. Then Manfrey acquired it as a speculation from the executors. Peter Wilson, the author, was killed in the blitz you may remember. Then Imperial Associated wanted to get the screen rights from Manfrey, and what do you think he did? Stipulated that I shouldn't have my original part, as had been planned, or any other part if it comes to that. I didn't know about it till Markstein told me on Friday. I was absolutely furious.'

George was looking like a punctured balloon. I cut in with a question to give him time to recover.

'What were Manfrey's motives?'

Yarnell smiled wryly.

'Well, his wife was a second cousin of mine and we were always pretty friendly. I can't see any other reason.'

'And where is Mrs Manfrey now?'

'Didn't you know?' he said. 'She was in the South of France when the Germans got there. She was interned. The last we heard of her, she was all right.'

'Well, about what happened yesterday morning,' broke in Wharton. 'Perhaps you'll tell us.'

Yarnell said Manfrey had looked very surprised to see him. Yarnell said placatingly that he wouldn't keep him for a minute and he was not calling strictly on business. Manfrey showed him grudgingly in and then asked if it was something about Pamela – Mrs Manfrey. Yarnell said it wasn't. It was a kind of errand of mercy. Then he spoke up for Roger Farnham, but Manfrey said there was nothing doing.

'Then I said I'd be going,' Yarnell went on. 'Then I turned as if I'd only just thought of it and I said, "By the way, why do you dislike me so much?" "Dislike you?" he said. "Aren't you rather flattering yourself?" Well, I couldn't say anything to that. What I did say was that he'd done a dirty trick over barring me from *Green Altar*– the sort of trick that was becoming associated with his name. That's when he simply ignored me. He pushed the bell for his secretary, Miss . . . er . . .'

'Lancing.'

'Miss Lancing and picked up his pen and went on writing as if I wasn't there. And that's all that happened.'

I don't want to labour an anti-climax. Twenty minutes later Yarnell had signed his statement and had gone.

'What do you make of it?' asked George, and almost pitifully. 'What *is* the bloody fellow? A thought reader, or what?'

George rarely swore, but I could sympathize. There he had been anticipating a deliciously ironical drama, and there had been Yarnell coming in and taking the whole show out of his hands.

'What made him change his mind?' asked Broad.

'Don't ask me,' George said. 'He's made his statement and gone, and that's the end of him.'

'You're not the only one who's disappointed,' I told George. 'All the same, I think it was perfectly normal that he should change his mind. The law's a terrifying thing to the layman. He realized he'd told us a lie and I admire his pluck in acknowledging the fact, even if it was only because he was scared we might find out for ourselves.'

'What *is* this?' glared George. 'Sermon for the Third Sunday after Trinity, or what?'

Broad, not used to those little exchanges between George and myself, cut in with the remark that Nevall was now our main stand-by.

'Which reminds me of something, George,' I said. 'Something I think will please you. May Clarke says she ought to know the voice of the man who was quarrelling with Manfrey. Suppose that man was Nevall. Would you care to suggest it to her?'

George frowned, then nodded, then went. It was five minutes before he was back.

'She thinks perhaps it might have been. Then she thinks it mightn't,' he told us indignantly.

'What experience of Nevall has she had?'

'Oh, he used to come here fairly often in the old days.'

'Well, I've got an alternative scheme,' I said. 'Nevall's playing in town at this very moment – in *The Careless Man*. You fix up a couple of seats tomorrow evening for you and May Clarke, and let her hear Nevall speak. Then put the same question.'

George frowned, then brightened.

'Why not?' he said. 'But you take her.'

'I've seen the play, and you haven't.'

'You can stand a second performance,' he said, and then was re-donning his antiquated spectacles. Then he went to the door and hollered for May.

'Mr Travers and I are going now, May,' he told her, with a kind of avuncular look over the spectacle tops. 'We may be in tomorrow and we may not. All we wanted to do was to thank you for your various kindnesses.'

She said it was nothing, but beamed all over her face. 'You go to the theatre much?' George asked her with another avuncular peer.

'Not lately, sir. I don't like the black-out.'

'What would you say if – as a small mark of appreciation – I met you here with the car tomorrow evening and we went to see –' He looked round at me. 'What was the play? A very good one, I'm told.'

'*The Careless Man,*' I duly prompted.

'That's it – *The Careless Man*. And no dressing up to the nines,' he warned her. 'Just your best bib and tucker and' – the avuncular look became positively roguish – 'just wash behind your ears.'

'Oh, sir,' she said. 'As if I shouldn't!'

There was nothing new till the Monday morning. George had paid a quick visit to the solicitors, and on his way back he dropped in to see me. Broad was at the inquest, which was going to end with a formal adjournment, and The Cote was more or less out of bounds that morning, with a conference there of parties interested in Manfrey's various enterprises, and, of course, the solicitors. Violet, I thought, would be having a great time.

'What's going to happen to the house?' I asked George.

'May's being kept on as caretaker,' he said. 'She's got a sister who was blitzed last year, who's coming back from the country to keep her company.'

'And what about Violet?'

'Don't know,' he said. 'Now Manfrey's gone I don't think she'll be keen on another secretarial job. Shouldn't be surprised if she follows up on Yarnell and tries to get him to work her a stage or screen job.'

Curious how we don't give other people credit for having the same perspicacity in things we've come to regard as our own peculiar property. I thought George had been a long way from an accurate summing-up of Violet, and yet there he was, hitting my own nail shrewdly on the head.

'By the way, we checked up on that Roger Farnham Yarnell said he was interested in,' George went on. 'Everything's O.K. there.'

'And nothing fresh about Nevall?'

'Never a thing,' he said.

'And who are Manfrey's heirs?'

'Nothing doing there,' he said. 'The heirs are two nephews, sons of two of his sisters. One's in North Africa and the other's a naval Commander somewhere on the high seas.'

'Any idea how much money Manfrey left?'

'Between twenty and thirty thousand,' George said. 'Not so much as you might have thought. Still it's better than a slap in the belly with a wet cod-fish.'

Then he began giving me advice and instructions about that visit to the theatre with May, and I let him run on. George has never quite accepted the evolution of myself from the apprentice stage, but it does me no harm to listen and it gives him pleasure to talk.

'What shall we do if she does recognize Nevall's voice?' he wanted to know. 'Try to get her to come to the Yard?'

'Why not this?' I said. 'The show starts at six-thirty, and I understand it's over at nine o'clock. Collona's little place will be open, so why not get her to have a bit of supper there, and you can happen to be there at the same time.'

George thought that a good enough idea and he left me to book a table. Then I had nothing to do with myself till the car came for me at about half past five. We picked up May at The Cote. I had to explain that Wharton had been detained, and that I'd come in his place. I think she didn't regard the exchange as any too good, but she soon got over her disappointment. She was pretty excited about the outing, for one thing, and even going to the theatre in a private car was a thrill.

When the car drew up at the theatre there was a quick conference. I swept May off her feet by saying that of course she must have something to eat before going back home, and it would be a pleasure instead of trouble. Then the driver was told to be outside Collona's in Langford Street at a quarter past ten, and into the theatre the two of us went.

We hadn't overdone things by getting too expensive seats, but May found the middle of the stalls a bit overpowering. By the time the curtain went up she was sitting there with as much aplomb as if it had been the gallery. Maybe the fact that she had met both Henry Nevall and the leading lady in what might be called the private life of The Cote had something to do with the complacency with which she settled herself in her seat.

I'm not going to bore you with an act by act story of the play. All I will do is give you a synopsis, and from that you may derive precious little satisfaction since a good play is not necessarily a good story. But *The Careless Man* was certainly original, even if it dealt with a lower middle class family and though its title wasn't too apt.

There was a mother whom we did not meet, and a family of two sons and two daughters, whose ages ranged from eighteen to twenty-five. The mother had been an interfering, overbearing woman who had made the life of the family a miserable affair. She had ruined, for instance, one daughter's love affair and put the second well on the way to divorce. She had hounded the youngest son into a job that he hated, and nagged the elder son for his greyhound-racing and dart-throwing hobbies.

But the mother was dead and the curtain rose on the evening after the funeral, with all the family taking a new breath and discussing the reorganization of their separate lives. The father – played by Nevall – was one of those mild-spoken and apparently colourless men, but the curious thing about him was that he gloried in no emancipation. He remained what he had been: quiet, easy-going and unambitious, and still feeling the invisible presence of the woman who had made his life a long subservience.

So while his children rejoiced in liberty and even turned it into licence, he remained the same. And that led to talk among the family, especially when he refused to fit himself into the schemes they had arranged for him. There were wonderings and whisperings in corners. This was remembered and that, and slowly the audience gathered what was at last in their minds.

And, of course, there was the natural revulsion of feelings towards the dead tyrant, viewed now in a romantic light and possessing virtues she herself would never have claimed. And so to the really great third act where, in spite of themselves, the family force things into the open.

'What if I did kill her?' says the father. 'If I did, it wasn't for me but for you.' Then he turns on them and shows them just what they are. Let them go to the police. Let them do what they like. Even if they don't the house is theirs, for he's going, and at once. Where to? That's his business, he says. That's the only secret he's been able to treasure for years, and the curtain falls with his exit.

I've made none too good a hand of telling you that story. I haven't conveyed, perhaps, the slowly growing change in that emancipated family and the as slowly growing tension as the truth dawns on them. I'd seen the play before, as you know, and yet I think I was more interested at that second seeing. As for May Clarke, you could scarcely hear her breathe, and when we came out and were walking the few yards to Collona's she was still in something of a daze.

'Well, what did you think of it?' I asked her.

'It was fine, sir,' she said. 'I don't know when I've seen anything like it. Made me absolutely miserable, though.'

Then she was asking what I reckoned the father was intending to do, and hoping he wouldn't have the police on his track. I gave it as my opinion that the family would never tell the police and that the father was going at last to have something of a good time. That cheered her up and it brought us to Collona's.

I spotted George as soon as we went in, and there was tremendous surprise. It is an unpretentious restaurant and we had quite a simple meal, with George asking May about the show. What had struck her most was that tremendous scene when Nevall had rounded on the family and had put them in their place, as she said.

'Nevall's got a very fine voice,' George said quietly.

'He has, sir,' she said, and then she suddenly remembered. She made as if to speak, but the words didn't just come.

'Anything strike you about his voice?' George said, his tone just as idly conversational.

'I hardly like to say it,' she said, 'but I'm sure it was him I heard with Mr Manfrey. When he shouted at that son of his it was just like what I heard.'

'That's interesting,' George said. 'He and Mr Manfrey quarrelling on the Saturday morning.'

He pursed his lips and then made what I thought was a false move. May wasn't the sort to be hustled.

'You thought a good deal of Mr Manfrey?' he asked her, leaning forward.

'Well, sir, he was quite a good master, taking him all round.'

'And you'd like to see us get the one who killed him?' That startled her, and George knew too late that he'd gone to work the wrong way.

'I don't know what you mean.'

'Well, it's simple,' he said. 'You say you're sure it was Mr Nevall who was quarrelling with Mr Manfrey at half past eleven on Saturday morning. All you need to do is sign a simple statement to that effect.'

'Oh, I couldn't do that!'

Wheedle as he might, George couldn't budge her. Then she thought of something else to make things worse.

'Would I have to give evidence if they had him up?'

'Just a matter of form,' he said. 'You wouldn't be in the witness box more than a couple of minutes. All you'd have to do was say you recognized his voice.'

That scared her finally off. She didn't change her mind about recognizing Nevall's voice, but she got to the stage of insisting that what she'd said had been in confidence. George didn't argue. It was well after a quarter past ten and he knew he was up against a brick wall.

We saw her off in the car and meanwhile had done our best to wipe Nevall from her mind.

'And what now?' I asked George as we strolled along in the dark towards Leicester Square.

'I'll slip up and see her in the morning,' he said. 'Maybe she'll feel differently after she's thought it over. And I might try the publicity angle. Get her to see her name in the papers and her photograph. That might fetch her.'

I said it might, though I didn't think it would. And there we left it. George was proposing to get to Hampstead at about ten o'clock and he'd call and report to me on the way back.

CHAPTER V
Here Endeth

As soon as Wharton arrived on that Tuesday morning I knew he'd had no luck with May Clarke. Whatever thinking she had done had only tended to make her even more scared of the witness box, and she had even withdrawn her statement to us that she was sure the voice in Manfrey's room had been Nevall's. Now she was saying that she wasn't sure, and pleading that she couldn't swear to something of which she wasn't certain.

George couldn't make up his mind as to what should be done about it. I suggested a call on Nevall and a certain amount of bluffing. George said he daren't go even that far on his own initiative. Rules of evidence were clearly laid down, and to deviate from them with a man with the possible influence of Nevall would be asking for trouble. Finally he said he'd have a word with what he called the Powers-that-Be, and he'd let me know the result.

It was at about three o'clock that afternoon when he rang me, and a few minutes later I was in his car and on the way to Gower Street.

'I don't want you to say a word except just the ordinary politenesses,' he told me. 'You just sit and look grim, if that isn't too much to ask of you. I'll do all the talking.'

That suited me, and it wouldn't be the first time I'd been the audience for George's Pooh-Bah. Also I realized it was going to be a ticklish business, and that his was the sole responsibility for the way things went.

It didn't take us long to get to Gower Street. Nevall was expecting us, and it was he who opened the door on the landing at the head of the stairs that ran up by the shop. He seemed quite at his ease, perhaps because he was doing most of the talking. He told us, for instance, that his man had been called up and he now had to depend on a daily woman who came in on five mornings a week. Most of his meals he had at a nearby hotel or at his club.

'You've got a perfectly charming place here, Mr Nevall,' I told him. 'So quiet too.'

He agreed that it wasn't a bad spot, though far too large for his now simple tastes. And while we were chattering like that, there was George like a silent menace in the background, aloof and official and ultimately not to be put off.

'Now, Mr Nevall, we'll settle this business of ours and then leave you,' he broke in. 'You're a busy man and so am I.'

Nevall hastily indicated a chair and I found one for myself. Now that George was coming to that unknown business which he had mentioned, Nevall seemed suddenly less assured. He brushed imaginary dust from his jacket with his fingers, and as George began to speak, those fingers were still fidgeting with this and that.

'I'll come straight to the point,' George said. 'What I'm going to say is entirely without prejudice, and the same applies to what you say too. Nothing underhand, Mr Nevall, and no trickery. A confidential talk and, I repeat, entirely without prejudice on both sides. You agree?'

'Most certainly,' Nevall told him. 'But isn't all this rather mysterious?'

'One-sided, up to the moment, if you like,' George told him. 'But to get back to last Saturday morning. By the original arrangement you were seeing Manfrey at eleven-thirty, whatever he wrote in his engagement book. But you didn't see him because you'd changed the call to the Sunday and he'd agreed. That is correct, so far?'

'Perfectly correct,' Nevall told him, though somewhat warily. He was now leaning back in the easy chair, his fingers slowly caressing his chin.

'You'd state that in any court of law on oath?'

'Why not?' He smiled almost amusedly. 'I'd swear in any court in Europe that I haven't spoken to Manfrey face to face for a good many weeks and that I haven't set foot in his house for as many months and more.'

'That clears the air,' George told him. 'And it brings me to the real reason for our visit. What I'm going to tell you is extremely confidential. I hope you won't take it amiss when I say that it's my duty to warn you –'

I break off there, though George didn't break off, because I want to convey something to you. He had said nothing to me of the line he was going to take with Nevall, and when he came out with that phrase about it being his duty to warn, I heard it with very much of a start. I also happened to be watching Nevall, and it startled him too, for his fingers tightened about his chin, and his eyes narrowed watchfully.

'. . . my duty to warn you of the consequences to yourself if anything gets out. I believe you to be a man of honour, and I'm sure you'll take the warning the right way. It concerns private information, as I said, and about what was heard in Manfrey's room at about eleven-thirty last Saturday morning. There was the sound of a violent quarrel. To be more explicit, it was a man's voice, and this man was apparently defending himself against some charge that Manfrey was bringing. Then the quarrel suddenly ceased, and that's the moment when we think Manfrey was killed. You're following me so far?'

'Certainly,' said Nevall, and strangely enough he now seemed merely inquisitive, as it were, and anxious to hear the rest.

'Now we come to the real point,' George went on. 'We have a witness. One who overheard some of that conversation. You've probably gathered that we must have had. But this witness is of the opinion that the voice she heard in Manfrey's room was your own.'

Nevall stared. He leaned forward.

'Would you mind repeating that?'

Wharton repeated it, and waited.

'Let me think this out,' Nevall said, and suddenly got to his feet. Then as quickly as if he had thought of something he sat down again.

'You yourself can't possibly credit that story,' he told Wharton bluntly. 'I'm not familiar with all the ways the law works, but I'm pretty sure that if you had a reliable witness you'd be putting me under arrest.'

'Not necessarily,' Wharton said. 'I'll go further and put more cards on the table. A single witness against an accused person more often than not means a cancelling out. That's one reason why I prefer to tell you in confidence about this witness and to give you the opportunity to make your own observations. Say, if you like, that we prefer your word to that of our witness.'

'That's very handsome of you,' Nevall said frankly. 'I'll take back a question I'd intended to put to you – whether all this wasn't some kind of bluff. As to my own observations, as you call them, you've had them already. I'm prepared to swear on any oath whatever, that except over the telephone I haven't spoken to Manfrey for over a month, and I haven't set foot in his house for a very long time. Just how long I can't at the moment say. A year or more perhaps.'

'That satisfies me,' Wharton said, and then Nevall cut in again.

'As for signing a statement to that effect, well, I'm quite agreeable.'

'No necessity, sir. No necessity at all,' Wharton assured him. 'All this has been without prejudice and I'm glad it's cleared the air. You anything to ask, Mr Travers?'

I said I couldn't think of anything, unless Mr Nevall had changed his mind about giving us the names of any people who might have considered the killing of Manfrey advantageous. Nevall shook his head.

'I *could* tell you one or two,' he said, 'but I'd rather not. That sort of thing is not much in my line. But I will tell you perfectly frankly that Manfrey's death wasn't wholly disadvantageous where I personally am concerned. If you wish details I can give them to you.'

Wharton waved them aside, and that was that. A couple of minutes later we were back in the car.

'What do you make of him?' he asked me.

'I think he was telling the truth,' I said. 'I also think he knows a damn sight more than he pretends. I'd even go so far as to say he's scared of us finding out just what it is he knows.'

'You think May Clarke was wrong?'

'If Nevall is telling the truth, then she *must* be wrong,' I said. 'Mistaken is perhaps a better word.'

And that, as far as I was concerned, was virtually the end of the Manfrey Case. Does that come to you as something of a shock? It came as still more of a shock to me, though the collapse of the Case was a bit less sudden. For all the things that remained to do were only in the nature of painstaking inquiry, and out of my province. And there was I with days left of my leave and nothing to do except ask George Wharton every now and again if there was anything new.

But everything was negative. No proof could be found that Nevall had left his flat that morning before the time he had stated. Nothing was discovered about Nevall personally to discredit his private reputation, which was that of quite a nice if somewhat colourless individual. Nor was any trace discovered of any other caller. That tweed jacket, too, was never found. The murderer couldn't have taken it, and substituted the alpaca one because there was blood on it, for practically no blood had even seeped from the wound. And in any case Manfrey hadn't been wearing that tweed coat when he was attacked.

Then I put up a theory which wasn't any good to us. Manfrey *had* expected some caller that morning. The previous night he had gone up to bed with the alpaca jacket on, and he had come down in it. Then remembering the caller he had taken the tweed coat out of the drawer or cupboard where he had put it, and had donned it ready for the caller. Something had happened to it when Manfrey was killed, and the murderer had made the substitution and had taken it with him. But as a theory, that was neither ingenious nor useful, if the jacket was not in our possession for examination and deduction.

But though there will be certain appendices to the Case, the last I heard about it before going back from leave was George's final theory, which was that some unknown caller who knew the house and its ways, had seen the last of its occupants leave that morning and had then rung the bell and been admitted by Manfrey. But though there were extensive inquiries into the ramifications of Manfrey's affairs, and one or two likely persons were questioned, nothing came of that theory. As for the final inquest verdict, that was 'Murder by some person or persons unknown'. As for the appendices which I mentioned, here they are.

In 1943 I was demobilized for reasons of health. There had been a nasty accident with a grenade, and after that pneumonia, and it was while I was convalescing from the latter that I happened to run across Benny Markstein.

'How's Victor Yarnell?' I happened to ask him. 'Don't you remember the last time I saw you, and your telling me about Manfrey playing him that dirty trick about *Green Altar*?'

'I remember,' he said, and frowned. 'He divorced his wife, you know, or rather she divorced him.'

'Really?' I said. 'And did he marry again?'

'Yes, and with what's known as indecent haste,' said Benny. 'And who do you think he married?' Then he shook his head. 'But you wouldn't know her. A girl named Lancing. I was at the reception and I thought I recognized her. She'd been with us for a time at Gerrards Cross.'

'What sort of a girl is she?'

Benny's lip curled.

'I don't think she'll be much use to Victor. Very showy, but –' He shook his head for the rest and then his expression changed. 'Did you know his first wife?'

'I didn't,' I said.

'A charming girl,' he said. 'Not as handsome as this Lancing woman, mind you, but very attractive all the same.'

He shook his head again. 'I can't make out what Victor was up to, leaving a woman like that.'

'Love is blind and a hell of a lot of other things,' I told him.

'You've said it, Mr Travers,' he told me feelingly.

So much for that little chat with Benny Markstein. When I mentioned the matter to George Wharton, I found that he already knew, for the Manfrey Case had merely been docketed, not abandoned, and anything that seemed to have a bearing was duly noted. But George didn't forget his prediction of well over a year before.

'Didn't I tell you she'd follow up Yarnell?' he said, referring to Violet Lancing. 'That woman was a thruster if I ever saw one. Didn't take the Old Gent long to sum her up.'

'True enough, George,' I said. 'And has anything else happened to do with the Case?'

'Never a thing,' he told me, and that again was that.

In the autumn of 1944 I was doing a whole-time job at the Yard, not through any merits of my own. But it was in an unofficial capacity that I had my next news of Yarnell.

It was first of all a bald notice in a casualty list.

YARNELL, LT V. – *Regt. Previously reported missing. Now reported killed in action.*

Then the following day there was an appreciation by a friend. But all it gave was a brief summary of his career, and as I was interested in the man generally and puzzled as to why he had joined up, I made it my business to run across Benny Markstein again.

Benny remembered our last talk about Yarnell. He spread his palms, shrugged his shoulders and reminded me of what he had said about Violet Lancing.

He didn't know the actual truth, he said, but he was certain that his guesses weren't far out. They were to the effect that that marriage had been a failure from the start. Violet had married him as a stepping-stone and not for his own sweet self, and that must have come as a shock when he knew it for truth. His contract with Imperial Associated had just expired, and less than two months after the marriage, he had joined up. Previously he had been deferred, so that the joining up was wholly voluntary. The whole thing was a tragedy, Benny said, and we left it at that.

'What's his new wife doing?' I asked him, and he seemed surprised that I didn't know. She had already had a small part or two on the stage, and then he was exasperatedly tapping his skull as if to force back something to his mind.

'Who was it told me?' he asked himself, and then clicked his tongue annoyedly. 'The older I get, the less I remember. But maybe it's that thriller of Tom Harris's at the Royalty she's in. Just a walking-on part, but it's something.'

Then in March of 1945 I happened to read a criticism of *The Parting Guest*, a new play at the Albany. It was Nevall's name that caught my eye, and he, it said, had been superb as the bishop. Then came the following:

> Violet Lancing more than justified the good opinions held of her by giving a devastating – or should it be ravishing – study of the love-lorn typist. Miss Lancing, unless I am uncommonly wide of the mark, is going to make the public sit up and take notice. All the same I shudder to think what would happen to British Industry if all typists were as gorgeous as Violet Lancing.

I didn't see that play. For one thing it was not in my special line, and for another I had no desire to witness a triumph, however minor, of the fair Violet. And I was not so sure that I shouldn't have thought of her not as fair only, but as fair and frail – if you get my meaning.

Maybe that was mere spite, but I didn't know. I thought of her career as I'd known it, and I thought of what Benny Markstein had told me. The British public, sitting up and taking notice, wouldn't know just what it had taken to get Violet Lancing where she now was. I was practically sure she'd been Manfrey's mistress, and I certainly hadn't any doubt that she'd taken

Yarnell from his wife. And to say that she hadn't actually killed Yarnell himself would be merely begging the question.

I got an ironic satisfaction about showing George Wharton that notice, and I expect he had it duly filed. He'd known about Yarnell's death, and he told me what I didn't know – that he'd been killed in Italy.

And that's the end. For the life of me I can think of nothing I've concealed from you. And looking back now I can honestly state that in my judgement it was sufficient for the police at least to have solved the problem of the killing of Manfrey. That it didn't was due principally to bad luck in the matter of intuitions – those little flashes of inspiration that come from nowhere, and make thick fog into broad daylight.

Perhaps you've had intuitions of your own. You may have beaten us at our own game and solved, to your own satisfaction at least, the murder of Charles Manfrey. But even if you have, there is just the possibility that your solution may be wrong, and you, too, may be glad of a Second Chance.

PART II

CHAPTER VI
A Case of Blackmail

IN THE JULY of 1945 I retired from my special work at the Yard, with the understanding that I should be on tap if at any time my services were specially needed. It had been agreed between George Wharton and myself that as soon as the European war was over, he would retire; but the consequent clearing up was a long business and he did not expect to be free till late autumn.

That suited my book exceedingly well. George and I were going into the private detective business, and it so happened that the premises in St Martin's which we were proposing to use were not free till about the same time. Then there would be certain alterations to make, and what with the operation of the £10 limit and the shortage of labour, we didn't anticipate getting settled in much before Christmas. But if there was a longer delay, then there was the chance of operating elsewhere, and I'll explain about that later.

George and I had gone into things pretty thoroughly, not that we considered there was an inordinate deal of risk. George had been careful all his life, not to say frugal, and I knew he had quite a substantial nest-egg in addition to what would be a really good pension. And he had the good sense to look at things from another angle – that of spending his leisure time. With luck he had a good span of life still ahead, and he is the sort that inactivity always frets and irks.

I was in very much the same boat, and when I say that my wife was all in favour of the scheme, it shows that she too had ideas about the use of my abundant and possibly fretful leisure. As for the capital I was able to put into the new business, there I touch wood and whisper in the strictest confidence that even if Beveridge and the Commissioners of Inland Revenue do their worst, I shall still be reasonably safe from the workhouse. In any case, as my wife has fortunately money of her own, I can call myself something of a freelance financially.

But it took a good deal of preliminary inquiry and assessment before we decided that our enterprise was going to pay. I think that if we'd known we weren't actually going to lose money we'd have been satisfied, but prospects were very much better than that. The prestige of George's name would put business in our way. Thanks to family connexions and a private pull, we should be handling the inquiry business of one of the largest Fire Insurance Companies. And both of us had the idea that there would be a lot of business involving inquiry about missing persons. Men might have been officially reported missing, but their relatives would still have hope of life, and in the chaos of Europe there would be hundreds of men whose appearance would be something of the nature of a resurrection.

And we had yet another sheet anchor – Bill Ellice. Bill had owned the Broad Street Detective Agency for about thirty years, and though a small concern it was a thriving one. I had used it on various occasions and had confidently recommended it, and I had come to know Bill Ellice pretty well. One sign of its stability was the fact that throughout the war it was about the only agency of the kind that consistently advertised, though in its modest pre-war way.

Things get around, heaven knows how. Bill had heard about me and Wharton and I'd heard that he was selling his agency, and so we got together, and the upshot was that I secured an option. That meant that if we couldn't open in St Martin's, we could carry on in Broad Street, but what we were hoping to do was to open as originally intended, and to make Bill's agency the nucleus of the new one. There would be modifications, of course. Bill had undertaken anything, divorce cases included, even if they'd formed no great part of the business. We were definitely cutting out divorce. And not because we were superior or too pure minded. It was only that it isn't too good an advertisement for a high-class agency when the public reads in its newspapers what the detective saw through the keyhole.

Bill and I knew and trusted each other. He knew and I knew that we should buy the business, option or no option, and that's why I became a kind of apprentice, and began spending quite a lot of my time in Broad Street. Bill hadn't any objections. He was short-handed for one thing, and a gregarious soul for another, and it was an unspoken part of the bargain that I should learn the business from inside. So he was pleased and I was pleased. You too will be pleased, if only to learn that here end the preliminaries. Now you know the lie of the land, we're ready for the affair of the frightened lady.

On a certain evening in late September, my telephone bell rang. It was Bill Ellice, wanting to know if I was busy. If I wasn't, then he'd slip along and see me. I asked him if he'd had a meal, and he said he hadn't, so I told him to come along at once and have a meal of sorts with me.

Bill was a heavily built man of about sixty-five: far more shrewd witted that his weight suggested, and with as good a business head as I've known. He didn't look at all worried when he came in, and that naturally made me wonder what had made his visit so urgent. Then as soon as the two service dinners arrived he told me.

'A pity you weren't in this morning,' he said. 'Then you'd have been in on this from the start. It's a blackmail job, and I don't like it.'

'You mean this particular case, or blackmail generally?' I asked him.

'Both,' he said. 'I got myself in bad once with the police over a blackmail case, and it taught me a lesson. And black-mail isn't a matter for a private agency, Mr Travers, if you ask me. It's a matter for the police, and the police only. The law gives secrecy and protection, and that's what we can't do. And I don't like it in what you might call an ethical way. An unscrupulous firm handling a blackmail case might get information which might lead to more blackmail. Bleeding the client with high charges, for instance.'

I quite agreed.

'That's why I thought I'd come and see you and get your advice,' he said. 'You're in a stronger position than I am. I know I'm pretty well in with the Yard, but you're right in. And you'd have Superintendent Wharton's backing.'

'I wouldn't be too sure,' I said. 'But the actual case, Bill. What was it?'

'It began this morning, at about ten o'clock,' he said. 'I answered the phone and there was a woman on the line. Educated voice and all that, and quite young by the sound of her. Say in the thirties.'

Then he was bringing out his pocket book and handing me a sheet of paper.

'Just before I came away I wrote down the conversation as near as I could remember it. You read it for yourself.'

B.E. Yes, madam. This is the Broad Street Detective Agency. The managing director speaking.

X. Can one rely on your firm working in very strict confidence?

B.E. Confidence – secrecy if you like, madam – is the one essential thing. You can rely on us as you'd rely on your doctor or your lawyer, or a priest.

X. Then you'd be prepared to look after the interests of anyone who was being blackmailed? *(She lowered her voice so much there that I only just caught her words.)*

B.E. Most certainly. But you understand that I should first of all have to ask you for a personal interview.

X. Yes, of course. And when could you see me?

B.E. That's for you to say, madam. Our time is entirely at your disposal.

X Ten o'clock tomorrow morning?

B.E. Very good, madam. Ten o'clock tomorrow morning, and I'll see you personally. And would you mind giving me the name? In the strictest confidence, of course.

X. Upson. Mrs Jane Upson.

B.E. Thank you madam. And the address?

X. 5 Selkirk Street, Westminster. It's just off Great Smith Street.

That was all. Bill said she had hesitated before giving the address, and he'd put that down to a natural disinclination to tell too much at one time. Then later in the day he'd given the whole business a good deal of thought. Finally he'd sent a man of his – and a good man at that – to see what kind of a place 5 Selkirk Street was, and to pick up anything useful about Mrs Upson.

'And what do you think happened, Mr Travers?'

'There was no such place and no such person?' I ventured. He shook his head.

'Not quite so bad as that. But that Number Five was a tobacconist's. Just an accommodation address where people can get their letters.'

I gave a Whartonian grunt.

'A bit fishy. Very fishy, in fact. And what's going to happen, do you think? She won't turn up tomorrow and you'll hear no more about her?'

'I don't know,' he said. 'Somehow I'm inclined to think she'll turn up all right. If she does, what do you advise?'

'Hear all she has to say,' I said, 'and then if you feel that way, turn the case down.'

'Yes,' he said, but rather reluctantly, as if he didn't want after all to turn away what might be good – and safe – business. 'But why shouldn't you come along, Mr Travers, and hear what she has to say? You can be in that inside room. You'll hear everything there, even if you don't see much.'

'Isn't there a buzzer through to your secretary's office?'

'There is,' he said, and gave me an inquiring look.

'Then what about this,' I said. 'I'll be there and listen to what she has to say. If I think the case is worth going on with, I can arrange a system of calls to tell you so. And one other thing. If she gave you a phoney address, she might have given you a phoney name. Why not have a man ready to tail her as soon as she leaves your office?'

Ethical was a favourite word of Bill's and he didn't think that particularly ethical. I thought so too, though what I said was that he could not afford to be narrow-minded. He needed protection against his client, and if he took the case there would soon come a moment when he'd have to ask her to be far more frank. Knowing her real name and address would be a good lever. It could even be a good reason for deciding after all not to undertake the case.

That was how we left it, and when Bill went home I began thinking things over for myself. And I had to acknowledge, if with not too many twinges of conscience that like the famous Frenchman I'd used a good deal of speech to conceal as much thought. Strictly speaking I ought to have advised Bill to have nothing to do with the case, but the Old Adam of curiosity had been too much for me. That was why I was feeling a positive excitement as I made my way towards Broad Street the following morning.

Well before ten o'clock we'd perfected our system of signals. I would buzz the secretary and she would buzz Bill. Two quick buzzes meant he was not to touch that case with a ten-foot pole. Four meant carry on, and it was to involve a message back to the secretary which she'd understand as a signal for the man to stand by who was to be on the client's tail.

As for the little room in which I was to be posted, its one window overlooked the cobbled yard of a wholesale ware-house. But the door into Bill's room had panels of three-ply, and we found that every word spoken in his sanctum could be distinctly heard by me. Ten minutes before zero hour found me installed, and I was to have a quarter of an hour to wait. And somehow I wasn't quite so enthusiastic, for it seemed to me in the quiet of that room and in the cold light of morning that I ought to have advised Bill from the beginning to have nothing to do with that client, and if that client was as untrustworthy as she had shown herself in the matter of the false address, then Bill might find himself badly let down. Such a client might even bring false accusations against him and his firm. Even if that didn't embroil him with the police, it would be damning publicity in a court of law.

Hitherto I had had the law behind me, and I had even been the law itself, and that had made me sure of my way. Now I was a private citizen, and if anything happened to Bill, then the responsibility would be mine. And yet that insatiable curiosity of mine was still keeping me back, and I was telling myself that it was folly to close down on a client while things were perfectly safe, and before that client had disclosed anything whatever about the nature of the blackmail. It might be something perfectly trivial, though lucrative enough from Bill's point of view. And then before I could make up my mind to take a belated action, I heard Bill's voice.

And since I didn't see his client, perhaps it will be better if I give the conversation as I took it down in shorthand. Action will be only deduced, but tones of voice were naturally clear enough to me. I should add that Bill has a perfect bedside manner. He is quiet, sympathetic, and exuding nevertheless an air of absolute competence and optimism.

B. Mrs Upson? . . . Very pleased to see you. Will you sit down? I'm Ellice, by the way, the managing director. I expect you recognize my voice.

C. Yes, I do.

B. And about this work which you were good enough to ask us to undertake for you, Mrs Upson. Would you like to tell me precisely what it is?

C. *(After a definite pause.)* You can really assure me that everything's going to be in the strictest confidence?

B. Even stricter than that, Mrs Upson. I shall probably handle the matter myself. If I need help then it will be by an employee I can trust as I'd trust myself. Even if you came into this room, Mrs Upson, and confided in me that you'd committed a murder and were being blackmailed in consequence, that would make no difference to me. I might decline to handle the case, but what you'd told me would never get outside this room. That's the only possible way a business like this can be run. Absolute confidence on both sides.

C. *(With a little laugh.)* Oh, but it's nothing so serious as that.

B. I'm sure it isn't. I was merely quoting an extreme case. But perhaps you'd tell me all about it in your own words.

C. Well, it's about something to do with my husband and myself. *(Another little laugh.)* Perhaps I was indiscreet, but I wouldn't like my husband to know. I didn't think anybody knew, and then, the day before yesterday – in the early evening it was – someone rang up. It was a man's voice and I haven't the faintest idea who it was, and he told me everything I'd done. It absolutely frightened me to death.

B. The man himself. What sort of a voice was it? Educated, for instance?

C. Oh yes. But it was sort of thick, as if he had a cold.

B. I see. And then he proceeded to utter threats?

C. Well, not really. When he'd finished telling me what he said he knew, he said I'd know more next morning, and then he rang off. Oh yes, and he said I'd better have a night to think things over. Then in the morning there was a letter.

B. You've brought it with you?

C. I'm sorry, but I was so frightened that I burnt it. I did copy down something it said – that I was to put a notice in the *Daily Tribune* if I agreed to what he said. It was 'Terms accepted – Polly'. In the Personal Column, of course.

B. Any mention of money?

C. Yes, it said I must be prepared to hand over in small notes the sum of five hundred pounds, and in the course of the next few days.

B. And what was to happen after you'd put the advertisement in the paper?

C. He was going to telephone me.

B. I see. I think I've got the general idea. And that brings me to a very important matter. You and I have got to talk to each other, Mrs Upson, as doctor and patient. If you keep anything back, then it's impossible for me to look after your interests. This business for which you're being blackmailed, for instance. Exactly what did you do? . . . Don't be alarmed, Mrs Upson. Morals don't interest me. The only thing that does interest me is protecting you against blackmail.

C. Well, it wasn't anything very serious. But my husband's a very jealous man, and I'm sure he'd absolutely break up our home.

B. Let's be frank. If he had the information, it would give him grounds for divorce?

C. Well, perhaps, yes. And I couldn't stand the scandal. I'm doing some very important work, and it might mean losing that, too.

B. You're not inclined to throw yourself on the mercy of your husband?

C. Oh, but he wouldn't believe me. He'd simply go raving mad. You've no idea how he acts.

B. Well, I propose something else. I hope you'll understand why I'm doing it, Mrs Upson, because it may sound remarkably foolish to you, my turning away a client.

C. But why should you do that?

B. I'm not, Mrs Upson. What I'm advising you to do is to go direct to the police. Everything would be confidential and they'd protect your interests.

C. But I can't do that. The letter warned me against going to the police. I tell you I was absolutely at my wits' end, and when I saw your advertisement, it was just like a god-send. Besides, even if I did go to the police and they caught this man, I'd have to go to court and someone might recognize me. And my husband would be bound to find out. I even believe he's had people following me already.

B. Your husband may know you're here in this office at this moment?

C. *(Another little laugh.)* Oh, no. I didn't mean that. But I do think he had me followed before, and if he was suspicious about anything, he'd do it again. That's why I took such precautions to come here this morning.

B. I see. . . . A remarkably ticklish business.

(That was when I pushed the buzzer four times. Almost at once came the buzzing in Bill's room.)

Excuse me a moment, Mrs Upson. . . . Yes? . . . Yes, you can get on with it. . . . Simply say I'll see him later. Sorry about that interruption, Mrs Upson.

C. It's quite all right.

B. About the best thing to do. I think I'd better insert that notice in the paper for you. That will take that much off your mind. You agree?

C. Yes, I'll be very glad.

B. If I get on with that at once, the blackmailer will almost certainly ring you tomorrow morning. I shall rely on you to get in touch with me immediately after. You agree again?

C. Yes, of course.

B. After that we can decide on our next actions. What will probably happen is that he'll suggest a place of meeting where you can hand over the money. That means that I should be able to get hold of him. But that will be for me to work out. The real thing is, what do you wish me to say to him once I've got him. We'll take it, by the way, that getting him, as I put it, involves a knowledge of his identity. All the same, what line do you wish me to take?

C. I hardly know – really. But if you knew who he was, couldn't you threaten to go to the police unless he gave assurances that he'd drop the whole thing? And, of course, make sure he didn't go to my husband out of spite.

B. Yes, I think that might be managed. It would have been easier, of course, if you'd kept his letter. And that's one thing I must impress on you, Mrs Upson, as your adviser. If he ever writes again, even if it's only a tiny note, see that I have it at once.

C. I will. I promise you that I will.

B. And when he telephones, make an effort to remember every word he says. By the way, could you let me have your telephone number in case I want to get hold of you in a hurry? You can rely on me being most discreet.

C. Oh, but I couldn't. I daren't risk my husband hearing anything. And I don't trust the maid. And, of course, *I'm* out a good deal.

B. Well, perhaps we can get over that. Meanwhile I shall be expecting to hear from you the moment this man rings you with any definite suggestions. Oh, and one other rather personal question. *(It was a wily one, bringing the lady to the matter of payment.)* While I'm not suggesting that there's the slightest chance of this blackmailer getting five hundred pounds out of you, or even a penny, could you raise that five hundred pounds if you were put to it? Say if we had to use it as a kind of decoy?

C. *(After quite a pause.)* Perhaps I could. You'd have to wait a day or two, though.

B. That would be all right. . . . And that, I think, Mrs Upson, seems to be about all, for the moment.

C. *(After a shuffling of chairs.)* May I pay you now for my visit, Mr Ellice?

B. *(A smile in his voice.)* Well, we don't do business just like that, Mrs Upson. It's usual to pay a preliminary retaining fee. In your case, ten pounds. After that, and when the case is settled to your satisfaction, we agree on a final fee. If the case takes longer than we've anticipated – and I may say I'm not expecting that in your case – then we might have to ask you for a small refresher.

C. I think you're very reasonable.

B. *(A pause, and Bill counted ten pound-notes.)* Ten pounds, Mrs Upson. Thank you. You'll trust me in the matter of a receipt. I'll give you a written one now, if you prefer it. You could deposit it at your bank.

C. It's quite unnecessary, I assure you.

(The voices began to recede. I clapped my ear to the panel and just caught the last words.)

C. Mr Ellice, you *will* keep this most confidential, won't you?

B. I assure you, Mrs Upson, that everything is as secret as the grave.

C. And if this awful man starts making what he calls disclosures to you, you won't listen to him?

B. *(Grimly.)* Don't let that worry you, Mrs Upson. I know how to handle that sort of character.

That was all I heard. Bill must have seen her out himself, but when he came out I didn't budge in case she came back to tell him some afterthought. When he coughed violently, I took that as a sign that I could appear.

'What'd you think of her?' was the first thing I wanted to know.

'A very smart women,' he told me. 'Not yet thirty, or very little over. Very smartly dressed. Almost a lady. Looked like one but didn't just talk like one, if you know what I mean. Struck me as trying hard, though.'

'And what about telling you the truth? What did you think about that?'

He smiled sarcastically.

'Truth, you say? I think she was a liar to the fingertips.' Then he thought of something to ask me. 'If you hadn't pushed that buzzer I should have told her I couldn't take the case.'

'You mean, why did I push the buzzer?' I said. 'It was like this, Bill. I thought she was a liar, and I'm interested to know just what lies she told. Also this doesn't strike me as very much of a blackmail case. I don't mean that blackmail isn't always a nasty business. What I mean is that this looks like being nothing very involved. The lady's been carrying on with another man, that's all.'

'If she's telling the truth.'

'Exactly,' I said. 'I think you should go so far as finding out if she has. And don't forget you can turn the case down at any moment you like.'

We argued a bit more and then I asked who was trailing the lady. Bill said Tom Bruce. Tom was a good man who didn't look like the ex-detective he was. Bill had had him ever since Dunkirk when Tom had been invalided out.

I pottered around for the rest of that morning, expecting that at any time Tom would be back. Then I went out to lunch and when I returned Tom still hadn't arrived. At three o'clock, and just when I was leaving for the day, he turned up.

'What luck?' Bill asked him.

'I lost her,' Tom said laconically.

'My God, no!' Bill said. 'How the devil did you come to do that?'

Tom said she'd taken a taxi near Camomile Street but he'd been lucky enough to grab another. She'd got out at Selfridge's and he'd followed her through various departments. Then she'd worked her way right back to Oxford Circus, pausing to look in every window that attracted her, and finally she'd done the same all down Regent Street, and then she'd gone into Swan & Edgar's. It was then about a quarter to one, and he followed her to the restaurant. Unfortunately she secured a seat nearer the lifts than the one he was able to get, but he'd eaten his own lunch at leisure and had managed to keep an eye on her. When his lunch was over he'd paid the bill but still hung on over his coffee. Then some people came between his table and hers and had stood there looking around for a table. When they moved, she'd gone.

At once he'd made his way to the lift and so downstairs, but there was never a sign of her. Then he had a brainwave. He went back upstairs and found a seat at the very table she'd occupied, and he ordered another lunch.

'Not so hot, the lunches you get anywhere nowadays,' he told us with a grin. 'Didn't inconvenience me too much having a second go. And I hung on till I was the last one at that table and I could chat with the waitress. I described the lady and sort of wondered if I'd known her. And what do you think. This waitress fell for it like a ton of bricks. She knew the lady all right because she was a theatre-fan. She's an actress. Name of Violet Lancing.'

CHAPTER VII
Developments

I SUDDENLY FOUND myself with my glasses in my hand, and giving them an involuntary polish. Maybe that had been the safety valve that had kept me from giving a start of surprise, for neither Bill nor Tom Bruce noticed anything. And I had the sense to keep my mouth shut.

'My God, what a liar!' Bill was saying. 'And telling us she was a Mrs Upson. But wait a moment though. She might be married to a man called Upson. These actresses stick to their maiden names.'

'She's not married,' Tom told us. 'She's a widow. Married an actor called Yarnell who was killed in Italy.'

'How do you know?'

'I looked her up in the telephone directory,' Tom said. 'Welford Mansions is where she hangs out. That swagger block of flats just off Great Smith Street. Two hundred and fifty a year, the smallest ones. Hers is about half way, and that's three hundred. One of the commissionaires told me. I knew him when he was at the Union Jack Club earlier in the war. He was demobbed, like me.'

'Good work, Tom,' Bill told him. 'Anything else?'

There was nothing except the theatre at which Violet was playing, and the name of the play.

'See you later then, Tom,' Bill said, and gave a satisfied grin. 'Go and get yourself another lunch. Mr Travers and I are going to talk things over.'

I didn't want to do any talking. What I was realizing was that we might be handling dynamite, and my duty was to let Bill in on the Manfrey Case and then induce him to give me permission to discuss the whole thing with Wharton. And yet I couldn't quite bring myself to that. There was the itch to know just a little bit more. And I speciously assured myself that whoever was blackmailing Violet Lancing was probably doing it on grounds that had arisen long after Manfrey's death. Violet, a go-getter and gold-digger if ever there was one, was always likely to overstep the mark and so run headlong into trouble.

'Well, what do you think of her?' Bill was asking me.

'Damned if I know,' I said. 'Your judgement was pretty accurate though. She's certainly a fluent liar.'

'Seems to me we've got two things to consider,' Bill said. 'First of all, is there any truth whatever in her statement that she *is* being blackmailed.'

'I think so,' I said. 'We must give her the benefit of the doubt. And why should she have let you put that notice in the paper?'

'Ask me another,' Bill said. 'For all we know there may be something phoney about that. Still, we'll say someone is threatening to blackmail her. Then what about that husband yarn. What are we going to make of that?'

'That she's being blackmailed for quite a different reason,' I said. 'But tell me first. Did she strike you as being frightened? Nervous, shall we say?'

'Oh yes. She was nervous enough. The more pat she spoke, the more nervous she was underneath.'

'So I thought,' I said. 'And there was one thing that struck me as highly suspicious – when she said that if you caught the man – let's call him X – and if he started to make disclosures, you were to swear to shut his mouth or keep his disclosures to yourself. You get me?'

'I think so,' he said. 'If X opens his mouth, then we discover that his threats have nothing to do with a husband. That makes her a liar to us, and it tells us the real reason for the blackmail. That's what she's scared of.'

'Well, how do you feel about things?' I asked. 'Like to give her the go-by?'

That was just a salve to my conscience. I'll own now that if he'd said yes, then I'd probably have found some way to make him change his mind. But he didn't say yes. What he did was scowl.

'Damned if I like her getting away with it like that. I don't like being made a fool of by a woman like her.'

'Right,' I said. 'Let's give her a bit more rope. See if she rings you up when X has seen the notice. That'll give us time to think things over. When and if she communicates with you again, then you've always the option of turning her down or going on just a little bit further.'

'Yes,' he said. 'Probably that's the best. But what about trying to get any more information about her?'

'A bit dangerous, I think. I wouldn't do it at her flat. The theatre, perhaps. And if Tom does it, he'll have to be damn careful. He ought to disguise himself a bit so as not to be connected with the man who questioned that commissionaire. You don't know commissionaires. He might have told her that a friend of his was very interested in her. Commissionaires are chatty people and the occupants of the flat will like talking to them.'

We talked that over and decided that Tom should try his hand at the theatre, though whom he was to question would have to lie wholly within his judgement. I promised to look in next morning, and Bill said he'd telephone me if anything arose meanwhile.

I was at Broad Street at ten o'clock the next morning. Nothing had happened by eleven o'clock, and as the time went by a faint depression settled on Bill Ellice's office. Then I went out for a coffee and when I came back twenty minutes later, the secretary warned me that Mr Ellice was on the telephone.

'Is it You-know-Who?' I asked her, and she nodded.

I waited there till she gave me the word to go through. Bill was looking pleased with himself. What had happened was this.

Violet Lancing had been ringing from a call-box, she said. Bill asked her at once if she was sure she had not been followed, and she said she had taken precautions. But as soon as she began to say what X had just told her over the telephone, Bill said it was far too dangerous to talk with a possible someone to listen in on the line. Could she come to his office at once? She said she could, and she'd take a taxi immediately. She added that she simply had to see him in any case because she was desperately frightened.

'She might be here in a matter of minutes then,' I said. 'But do you know what I've been thinking, Bill? Suppose there's any truth in the fact that she's been carrying on with some man. We know there isn't a husband to be scared of: at least I haven't seen anything in the papers about her marrying again.' I realized there that I had let slip more than I intended, and I hurriedly added that actresses' marriages were always news.

'So the man she's scared of is someone who can do her harm in her profession,' I went on. 'His revelations might cause a scandal that would make her name mud. And I think that X — the man who's just rung her up — is actually that man she's been having an affair with.'

'Could be,' said Bill.

'Take that cold he's supposed to be suffering from,' I said. 'The cold that made his voice sound thick. That wasn't a cold. It was just X disguising his voice. And he had to disguise it because it was a voice that otherwise would have been perfectly familiar to her.'

'Sounds good sense to me,' Bill said as I got to my feet, ready to get along to my hidey-hole. 'But why shouldn't you stay on here? I'll tell her that her case is more complex than we thought and I'll introduce you as my partner.'

'I don't think she'd talk so freely,' I said. 'Maybe some other time.'

I got into that inner room just on the dot. Once more here is the exact conversation, or at least the relevant parts of it.

B. Good morning, Mrs Upson. Very nice to see you again.

V. Mr Ellice, I'm terribly frightened.

B. No, no, no. You mustn't talk like that. We're here to see that you're not frightened. Just ease your mind now and relax. Tell me all about it.

V. Well, that man rang me up just before I rang you.

B. Excuse me. Same man and same voice?

V. Oh, yes. His cold sounded worse, though. But it was the same man.

B. And you've still no idea who he was? You couldn't even make a guess?

V. I haven't the faintest idea. I only wish I had.

B. Well, sorry to have interrupted you, Mrs Upson. Carry on please.

V. Well, he said I was to meet him in Victoria Street to-morrow morning. At ten-thirty sharp, on the pavement outside Massey's book-shop.

B. Let me see. That's what I might call the station end, isn't it?

V. Yes. About three-quarters of the way down. And I was to have the money with me. Five hundred pounds in pound-notes.

B. Excuse me, but do you now actually have the money?

V. *(Hesitatingly.)* I think I shall have it by tomorrow morning.

B. That's all right, Mrs Upson. Don't worry yourself about the money. I'll attend to all that. *(A laugh.)* I don't mean I'll find the money for you. What I mean is that it mayn't be necessary to use actual money as a decoy. But I'll go into that later. And did he say anything else?

V. Yes, he did. I said, what guarantee was there that he wouldn't go on demanding money after I'd given him the five hundred pounds. For all I knew he might go on demanding money all my life and I should simply be a beggar. And then he said the most extraordinary thing. *(A pause.)* That's what frightened me. I thought for a moment I was simply going to flop down in a faint.

B. Yes?

V. What he said was that I should have every guarantee that once the five hundred pounds was paid, I'd never have to pay any more. I said how could I know that, and he said that as soon as I saw him I'd know he was speaking the truth.

B. Very interesting. And what then?

V. Well, he didn't let me get in another word. He just repeated the instructions, and rang off. Oh, yes, and he warned me about going to the police.

B. *(Very cheerily.)* Well, Mrs Upson, there's nothing to be frightened of there. If you ask me, it's the man himself who's more scared than we are. But just one question. When he said you'd recognize him, and that that'd be sufficient guarantee that he wouldn't keep on trying to extort money from you, did that give you any clue to who he was?

V. It didn't. I still haven't the faintest idea.

B. Then tell me something else. You seem pretty sure that the voice was a man's. Think it over for a moment. Could it possibly have been a woman's? I've heard impersonators on the wireless and seen people like Florence Desmond on the stage who make no bones whatever about imitating men. Close your eyes and you wouldn't know it wasn't a man.

V. That's an idea. I never thought of that.

B. Very well, then, Mrs Upson. Why not think a little more? If it's a woman who's trying this blackmail game, have you any idea what woman it is?

V. *(After quite an interval.)* I haven't – at the moment. But women like me always have heaps of enemies.

B. Well, perhaps something will occur to you. If it doesn't it's no particular matter. And about tomorrow. I'll get our plans worked out and you can rely on everything being absolutely in hand by the time we meet. I suggest the Victoria Cinema at ten o'clock sharp. That will give us a clear half hour.

V. *(Definitely nervously.)* And do I bring the money?

B. No money. Your handbag – yes. That will look as if the money is in it.

V. *(Very nervously.)* You're sure there won't be a scene?

B. My dear Mrs Upson. I assure you that you won't even know what's happening. You'll have nothing to do with it. Everything's in our hands. That's what we're here for. No scenes, no worry, no nothing. Tomorrow morning then, at ten o'clock sharp outside the Victoria Cinema. And may I impress on you most earnestly the need for secrecy. Make sure you're not followed. And if I may make a suggestion to such a pretty woman – you'll pardon my saying so – I should wear one of those hats with veils, if you have one, and sun-glasses. Anything you can think of that might disguise your personality.

V. It sounds quite thrilling!

B. Well, it's nice to hear you say so. Keep up that optimism, Mrs Upson. We're paid to do the worrying, and, believe me, we're not worrying yet.

(Movement of chairs and voices fainter.)

And if I should want to communicate with you urgently before the morning, how do I get you?

That was all I heard. In a few minutes Bill was telling me that she'd said he could ring her up at any time before five o'clock or after ten at night at a friend's flat. The number she gave was her own number.

'She sounded badly scared,' I said.

'She's scared all right,' Bill said, 'even if she has got sense enough to keep on lying. That hunch of yours seems to have been right, by the way. If not, why did X say she'd recognize him?'

'I don't know,' I said. 'But tell me. Was she, as far as you could gather, telling the truth when she said she still had no idea who X was?'

'That's about the one thing I'd swear she was telling the truth about.'

'Then the theory doesn't look so good,' I said. 'I doubt if a man with whom she'd been so intimate as that could disguise his voice sufficiently well. Not that it matters two hoots. But why did you suggest X might be a woman?'

'Sort of natural sequence,' he said. 'If she wasn't sure of the man, then it might have been a woman.'

'And what were her private reactions, as far as you could judge, when you said it might be a woman?'

Bill pinched his chin reflectively.

'I rather think I had a lucky shot. She gave quite a start, just as if she knew the very woman who might fit. Either that or she was play-acting. Making me think it might be a woman when all the time she knew it was a man.'

'Damn all liars,' I said fervently, and Bill was with me. Then we left Violet Lancing to stew in her own juice, and settled down to the campaign of the following morning. The upshot was that after lunch we decided to reconnoitre Victoria Street and to make the final plan when we'd surveyed the ground. There was some argument as to whether or not Tom Bruce should be taken with us, and finally we decided against it. In any case Tom said he wanted to be at the theatre by four o'clock as he thought he had a contact that might produce some information.

Bill and I took a bus as far as the Army and Navy Stores. Then he crossed the street and I continued along on the left. If either of us saw anything interesting, he was to give the other the high sign. That was why we'd decided against bringing Tom Bruce. Three people would have been more conspicuous than two individuals on opposite sides of the road.

There were remarkably few people on the pavements. Victoria Street isn't a shopping centre like the streets of the West End, where all the women of the suburbs seem daily to be decanted for the purpose of window gazing. Bill was carrying an attaché case and looking like a professional man making his leisurely way towards an early train home. I had on what might be called my West End garments, walking cane and suede gloves complete, and I, too, strolled like a man of leisure.

Bill passed Massey's book-shop and then turned back as if he'd noticed something interesting. For quite a few moments he looked at the books in the outdoor racks, and I guessed he was using the window as a mirror in which to see my side of the street. Then I happened to notice something. I made as if to cross the street, then changed my mind, but the turn allowed me to lift my eyes upwards. What I saw was quite interesting. Another moment or two I had my handkerchief out and was blowing my nose. When I saw that Bill had spotted that high sign I turned into the passage way between two shops, and made my way up the stairs. On the landing was a notice, with arrow pointing left – Daffodil Tea-rooms.

When I got inside, everything was better and better. The main room had two large windows looking over Victoria Street, and one was at one end of the wall and the other at my far end. A table at one window was occupied, but I secured one at the other. Within a couple of minutes Bill had joined me, and we ordered a pot of tea for two and toasted tea-cake.

Bill's eyes roved professionally around, and then he gave a satisfied nod.

'Marvellous. Couldn't have been better if we'd built the damn place ourselves.'

It certainly was the most amazing piece of luck, and it didn't take long to work out a plan of campaign. Bill would meet Violet Lancing as arranged and he'd bring her at once to the tea-rooms. The proprietor or manageress would have to be interviewed so that both window tables were reserved. He and Violet would be at the far table and Tom and I would be at the other. Tom she didn't know, and as far as Bill knew, she didn't know me, but I was making my own plans in case her memory should be sufficiently retentive to recall the spectacled, spindle-shanked individual of three years before.

There we would all have coffee and wait till zero hour. Violet would simply have to point out to Bill the person who arrived at Massey's book-shop at half past ten, and then Bill would give the high sign for Tom to nip down and get on the trail as soon as X grew tired of waiting. Bill might or might not come down too. It depended on whether or not Violet would recognize X, and go so far as to give a name, and even an address. All Violet would then have to do was to go about her lawful occasions.

So much for that. Back we went, and by separate ways, to Bill's office. There wasn't anything special to do, so I left, and I was so keyed up that I knew there was nothing for the rest of the evening but a cinema show to keep my mind off things.

I don't know if you're like me, but when I'm excited all about something, a little snatch of tune – it may be – will keep running maddeningly through my head and driving me nearly frantic. Where it comes from heaven knows, but perhaps from the casual whistling of a passer-by, but come it does, and the hard thing is to get it to go again. But it wasn't a snatch of tune this time. It was a quotation. Something I'd committed to memory as a schoolboy. Something from *Julius Caesar* that had struck me as apposite, and a direct reference to myself and the way I was getting keyed up before the main climax and event.

> *Between the acting of a dreadful thing*
> *And the first motion, all the interim is*
> *Like a phantasma or a hideous dream:*
> *The genius and the mortal instruments*
> *Are then in council; and the state of man,*
> *Like to a little kingdom, suffers then*
> *The nature of an insurrection.*

Perhaps that's too highbrow for you. And you may wonder why *Julius Caesar* has cropped up again. If so, I assure you it was not by design. That quotation just happened to come, and that's all I can say. And yet it struck me at the time as rather a remarkable thing, and especially when my mind went instinctively back to the events of three years before, and the circumstances under which I'd first come into contact with Violet Lancing.

You too may remember. There was the dead Manfrey, face to the ceiling, and like the dead Cassius on the bloody field of Philippi. There was Nevall, the perfect Brutus, and so it was easy after all to trace the way that that quotation had intruded itself upon my mind. But the cinema rid my brain of it, and when I came out I was thinking only of an evening meal. Then I remembered the Case again, and I made up my mind to call at Broad Street and see if Tom Bruce had returned.

He'd actually been in since six o'clock and I found him there on duty till Ellice returned at eight.

'Any luck, Tom?' I said.

'Not a lot, Mr Travers,' he told me. 'The boss's orders were to be too darn careful or I might have got a bit more.'

What he'd picked up was useful but far from sensational. Violet Lancing was far from popular. It was said she gave herself airs, and it was also hinted that she was no better – as they say – than she might be, even if the name of no particular man was mentioned. She was said, too, to have ingratiated herself with Henry Nevall. It was even said she was setting her cap at him, but the feeling wasn't reciprocal, as Tom put it. There was talk about how she kept up that three-hundred-a-year flat. It was true she had only had it for six months, but she had only her salary and the modest pension for her late husband.

That jumble of rumour and scandal didn't amount to much, as Tom himself had to admit. I left him holding the fort and went off in search of a meal. Then I spent an hour or two at my club, and it was latish even for me when I finally turned in. And then that cursed quotation came back to my mind.

Between the acting of a dreadful thing
And the first motion . . .

So it went on for what seemed hours, though it probably wasn't more than minutes. I remember assuring myself that murder *was* a dreadful thing, and then I must have dropped off to sleep. When I woke the sun was shining, and now that zero hour had come, all the introspections had gone and I was feeling fit as a flea.

CHAPTER VIII
The Unexpected

JUST AFTER ten o'clock I was in the Daffodil Tea-rooms with Tom Bruce. Very few people were there, but in a short time they began to drift in, business people mostly with a sprinkling of shoppers. At ten minutes past, Bill came in with Violet Lancing and made for the left-hand window table.

After three years I was seeing Violet Lancing again and she seemed to me to have altered very little. I took a quick look at her from behind my newspaper, and it seemed to me, too, that she'd done precious little in the matter of disguise. It was true she had a perky little hat with a kind of veil that hung like a semi-circular cover for forehead and eyes, but she wasn't wearing glasses. Everything about her was very chic, and I guessed that she'd found it just too hard to make a sacrifice of glamour.

'Some dame!' Tom said out of the side of his mouth. From the pictures and crime magazines he has acquired what he regards as a vocabulary suitably tough.

Bill ordered coffee and the two settled themselves at their table, and they were seated parallel to the window. That meant that Massey's book-shop just across the road was in full view, but by sitting slightly back from their table they themselves were invisible from the street. Violet had her back to us, and I ventured to change places with Tom. In that way I had her back at least under my eye, and Tom could concentrate on watching the opposite pavement.

The time began to pass quickly at first. More and more people were coming in for coffee, and on the pavement across the road was a steady trickle of pedestrians. Tall buses would go by and obscure the view, and after the green lights had gone on just down the street, there would be a quick surge by of traffic. Then the first likely customer stopped at the boxes of books, but he was an old white-haired man and hadn't the look of a black-mailer, and in another five minutes he had made a purchase and passed on.

There was chatter in the room and the air was getting blue with smoke. Still seven minutes to zero hour, and I began looking at the various tables, even if I hadn't time for my favourite hobby of trying to place this person or that in some particular trade or profession, or to judge from a snatch of conversation the part of England from which the speakers had come. In fact I saw only one person who really interested me, and he had only just come in. He was a tallish man who looked about forty, though maybe the black beard and his glasses made him look older than he was. As he was wearing quite a new sports coat with flannel slacks, I decided that he was a naval man on leave or recently demobbed. But his face looked rather too pale for that. It hadn't what I might call the tang of the sea, and just when I was debating the point, Tom leaned across the table.

'You don't often see a dame interested in books!'

A woman, tallish and slim and fairly young by the back of her, was examining the shelves of books that ran above the boxes. I glanced at my watch, then slid a two-shilling piece across to Tom.

'Three minutes to go. You'd better pay the bill.'

Tom cracked his fingers and the waitress came up. I was watching the woman. Every few moments she would give a quick glance each way along the pavement, and then she would be moving slowly along the shelves of books again. Traffic streamed by, and when the view was clear again she was still there. Then she turned and I saw her full face. About thirty, she looked. Neatly dressed and quite good looking. Violet was leaning slightly forward, doubtless at Bill's suggestion, and was looking at her too.

The woman turned back to the books.

'What about getting downstairs, Tom?' I said. 'She seems to be the only likely one.'

Tom moved off. Zero hour had passed, and everything had been far different from what I'd imagined it. Even that woman now seemed something of an anti-climax, for she suddenly selected a book and went into the shop. A minute or two and she was out again. A look each way along the pavement and she moved slowly off, towards Westminster. And then she did a queer thing. Twenty yards along the pavement was an open door between two shops. That's where she halted. She gave a glance at her wrist-watch and then took up her stand half in the doorway and half out. Under cover of looking through her book she was keeping a look-out along the pavement.

That was when I knew she was X. It was almost ten minutes past zero hour but she had not given up hope. Anything might have happened to delay the expected victim, and there apparently she was determined to stay till it was obvious that the victim had refused to play ball. So I changed my seat again so as to have her in better view, and it was just as I was on my feet, my back to the room, that something happened.

In the chatter of that room I had heard nothing, but what I was aware of was a movement inside the room. People were getting up and one or two were moving towards Bill's table. A hurrying waitress obscured my view, and then I saw that Bill was kneeling. His arm was round Violet and it looked as if she had fainted. People were surging round, and I heard Bill hollering for them to stand back.

I made my way towards the door and waited for a minute. The manageress was pushing her way through, and carrying a glass of water. A waitress came back my way.

'A lady taken ill?' I said.

'Only a fainting fit,' she told me. 'Her uncle says she often has them.'

There seemed nothing I could do, and the last thing I wanted was for Violet to come round and to open her eyes on me. Mind you, I did have some preposterous idea of saying I was a doctor and so getting to the table and the patient, but just in time I remembered that the longer Violet was unaware of me, the better for the Broad Street Detective Agency. And Bill seemed to have everything in hand, so I slowly made my way down the stairs and out to the street.

I didn't see Tom, but I did see something that interested me, if only for a moment. The woman was still there, and who should be speaking to her but that supposed naval man. But he was only asking the way to somewhere, for she stepped out to the pavement and pointed. He raised his hat as if in thanks and then moved on. Then he began sprinting as a bus passed him. At the bus-stop, some thirty yards on, he boarded it, and when I looked back towards the woman, there was no need to have looked back at all, for she was now almost at the bus-stop and walking on towards Westminster. Twenty yards behind her I caught sight of Tom Bruce.

What to do with myself then I didn't know, so I began walking slowly back towards Victoria station. Then I crossed the street, bought a morning paper and, with my back against the door of a closed shop, began to look through it. With an eye to spare for the entrance to the Daffodil Tea-rooms, I must have waited a good ten minutes before Bill appeared, and Violet with him. Holding her arm, he guided her across the street and there they waited for a minute or two. Then he hailed a crawling taxi, saw her in, and stood watching till the taxi had disappeared.

I had been making my way towards him, and when he turned he saw me. But he gave me no sign and simply walked past me. I turned and followed. On the corner by the station he halted outside a restaurant and then went in. In a couple of minutes I was at his table. He had ordered more coffee and I was having an ice-cream.

* * *

'You're as wise as I am,' Bill told me perplexedly. 'What made her pass out like that I don't know. She just gave a sort of moan and over she went.'

'Genuine, was it?'

'It was genuine enough,' he told me grimly. 'Her face went white as a sheet. Took us a good ten minutes to bring her round, and then we had to take her to the manageress's office.'

'Could it have been the sight of that woman who was looking at the books? The one Tom is now tailing?'

'Don't think so,' he said. 'Funny about her, though. I asked her if she recognized her, and she said she didn't. Now I come to think of it, I could almost swear she did. She gave a sort of start and a lift of the eyebrows that time when she turned full face towards us. And she couldn't rest content. She had to keep looking at her.'

'We'll know more, when we hear from Tom,' I said confidently. 'But that doesn't explain why she fainted. That woman had gone clean out of her sight by then.'

'I know,' said Bill. 'All I can think is that she suddenly remembered something. Recognized the woman, perhaps.'

'And what was Violet like when you met her?'

'Very windy,' he told me. 'I had the devil of a job to get her to that tea-shop. Told her she'd be dead safe there. See everything and not be seen. But she got a bit nervy towards the half-hour. Perhaps it was that repression that made her pass out.'

'And where's she gone now?'

'Ostensibly home. She wouldn't let me accompany her, and for pretty obvious reasons. I kidded her that everything was well in hand and she probably wouldn't have any more trouble. Put on a mysterious act for all I was worth.'

'And she believed you?'

Bill made a bit of a grimace.

'Not so that you'd notice it. A bit too much like reciting *The Wreck of the Hesperus* to a deaf-mute and waiting for applause. Expect she was feeling none too fit, though.'

'And what's arranged?'

'Oh, that we'll notify her when there's anything to report. But you bet your life she'll be ringing up before the day's out. Or in the morning at the latest.'

There was nothing much else to talk about, and it would have been far too dangerous to reconnoitre Victoria Street for a possible sign of Tom Bruce, so we took a bus for Liverpool Street. When we got to the office, nothing had come in from Tom, so Bill went off for an early lunch and I held the fort. When he came back I went to lunch. At two o'clock there was still no word from Tom. At a quarter past the telephone bell went and there he was on the line.

I took the call because Bill happened to have just gone to another room to look up something in the files.

'Travers speaking, Tom. Where are you speaking from?'

'A call-box, top of Victoria Street. I've tipped a paper man to keep an eye on that dame for a couple of minutes.'

'Here's Mr Ellice now,' I said, for Bill had come back. Bill waved for me to carry on.

'Right-ho, Tom,' I said. 'Tell us what you know.'

'Where do you think that dame went to?' he said. 'Only about a couple of hundred yards up. Went into a ladies' hairdresser's, smart looking place named "Rhoda".' He spelt the name for me.

'I reckoned she was going to have her hair fixed, by appointment or something, and that was why she was hanging around that book-shop, just to pass the time. But I reckoned I'd better keep an eye on her when she came out, but she didn't – not till half an hour ago. And she hadn't been having her hair done. I got well behind her and I could tell that.'

'Where'd she go?'

'To a little restaurant at the bottom of Whitehall. She was in there about twenty minutes and then she came out and went back by bus to the shop. Reckon she's employed there, or something.'

'You hang on,' I said. 'I'll be along in a few minutes. Where can I pick you up?'

'Just inside that left-hand turning past the Army and Navy,' he told me.

'Right,' I said. 'I'll be along inside half an hour. If you've gone – well, you've gone, and you can get in touch with us later.'

When I told Bill about it, he said it was the best thing to be done.

'A high-class hairdresser's,' he said. 'Trade name of Rhoda. I know the sort of place. My wife goes to one at Finchley called Patricia.'

'Wait a minute, Bill,' I suddenly said. 'I've got an idea.'

I thought it was a thundering good idea. Even Bill said it wasn't so bad.

'What is she, employee or principal?' I asked him.

'Couldn't say,' he told me. 'Those girls they employ in those high-class places are smart as mannequins. Mind you, she struck me as a superior kind of type, the little I could see of her.'

'I wouldn't be surprised if she isn't Rhoda,' I said. 'An employee wouldn't be able to slip out at ten-fifteen in the morning in order to hang around looking at books, and within sight of the shop.'

'All the better for your scheme,' Bill told me, and as no further exploration seemed necessary, I pushed off by bus. Then no sooner had I boarded it than I remembered something, and at the very first stop I got off again.

Liars should have good memories. Once upon a time, during my association with George Wharton, I jibbed badly at lying, even if I secretly admired the superb capabilities of George. Witnesses lied, as George would point out, and it was not only necessary but vital that lies should be countered with lies. I, younger and remarkably callow, thought that was hardly cricket, but in the course of time I became – in the sacred name of justice – a liar almost as accomplished as George himself. That was why I had been lying to Bill Ellice with scarcely an inward blush. As far as Bill knew, I knew nothing of Violet Lancing, and had never clapped eyes on her till that morning in the Daffodil Tea-rooms. But even comparatively white lies like that needed to be backed by a good memory.

What I'd forgotten to work out was this. If the unknown woman whom I was shortly hoping to interview was X, then

X would soon be in touch with Violet, if only to put on more pressure after the let-down of that morning. Suppose my call at 'Rhoda' aroused suspicions, mightn't that call be mentioned to Violet? Mightn't I be regarded – unlikely though I looked – as an emissary of the police with whom Violet – in spite of warning – had probably been in contact? And to describe me might be to recall to Violet the Travers she had met in the Manfrey affair at The Cote. And what the results of that might be I couldn't imagine. What they would certainly do would be to scare Violet into six fits, and they couldn't do the Broad Street Detective Agency any good, either.

So I slipped across to my flat and told my taxi to wait. You'll laugh at me perhaps, when I say I did a bit of disguising. That sort of thing sounds melodramatic or rather like playing at Red Indians, and altogether hopelessly *démodé*. But I slipped in a couple of cheek pads all the same and I fixed a wispy kind of moustache above my tooth-brush one, and I put on an old pair of rimless spectacles instead of my huge horn-rims. And since the proof of the pudding is said to be in the eating, let me tell you that when I came up to Tom Bruce – and wearing a different suit and with a pronounced stoop to my shoulders – he merely gave me an interested look and let me go by him. And he was very impressed when I made myself known.

'What about your slipping off for a spot of lunch?' I suggested.

He said he'd had some. While the unknown lady was in the little Whitehall restaurant, he'd bought some sandwiches and had eaten them outside. I gave him an outline of my scheme and then moved on.

It was a smart looking shop, as Tom had said, even if there wasn't a reception room. What one did was to step straight into an ordinary shop with a counter at which a lady assistant was presiding over a multiplicity of what I class as cosmetics.

'Are you the manageress?' I smiled at her, and tried to look pleasant but somewhat senile.

'Oh no,' she told me, quite pleased all the same.

'Is there any possibility of seeing her?'

'Well, there isn't a manageress,' she said. 'It's Mrs Yarnell you'd have to see.'

I don't know what else she said. I think it was that Mrs Yarnell was busy, and mightn't be able to see anybody. What I do know is that I was mentally all out for a minute after she'd mentioned the name Yarnell.

'Was it very urgent?' the assistant was saying.

'In a way – yes,' I said.

She disappeared for a moment and I heard her passing the message on. A minute and there was a return message that I didn't hear, and then she reappeared.

'What name was it, please?'

'Colonel Harrison,' I said.

Back she went and when she next reappeared it was to ask me to wait a minute or two. I was finding my heart thumping inside my ribs. Mrs Yarnell. Victor Yarnell's wife or I was a Dutchman. The woman whom Yarnell had divorced to marry Violet Lancing! And that meant a new harking back to the murder of Manfrey, or at least it seemed so in the minor panic that was now possessing me. Violet Lancing being blackmailed by Yarnell's ex-wife. Dynamite wasn't the word for it. And unless I could lie pretty furiously and convincingly, Bill Ellice was in for a bad time with the police.

There was a sound of approaching steps, and Rhoda Yarnell appeared. She was the woman I had watched that morning, there wasn't a shadow of a doubt about that, and a charming, if highly business-like woman she looked. When she spoke to me I was recalling what Benny Markstein had told me about her.

'You wanted to see me?' she said. Her voice was what I might call a cultured contralto, and her smile was most attractive.

'It's about my wife,' I said, and tried to put a Blimp-like quality into my tone. 'We've just got back to London and her old hairdresser in Bond Street has been bombed out. Last night we were wondering where she could find another. She's very particular, by the way, and as I was going by your – er – shop, I thought how nice and attractive it looked.'

'That's very charming of you,' she said. 'We shall be delighted to be of service to Mrs Harrison. I do advise, though, that she rings up in good time for an appointment. We're most frightfully rushed these days.'

'Expect you are,' I said gruffly, and: 'Well, that's very good of you. I'll report to my wife and I expect she'll be ringing you up.'

An interchange of smiles and out I went. But as I made my bowed, decrepit way back towards Tom Bruce, I was feeling none too happy. Yarnell's wife and Violet Lancing, I said to myself again and again. Everything *must* hark back to that Manfrey affair, and if so Wharton ought to be told everything, and at once. And then the devil was at my ear again.

Need things go back to the Manfrey Case? Rhoda Yarnell had good enough reasons for hating Violet Lancing, and surely a hair-dressing saloon was a hotbed of scandal. Customers would talk, and maybe Rhoda Yarnell had picked up something about Violet that could form the basis of a blackmail campaign. And then on the other hand I was telling myself that Rhoda Yarnell didn't look like a blackmailer. Or did she? When I came to think back to that brief interview, it seemed to me that her looks and manner, however charming, had had beneath them a cool efficiency that amounted to hardness. Or was it more of an observant wariness: the kind of wariness that would come when that assistant had told her that a man was wishing to see her urgently. After the morning's débacle, mightn't she have assumed that that caller was from the police?

Then as I neared Tom Bruce I had sense enough to realize that speculation was a waste of time. The whole thing boiled down to simple alternatives. Rhoda Yarnell had been at Massey's book-shop that morning either by chance or design. If by chance, then the long arm of coincidence, as they call it, had stretched out once more. If by design, then it was my clear duty to advise Ellice to have nothing further to do with the Case and either through me or directly to report the facts in confidence to Wharton.

Then as I turned down that side road where Tom was waiting, I had an idea.

'I know who she is, Tom,' I said. 'She's the owner of the shop, and the name's Rhoda Yarnell. Does that convey anything to you?'

It didn't.

'I just wondered,' I said. 'But there's no need for you to wait here till she leaves the shop this evening. She mayn't go till half past six or so. What about my staying here while you slip along to a telephone. Her name ought to be in the directory. Not the shop but her private address.'

He wrote the name down and went off. I'd told him to get himself some tea, but all the same he was back inside the half-hour. And there wasn't a trace of any Rhoda Yarnell in the book, he said, or of R. Yarnell or Mrs R. Yarnell. So there wasn't anything for it but to wait.

I went back to my flat. That disguise business had been amusing enough but I didn't feel like giving an exhibition before Bill Ellice. Then when I'd reduced myself to the normal and commonplace once more. I had a bit of a breather while I wondered just what I ought to report to Bill. It seemed to me that I'd rather tied myself in knots, and I'd either have to make something of a clean breast or go on telling the same white lies. Then my eye happened to fall on the telephone, and with a sudden access of either bravado or desperation, I dialled the Yard and asked to be put through to Wharton.

I was kept waiting for a time, and then a certain Inspector whom I knew came on the line.

'That you, Mr Travers? Sorry to say the Super isn't in. He's been in South Wales this last couple of days.'

'When's he due back?'

'Tomorrow afternoon at the latest. Any message?'

'Yes,' I said. 'You might be so good as to say I rang him on rather urgent business.'

I couldn't help beaming all over my face. We're told that the way of transgressors is hard, but there was I, absolutely in the clear. If Wharton gave me one of his famous glares and demanded why he hadn't had all the facts reported to him as soon as the name of Violet Lancing had cropped up, all I had to do was to say with pained astonishment that the last thing to do was to tell those facts to all and sundry. He was the only man who should be told, and we were keeping our mouths shut till his eagerly awaited return. And if that wouldn't make George wag his tail, then – to use a favourite remark of his own – my name was Robinson.

And there was another amazing stroke of luck. If George wasn't due back till the following afternoon, then we had that extra time in which to go on with the Case. Not that I expected anything dramatic to turn up. Still, you never knew. All the same I wouldn't overplay my hand. What I would do was spill the beans to Ellice in the morning, provided of course that there were no alarming developments meanwhile. A white lie or two either way wouldn't matter, and in the morning I could always say that I'd only just become aware of the significance of the name Yarnell.

So I rang Broad Street at once, and all I told Bill was that the woman under suspicion was definitely the proprietress of that hair-dressing establishment. I added that her name wasn't in the directory and that Tom was going to tail her to her private address, and then before he could begin asking questions I added finally that the rest could keep till I came along in an hour or so's time.

CHAPTER IX
End of the Rubber

'THAT NAME Yarnell seems vaguely familiar somehow,' I was saying to Bill Ellice.

Bill frowned. 'Well, it's not all that uncommon. A smart, clever woman, you said?'

'Yes. Not a glamour wench like Violet. Much more of a lady. Just that poise that makes all the difference. A nice voice too. And she didn't have to be careful over accent or aspirates.'

'You're a regular poet,' Bill told me, though what he probably had wanted to say was that I'd certainly got the gift of the gab. 'All the same, whatever she is, she's a blackmailer. It's fifty to one on it. And we're in the devil of a hole.'

'How?'

He looked surprised.

'Well, we've got to get results, haven't we? Even if we're pretty sure that the Yarnell woman is X, we can't very well force an interview and bring any charges. There'd be hell to pay if we happened to be wrong. And she'd only deny it, so where'd we be? We've got to get a damn sight more on her than we've got up till now.'

'I've thought of something,' I said. 'It mayn't help, but then again it might. About Rhoda Yarnell's voice. It's what they call a velvety contralto. Just the sort of voice that might have been manipulated to do that telephoning to Violet Lancing.'

'It must have been,' Bill said, and then began frowning again. 'But the thing is, what next? Surely she'll have to get in touch with Violet Lancing again? She won't let the whole thing drop just because Violet funked it this morning.'

'If she calls round to see Violet personally tonight, then Tom will be on her tail,' I said.

'Let's hope he is,' he said. 'Something's got to happen before tomorrow morning or we'll have to lie like hell when Violet rings up. Even then we can't go on bluffing for ever.'

'There is an alternative,' I told him. 'You've got Violet very much where you want her. If you told her, for instance, exactly who she was and where she lived: told her in so many words, in fact, that she'd been lying like hell to you, then she'd be in a bit of a dilemma. That'd be the moment to tell her what you've found out about Rhoda. You could practically demand that she told you the whole truth for once. What the blackmail was really based on, for instance, and where exactly Rhoda came in. She wouldn't have time to think up lies if you sprang it all on her like that. Even if she did think up something on the spur of the moment, you might still gather a good deal from her reactions.'

'I don't like it,' Bill said. 'Not yet. Tom might pick up something tonight, then we can talk things over in the morning.'

'I've got another idea,' I said. 'Mind if I do some telephoning?'

Bill waved a hand and I rang the theatre. The box-office answered me.

'I know I'm a bit late,' I said, 'but I've seats for this evening and we weren't using them because a friend told us that Miss Lancing wasn't in the show any longer. Would you mind telling me if that's true?'

'It's not true at all,' the girl said. 'Miss Lancing wasn't playing at the matinee because she was taken ill. But she's better now.'

'And playing tonight?'

'Of course!'

'There we are,' I said to Bill. 'She certainly had a shock this morning but she's got over it now. Or else she's too jealous of her understudy to be away for more than one performance.'

He was too polite to say that he hadn't an idea of what I was getting at, so I explained.

'If Rhoda Yarnell wants to see Violet personally, and if she doesn't leave the shop till about six, then she'd have to go to the theatre, or else see her when the show's over, and that might be pretty late.'

'I hope to God she does see her,' Bill said fervently. 'That'll tie the two women up. If I work that stunt you suggested, it will give me a big lever.'

And then the telephone went. Bill grabbed it almost before it had rung.

'Yes? . . . Oh, it's you, Tom. Where are you speaking from? Rainsford? Good lord!' Rainsford by the way isn't the real name of that North London suburb.

There were various noises from Bill's end and then: 'Hang on a minute, will you?'

He glanced at his watch.

'A quarter to seven. Tom says she left Victoria Street before half past five. Took a bus to the Leicester Square Tube and went through to Rainsford. He followed her home and now he's ringing from near the Tube Station. Wants to know if there're any orders.'

I could only frown in thought. Bill went hurriedly on.

'She *didn't* see the Lancing woman. And Bill says she hasn't done any telephoning since she left the shop. That puts us in a jam.'

Bill was a far too conscientious soul, though I didn't tell him so. But he looked so worried that I had to do something.

'Tell him I'll meet him outside the Tube Station as quick as I can make it. Hear what he says.'

'That's real good of you,' Bill told me when he'd hung up. 'Nothing like hearing from Tom first hand.' And, as I began putting on my overcoat, 'If anything happens, give me a tinkle at Finchley.'

'That's it,' I said. 'You get home and get your slippers on. Tom and I'll soon have everything in hand.'

Bill looked almost cheerful as I went out. I shouldn't have been so cheerful myself if I'd known what was going to happen.

I had to change twice and best part of an hour had gone by when I came out at Rainsford Station. Dusk was in the sky but it looked like being a superb moonlit night. Tom said there was a little café open just along the road.

'Not your class, Mr Travers, but it's a bit nippy tonight.'

'Class be damned,' I said. 'Any port in a storm.'

So we found a seat by ourselves in the café, and I ordered a pot of tea and two plates of fish and chips. The flavour was pretty pronounced, but I was so hungry that most of my portion had gone by the time I couldn't help being aware of it.

'Just one of them little detached houses,' Tom was saying. 'About a quarter of a mile from here. Built just after they brought the Tube out here, I reckon.'

'Why no telephone?' I asked.

'She's only had it about a couple of years,' Tom said, 'and they didn't put in any new telephones during the war, not unless it was national importance. Now they've got so much in hand that she's got to line up in the queue, like the others.'

'How did you find all that out, Tom?'

'Ways and means,' he told me with a bit of a grin. 'Soon as the guv'nor said you'd be here in an hour or so, I thought I might as well have another dekko. Happened to do a good turn to a maid in the next door house.' The grin grew more broad. 'Taking her to the pictures next Saturday – I don't think.'

'Anything else did you learn?'

'Nothing else,' he said. 'Didn't do to be too inquisitive.'

'Well, it doesn't look as if you can do any more good tonight,' I told him. 'I'll just have a look round for myself, and you might as well slip off home – whichever one of your homes you're going to. I'll report to Bill. He's just a bit worried, so you'd better keep out of his way till the morning.' He drew me a rough map on the back of the menu and it looked as if I couldn't miss the house. 'Homestead' was the name, and it was the second on the left in the road. Then we parted at the Station and I pushed on. But not in any hurry. It was true that I hadn't any comic disguise but my six-foot-three is reasonably uncommon, and to disguise that with a stoop would have been merely to call attention to the Colonel Harrison of that afternoon. Not that I was intending to run any risk of Rhoda Yarnell getting even a glimpse of me. All I wanted to do was to get the lie of the land.

The moon was well up so I kept to the shadowed sides of the roads. And when I came to 'Homestead' I had a piece of luck, for that was on the shadowed side too. I walked slowly past it to almost the end of the road, and then I turned back and passed it again, changing the tempo of my steps.

It was quite a small house. Three bedrooms, perhaps, with sitting-room, dining-room, and kitchen, and all on the small side. It had a low wall and a privet hedge in front, and the usual crazy paving path led to the front door. Narrow flower beds ran alongside it, and on each side of them were strips of lawn. A side gate led apparently to a back door, and there was a kind of recessed blackness that might have been a garage.

Now there was nothing unusual or unexpected about any of that. What was unusual was this. Whereas the rest of the houses in that road – and they were all much of a muchness – had what

I might call pre-war lighting, 'Homestead' was as dark as hell's gates. And that didn't mean that there was nobody in the house, and I'll tell you why.

So much did that darkness intrigue me that at last sheer curiosity got the better of me. I gently opened that side gate and made my way noiselessly across a strip of lawn till I was near a window. Then I saw that curtains were drawn, just as in the old black-out days, and as soon as I knew that, I turned quickly to get back to the road again. Then I saw that along the boundary fence ran a narrow shrubbery. I don't quite know why, but I slipped into that instead. What looked like a dense lilac bush shielded me, and when I moved the branches back, I had the front of the house in full view.

What I was expecting to see I don't know, but I hoped perhaps that someone would come in or go out. But ten minutes went by and nothing had happened, and then it seemed to me that I was wasting my time. What I should have liked to do was to take a look at the back premises, and listen perhaps at windows. Or if I even caught a chink of light it would at least prove what I wasn't sure of – that Rhoda Yarnell was still in the house. And then, when I was debating what to do, something happened.

There was a sound like a faint creak, and in the blackness to my right. I gently eased forward and out of the blackness a definite new shadow emerged. It halted and merged into the shadows of the house, and soon I was wondering if my eyes had deceived me and there was nothing there at all.

Steps went by on the road, and in a few seconds there was silence again. Then I saw the man clearly as he suddenly appeared at the angle of the house. A short, stocky man, he looked, and then, almost at once, he was at one of the front windows. He stooped, ear against the very glass. Then in the distance was the sound of feet again, and men talking, and at once he was back in the shadows of the house corner. The feet and the voices went by, and at last there was silence again.

Who that man could be was utterly beyond me. That he was interested, and surreptitiously, in Rhoda Yarnell was absolutely certain, and suddenly I made up my mind. With-out making any noise that would cause alarm within the house itself, I would challenge that man. There was every reason why I should challenge him. To him I should be just the ordinary citizen who has seen something suspicious – someone loitering with intent: a likely burglar making a preliminary investigation. I gently eased myself out and then tiptoed towards the darkness which I now knew to be really a garage. Well in the shadow I halted. Along the road was the sound of a woman laughing noisily, but where I stood was a silence in which I was straining to listen.

Then there was a sound by the garage corner. Someone had moved and there was a creak as of a shoe.

'What're you doing there?' I said, and lowered my voice to a fierce whisper. 'Come on out of it! Let's have a look at you.'

He was on me before I got that last word out. As he suddenly loomed up in front of me I saw his face. Not clearly perhaps, but well enough to know him again. It was a fattish, clean-shaven face, the eyes deep-set. That's all I know. What he did was to catch me clean in the wind with a short-arm jab that doubled me up. Then, and it must have been in the follow-up in the same split-second, he caught me one on the jaw and out I went.

I don't know how long it was before I came round but it was no more than a matter of a minute or two. My jaw felt as if it was cracked and there was the devil of a pain in my short ribs, but by the mercy of heaven my glasses were not smashed. Then as soon as I remembered what had happened I had a sudden alarm. But never a thing was missing from my pockets and my wristwatch – quite a valuable one – was still in place, its glass unbroken.

I didn't stay where I was to do my thinking. Nothing had apparently been heard in the house and as soon as I was sure there were no sounds, I made my way across the grass again and out to the road. A few yards along I dusted my overcoat and pressed a nasty dent out of my hat. Then I walked slowly on towards the station.

What that attack on me meant I had no idea. The man wasn't a burglar, that was certain, or he'd have helped him-self to my wallet and watch. And he hadn't looked like a burglar. A burglar on the job doesn't wear an overcoat and bowler hat, or so it seemed to me. And that listening at the window of the house was out of character too. If then the man was some sort of snooper, just what was his object? To that there was no answer, though one thing stood out a mile – that there were more ramifications to that blackmail business than had as yet appeared on the surface.

But when I asked myself what the man had intended to do if after his listening he heard no sound in the house, I had a sudden idea. There was one thing I *could* discover – whether or not the house was empty: whether, in fact, Rhoda Yarnell had left it while Tom and I were having that meal.

So as soon as I got to that telephone box which Tom had used, I rang the police.

'I was just going down Roseland Road,' I said, 'and I saw something suspicious at a house called "Homestead". A man was acting suspiciously in the garden and when I challenged him, he bolted. The house looked to be empty – so it might be worth your while to have a look.'

'Who is it speaking?' I was asked.

'Never mind that,' I said. 'I'm a perfectly respectable citizen who doesn't want to waste time in court if you make an arrest.'

That was all, and I began making my way towards 'Homestead' again. A car came hurtling round the corner and drew up outside. Two plainclothes men went to the front door and I delayed my passing accordingly. The door was opened almost at once, and the woman who opened it was almost certainly Rhoda Yarnell. But I didn't stay to make sure. It was enough for me that she'd been in that house ever since Tom had seen her enter it. And that made it even more important to find an answer to the question why the windows had been so completely and effectively blacked out.

A few minutes later I was in that call box again and ringing Bill Ellice at his private address.

'No news that won't keep till the morning,' I told him. 'Everything's well in hand, so treat yourself to a good night's rest.'

In any case I didn't see what I could tell him. Certainly not about that curious attack on myself. That would have to be reserved for Wharton. And I wasn't going to give him even a hint of what I was going to tell him in the morning – that I'd remembered who Rhoda Yarnell was. But he seemed satisfied to leave things like that, so as far as I was concerned, everything in the garden was lovely. Even my jaw wasn't cracked, and when I wiggled it it hurt a bit and no more. And if I didn't take too deep a breath, my belly wasn't so bad either. And when I tackled my breakfast the following morning, the jaw was practically normal. In a day or two's time there'd be on my belly a green and yellow circle as big as a plate, but the breathing was all in order again. If it hadn't been, it wouldn't have worried me too much. I was far too busy, getting ready the revelations I should soon be making to Bill Ellice.

It was only half past nine when I got to Broad Street. I had to wait a few minutes because Bill was interviewing a client. I asked the secretary if Tom had shown up.

'Mr Ellice has sent him on another assignment,' she told me. 'Something that came in by this morning's post.'

I used that as an opening when I got into the office.

'Sally tells me you've taken Tom off the Lancing job, Bill. Any special reason?'

'Read that,' he said, and passed me a letter.

Dear Mr. Ellice,

I have decided not to take any further action in the matter, as I have discovered that it is all due to a misunderstanding. Everything is now cleared up, but I am very grateful to you all the same, and shall recommend you to all my friends. I also enclose another and final payment which I hope you will consider satisfactory.

Yours sincerely,

Jane Upson

PS. I hope you didn't think me too foolish yesterday morning in the tea-shop. I know that I fainted from sheer relief, though I couldn't tell you that at the time.

PPS. I rely on you to keep everything confidential. Again many thanks.

I read the letter through again, if only as a cover for thought. In some ways it was a facer. In others it was about the biggest piece of luck I could have had.

'How much was the extra payment?' I asked as I gave him the letter.

'Ten pounds in notes.'

'Not a bad little case – financially,' I said. Bill cut in with his own views, and his language was almost blasphemous. To hell with the ten pounds! What he didn't like was being made a fool of. That woman, getting away with a pack of lies. And thinking him simpleton enough to be taken in by the cheap flattery in that letter.

'Recommend me to all her friends – the hell she will! If she ever catches sight of me, she'll disappear as if the devil had kicked her endways.'

I had listened with what I hoped was a sympathetic if serious face.

'Do you know, Bill, I'm just realizing that this is the very best thing that could have happened. Remember what I told you yesterday? That I ought to know that name Yarnell? Well, I've now remembered why.'

Bill's eyebrows lifted.

'Remember the Manfrey Case?'

He remembered it, and where he didn't remember I could prompt.

'Well, I was in on it,' I said. 'Only from the outside, though. I happened to be on leave and Superintendent Wharton took me along as a sort of holiday treat. That's why I don't know all the ins and outs, except that the Case was filed. But this is what I do know.'

I told him practically everything I could have known, provided I'd been as much in the background as I'd made out. When I'd finished, his eyes were definitely bulging.

'My God, we've been handling dynamite!'

'You're right,' I said. 'And the fuse was burning.'

Then he wanted to know what was the best thing to do.

'I've made some preliminary inquiries,' I told him. 'Wharton's been away for a few days and he's due back this afternoon. What about my handling him? Provided I can guarantee that you and I will be in the clear?'

Bill's gratitude was so genuine that I felt a bit of a swine.

'Don't thank me, Bill,' I said. 'My advice got us in this mess and it's up to me to get us out of it. And I can. I wouldn't mind betting you that Wharton will want to give us a medal.'

'Medal be damned!' said Bill fervently. 'I don't want any medals. All I want is a clean bill of health.'

And there ended another phase of the original Manfrey Case. Maybe by now you've satisfied yourself that you really do know both how Manfrey was killed and the one who killed him. If so, the rest of the story will have no interest for you. Or perhaps you may be wondering if you are right after all, and in that case you may like to read on.

PART III

CHAPTER X
A New Game Begins

I WAITED for a call from George Wharton till nearly six o'clock that evening, and just when I was thinking of going out for a breather, what should he do but turn up at the flat. And he was in a very good humour. Whatever job it was that he had been doing had turned out pretty well, and now he was looking forward to a couple of free days for a belated clean up of his little kitchen garden. Something of an Indian summer had set in that morning and he didn't refuse a bottle of beer.

Everything was set fair for my story. George pricked his ears at the first mention of Violet Lancing, and then lugged out his huge notebook. But all through that long recital he didn't interrupt me more than twice, and then only because I hadn't made something sufficiently clear. But when I'd finished he began his questions. Maybe the knowledge that Ellice and I had thought him the only one competent to look after both the Case and our interests was putting him on his mettle. Perhaps I have told you that he has an amazingly retentive memory, and after that one hearing of the facts of the Case he seemed to get a better grasp of things than I had managed to secure in a close and even intimate acquaintanceship. And just a word to you about the questions he asked and the answers I gave. It's this: that they contain the whole solution of the Case. The pieces of the jigsaw were there, even if it was to take time and good luck to fit them together.

'Rather naive kind of blackmail?' was his first remark, about Rhoda Yarnell. 'Suggesting a meeting with the Lancing woman in broad daylight in Victoria Street. Trusting a good deal to chance, wasn't she? If the Lancing woman had communicated with the police, she'd have been caught red-handed.'

'I don't know,' I said. 'What could we pin on her? She'd have denied everything. And she'd have said she went to that shop to buy the book she did buy. And you bet Violet Lancing would have denied all knowledge of her.'

'That five hundred pounds. Did the Lancing woman actually have it ready?'

'Everything points to the fact that she did.'

'Five hundred pounds,' he said slowly, and as if he saw five hundred golden sovereigns on the table before him. 'That's a nice little sum of money, even in these times. Where'd she get it from? What's her salary?'

'Don't know,' I said.

'You don't know!' Then he gave me his first glare.

'You can't have it both ways, George,' I said and hurriedly filled his glass. 'We could have found out all that if we'd gone on with the Case. But we didn't, and I've told you why.'

He grunted and I knew the grunt for an apology.

'Then tell me something else,' he said. 'We know the Lancing woman's an even bigger liar than she was three years ago, but why did she call the whole thing off?'

'Gawd knows,' I said flippantly. 'You answered the question yourself when you said she was a liar. But if I chance what I think is a good guess, I'd say she's paid over the money, and she's satisfied she won't have to pay any more.'

'Perhaps you're right,' he said. 'If so it's a kind of family affair and the law can't butt in.'

'It'd have been hard work for the law to butt in in any case,' I reminded him. 'Everything depends on the evidence of Bill Ellice – and perhaps myself, which comes to the same thing. You can't expect Bill to betray a client, even if that client has turned him down.'

'There might be ways and means,' he said darkly. 'But that fainting business in the tea-shop. I can't quite get the hang of that. You say she'd had a good look at Rhoda Yarnell long before she fainted?'

'That's right. Rhoda Yarnell had even moved away from the book-shop by then.'

'And you can't suggest any reason?'

'None whatever.'

He scowled at the glass of beer, shook his head, and then took a swig.

'I've got an idea that that's the answer to the whole thing. Find out why she fainted, and everything'd be as clear as daylight. But going back to the Yarnell woman. I'm assuming it's a certainty she was the blackmailer. Then what information could she have had that was worth five hundred pounds?'

'Heaven knows,' I said. 'I've been racking my brains over that all this afternoon. All I can think is that it's something arising out of the divorce. Maybe she discovered that the Lancing woman had been her late husband's mistress before marriage. Maybe then she could have proved perjury at the divorce trial.'

'But that doesn't tie up with the Manfrey affair!'

'I know it doesn't,' I told him patiently. 'And that's another thing that's been worrying me, for I've got a hunch – as strong a one as I've ever had in my life – that the whole thing does tie up.'

You might not think that George, stolid and unimaginative as he chooses to look, would ever believe in anything so unsubstantial as hunches. But he does, and in his time he's had good reason. That's why my own mention of a hunch didn't meet with a snort or a glare.

'Let's hope you're right,' he said. 'But I've got an idea too. Why shouldn't her husband – ex-husband if you like – have written the Yarnell woman a letter before he was killed? My idea is, and so is Broad's – you remember Broad? – that Yarnell enlisted because he'd made a mess of things, and he'd come to hate Violet like hell. Wouldn't that make him try to sneak back to his first wife again?'

'Almost certainly yes,' I said. 'But what could he have told her?'

'There you've got me,' George admitted. 'But I bet he didn't live with a woman like that without finding out a few things. Or else why did he leave her?'

He frowned as if he had another idea.

'I never saw that Yarnell woman. There wasn't any need to. You say she's a smart, business-like woman. You'd call her a lady?'

'As near as makes no difference.'

'Funny,' he said, and shook his head. 'I mean taking an interest in that ex-husband of hers. Pretty much of a weakling, or so I thought him. Or am I rushing too far ahead? After all she didn't have anything to do with him as far as we know. She mayn't even have answered any of his letters, but that wouldn't have stopped her from profiting from any information that he'd happened to write. But wait a minute, though. Why did she take all that time before she took any action? Yarnell's been dead a year or two now.'

'Perhaps she didn't want the money before,' I suggested. 'Maybe the shop isn't doing so well as you'd think. Maybe it isn't her shop after all.'

'There we are then,' said George, and made a note in his book. 'There's one line of inquiry if we decide to reopen the Case.'

Then he was frowning, and shaking his head again.

'It *must* tie up with the Manfrey Case. Something keeps on hammering away at me that it must. What you might call two former characters suddenly crop up. And then there's that new element that comes in.'

'What element?'

He stared and then asked where my brains were.

'The man who assaulted you last night. He's the new element. Where's he come in?'

I said I'd told him all I knew and I'd no guesses left.

'Wait a minute,' he said. 'You do know why that house was blacked out.'

'Maybe I don't,' I said. 'All I can think of is that Rhoda Yarnell was pretty upset, scared if you like, after her client didn't turn up. If so it would be natural to shut herself up in the house with the windows blacked out and the doors locked.'

'Oh, no,' he said. 'Those windows were blacked out so that nobody could see who was in the house.'

'You mean there might have been someone else in the house beside her?'

'Logical, isn't it?'

'Then who was it? Violet Lancing?'

But George was getting to his feet and moving across to the telephone. He ruffled the pages of the directory and then found his number.

'Wait a moment, George,' I said. 'Were you thinking of finding out if Violet Lancing was at the theatre last night?'

'Why not?' he asked me.

'Well, if that girl in the box-office happens to mention the fact to her, mightn't that put Violet on her guard?'

'I don't give a damn if it does,' he told me. 'The more scared she is, the better I'll be pleased.'

He got his number and his answer. Violet had been play-ing as usual, and that was that. But the more we looked at it, and from the more angles, the more of a mystery that snooper seemed to be.

'Medium height, thick-set, and something of a bruiser,' George said. 'There was nobody in the Manfrey Case like that.'

It was a teaser. We couldn't even get as far as theorizing about who he was and why he'd been there, and when I make a confession like that, it shows that I at least was licked. Usually, right or wrong, I can find a theory for anything. George once said, and not nicely, that I was the only man living who could account at a second's notice for the larynx of Balaam's ass and the gullet of Jonah's whale.

'What about you having another look round tonight?' he suddenly asked me. 'I'll ring the local police and give them the office.' He chuckled. 'And keep your eyes skinned this time. And keep your distance and use your reach.'

'You're a cheerful sort of second, George,' I told him. 'But don't forget that the best pugilists don't wear glasses in the ring. Also I'm a man of peace.'

'Man of peace be damned,' George said. 'You're not going to sit down under what he gave you last night?'

'We'll see,' I said. 'But what about you? Are you advising the Manfrey Case should be officially reopened, or aren't you?'

'Don't rush me,' George said at once. 'There's got to be a good deal of thinking before I commit myself to that. Because I'm ringing up the police for you, that doesn't say we're going the whole hog. No,' he said, and shook his head warily again. 'I've got to have time to think this thing out. No panic, no hurry. Nobody's going to bolt. What's been done has been done and –'

'And two and two make four,' I told him. 'I could go on like that for hours, George. But tell me this. If you *had* re-opened the Case, what would you do?'

'What would I do? Well, I'd have both of those women under observation day and night. It mightn't be much good, but I'd cast the net for your pugilistic friend. I'd check Rhoda Yarnell's business and her bank account.'

'That's enough to be going on with,' I said. 'Have another bottle, George, and drink to a treat in store.'

'Not for me,' he said hastily. 'Jane expected me home an hour ago. Just a note or two and I'm off.'

He promised to ring the police as soon as he reached his house. Then I mentioned Bill Ellice again. Then as soon as he'd gone, I rang Bill up.

'Travers here, Bill. Just had a long talk with Wharton, and everything's O.K. Clean bill of health and a medal to follow.'

'You're not pulling my leg?'

'Honour bright, Bill,' I told him. 'He told me he'd got no use for inquiry agents, but you were the exception. And, what's more, Bill, there's just the chance that he may ask you to lend a hand if he takes things up himself.'

'That's pretty good of him,' Bill said. 'But would it be ethical?'

'Of course it would,' I said. 'You didn't give your word to Violet. You gave it to Mrs Upson.'

'By gosh you're right!' Bill said. 'Funny I didn't see it that way.'

I told him I'd be along some time the next day and that was that. Bill had sounded positively rejuvenated, and I was feeling on top of the world. And if I was feeling fine after having wriggled out of a tight situation, I said to myself, what heights of ecstasy would have been mine if my conscience had been clear all along? What a grand life that must have been, I told myself, never to tell the whitest of lies and to have a conscience like driven snow. A grand life indeed. I'd have to try it some time.

But I wasn't feeling quite so happy when I emerged into the moonlight at Rainsford. I suppose I've done a bit of scrapping in my time, but sighting a Hun at the end of a rifle or heaving a grenade at thirty yards is hardly the same as coming to grips at close quarters with a man who has a first-class knowledge of how to use his fists. It was those cursed glasses of mine that were worrying me: the damage to my eyes if a blow smashed them, and the fact that without them I'm even blinder than a bat. And if I did get near what George had called my pugilistic friend, I couldn't even indulge in a rugby tackle.

But I did take the precaution of going to see the local police, banking on the fact that George must have mentioned me quite favourably. From the attitude of the station-sergeant I gathered that George had surpassed himself.

'I suppose you can't tell us any more about why you rang us up last night?' he asked me.

I hinted that things were very much in the embryo stage, and that pretty big issues were at stake, and I promised that as soon as anything whatever could be let out, Rainsford should be the first to know. In fact, they might have to co-operate. Meanwhile a security black-out wasn't the word for it.

George had had the sense to imagine that 'Homestead' would have a back and a front, and when I left the station a plainclothes man went with me; a youngish chap called Adney, and he told me he was a bit of a runner. He also told me what had happened at 'Homestead' the previous night, for he had been one of the men I'd seen at the door.

Rhoda Yarnell had been scared at the mention of police. That didn't strike Adney as anything remarkable. Funny, he said, how people will be scared of seeing the police even when they come to help. A hangover, he suggested, from kids who're always scared of a policeman. But she eased up a lot when she knew why they'd come, only to get very nervous again when told of a man who had been hanging round the house in the dark.

'Did she let you inside?'

He seemed surprised at the question. There wasn't any need to look inside the house. Any attempt at burglarious entry would have been made from the outside and she insisted that she'd heard no sound whatever.

'It's very important,' I said. 'I can't tell you how, but I'd like to know if she showed any real disinclination to admit you to the house.'

'Now you come to mention it, she did,' he said. 'I mean, she blocked the whole doorway up and didn't even ask us in to talk things over.'

In any case he and his colleague had made a thorough examination of all windows and doors and when they'd finished Mrs

Yarnell told them she'd had a look inside and had seen nothing unusual.

'She didn't ask you in for a drink?'

'Not so as you'd notice it,' he told me with a grin.

'And that was the end of it?'

He said it was – virtually. She'd been assured that she could sleep in safety, though no special action was actually taken. For one thing the police weren't sure that the whole business hadn't been a hoax, and so the matter was left as a routine one for the constable on the beat.

By that time we were near 'Homestead' so we halted for a quick pow-wow. I could take the back, he said, and he would take the front, and as we'd be within hollering distance of each other, we might claim we were keeping in touch. I found it wasn't so hard to get around to the back. Three houses on was a passage that led to another and much wider passage between the back gardens of the two relevant roads. But when I got to the fence that formed the back boundary of 'Homestead', I didn't feel any too happy. That passage seemed very cramped. It didn't give me much elbow room if some local inhabitant came along on his lawful business and happened to wonder what I was doing there. So I found the door in the fence, intending to go through to the back garden, but that door was locked. And that was a curious thing. Why should a door be locked when it is the only one available for tradesmen? Rhoda, I decided, had locked it as soon as twilight was near.

We'd agreed that our watch might reasonably end at midnight. The stranger whom I'd disturbed the previous night had probably arrived by Underground, and presumably he'd have to go home the same way. The idea suited me, for I too would have to get back to town that night. And so, to make a long story short, I began my watch. Nothing happened, and soon I was bored to tears. The back of the house showed no chink of light and I might have been watching a mausoleum. And that went on till nearly eleven o'clock, by which time I decided to break the monotony and have a quick chat with Adney. But when I got round to the front there was never a sign of him. I walked along and then back. I even whistled softly, but still there was never a sign.

What had happened I couldn't imagine, so I moved a little way along the road and waited under some trees in front of an undeveloped plot, and then in a few minutes I saw him coming along.

'What's been happening?' I wanted to know.

The man had been there, he said, but he hadn't heard him because he'd been wearing rubber-soled shoes, but from his hiding place in the side shrubbery of the garden opposite the house he'd seen him come by, and the description tallied with the one I'd given. The man went slowly by the house and then came back. He gave a look each way along the road and then just as his hand was on the side gate, Adney emerged from his hiding place, and at that very second the man chose to have another precautionary look round. At the sight of Adney he bolted, and as Adney was also wearing rubber soles, I had heard nothing of the chase.

At any rate it hadn't lasted long, for the man had suddenly disappeared. And that wasn't difficult, with a short stretch of woodland between us and the station. Adney had looked round for a time and had done some listening, and then he'd decided to get back and report to me.

'Pity you didn't go straight on to the Underground,' I said.

'What a hope, sir,' he said. 'If he's living in town then he'd a choice of bus and train, besides the Underground.'

'I've got a hunch it's the Underground he's taken,' I said. So we started off walking briskly that way, and I told Adney I'd report back to the police if anything happened. When he wanted to know what about the following night, I told him I didn't know.

I had to wait for a bit at the Underground station, but there was no sign of my man on the platform. So that again was that, and pretty disappointing, too. For a second time that man had been on the job, and for the second time he'd been scared. Now it was a hundred to one against his having another try.

I reported to George in the morning. It's bad enough sometimes to gather anything from him when you're looking him clean in the eye. Over the telephone I had no idea what was in his mind. He did say he'd expected that second try and he also added that he doubted if there'd be a third.

'All the same I think I'd go along,' he said. 'If he was prepared to take a risk after you disturbed him the first time, it shows he's doing something he thinks it worth while taking risks about.'

'And still no official action?'

'Don't know yet,' he said. 'I'm seeing You-know-Who some time this evening. Might have some news tomorrow.'

I hadn't the least idea whom he meant by You-know-Who, unless it was an Assistant Commissioner, but George loves mysterious hintings. The Big Bugs, the Powers-that-be, and Some-of-the-Nobs are other names he gives to the same mysterious functionaries and superiors. But it wasn't bad news to learn that things were likely to move.

I did a job of work for Bill Ellice that took up most of my day. Then I rang Adney and dusk found me on the way to Rainsford again, and with as much real hope of catching our man as of meeting Hitler in Jerusalem. But Adney was optimistic enough, at least till just short of eleven o'clock. Nothing had happened and nothing had stirred. I had definitely seen a crack of light in an upstair room, and that looked as if Rhoda had gone to bed. It was just after that crack of light disappeared that Adney and I met in the passage way, and with the same idea in view, even if he left it to me to suggest that we might as well call it a night.

His way led towards the Piccadilly line station, and I want to make it clear that what I said was after I'd given him the tip. I'm not spreading myself about being particularly generous, but my experience has always been that any kind of tip is a good invest-ment. Many a time I've found myself wanting a spot of help and I've run up against someone who remembered, not me, perhaps, but a half-crown tip. I made Adney's more than that, and I will say that he didn't want to take it.

But as I said, it was after that and just when I was saying good night, that I had an idea.

'Mind you, we can't do it, Adney!' I said, 'but I'd like to have a look over that house tomorrow when Mrs Yarnell's gone to town. Suppose you haven't got a respectable burglar among your pals?'

'Afraid not, sir,' he said, and laughed.

And so to the sequel. I'd been round to Broad Street for most of the following morning, and it was just after I'd dis-posed of a service lunch that the telephone rang. I guessed it was Wharton, about to tell me what had happened at his conference. But it was Adney.

'There you are, sir,' he said. 'Been trying to get you for the last hour.'

The rest was put in rather vague terms, and I guessed he was telephoning from somewhere where he might possibly be overheard. What his news was amounted to this.

He'd thought about my burglar idea, and then as soon as he'd seen Rhoda Yarnell leave for town, he'd had a look round the outside of the house. To put himself right with the neighbours on each side he'd made inquiries there about what I might call burglary noises, and he'd shown his credentials. Then he'd examined Rhoda's ashbin that was standing by the back door. In it he found some stubs of cigarettes. There were two kinds, and one kind always had lipstick on the stub and the other kind hadn't. He'd also found a dirty screwed-up receipt from a local firm of wine and spirit merchants.

Now he knew the assistant in that shop and he had a word with him. What he learned was that Mrs Yarnell had ordered a case of light ale about a month before, and that was the first time she had dealt with the firm. Three weeks later – only a week ago – the order had been repeated and the empties collected.

'What do you make of it, sir?' Adney wanted to know.

'Well,' I said, and tried to make it dubious. 'It looks as if she'd had someone staying with her.'

'Just my idea,' he said. 'You don't think it could have been our friend?'

'But he was outside the house, trying to get in.'

'I know, sir,' he said. 'She might have kicked him out for some reason or other. Trying to get too fresh or something.'

I didn't say that that was preposterous and that he wasn't her type. What I did tell Adney was that he'd done a smart job of work and if he picked up anything else he might let me know. I added that if someone had been staying in the house for best part of a month, then there'd be the question of rations, so what about discreet inquiries at shops with which Mrs Yarnell dealt.

That was how we left it. What I didn't know then was that before a very few hours had passed I should have all the answers. And the way I got them was this.

CHAPTER XI
The Pugilistic Friend

THERE COMES A TIME in any case when – to give none too good an illustration – one knows for a certainty the value of x, and then the value of y. After that it is easy to find the value of $x + y$. But that isn't deduction: it's routine and axiomatic. What I did that afternoon when I sat down to think things over was something quite different. You can call it deduction or a first-class guess, but all I will say is that it was one of the few occasions in fifteen years of experience when things came out according to pattern. I should also add that when things did so turn out, nobody was more surprised than myself.

What I began thinking was this. That mysterious snooper at 'Homestead' had been definitely scared from the house. If he was interested in Rhoda Yarnell herself or in the unknown man who had been in the house, then he would now have to transfer his field of inquiry elsewhere. And since Rhoda Yarnell could be said to include the man, the only thing for him to do would be to keep a watch on her. My guess was that the man, whoever he was, had also been scared away, and if so a tailing of Rhoda might bring my snooping friend back to the man again. And if all that was correct, then by all the rules my snooping friend should be keeping the Victoria Street establishment under observation.

Mind you, I was utterly in the dark about everything else. I'd no idea what the snooper was hoping to find out, and I couldn't even make a conjecture. Wharton had called him a new element and I was thinking of him as an intrusive new factor into what had been a reasonably clear case of blackmail, and as such he was interesting me more than that case itself. So as soon as I'd told myself that his only logical course of action was to keep an eye on Rhoda Yarnell, I took a bus that deposited me at the Army and Navy Stores. I wore no comic disguise for, between ourselves, I'd no real confidence in the deductions I'd made.

I crossed to the other side of the street and made my way slowly towards the hairdressing establishment, squinting across out of the corner of my eye. Then on my side of the street I became aware of a man, well behind the newspaper he was ostensibly reading, and a few feet from a flower-seller on a camp stool, surrounded by masses of chrysanthemums. The man had his back against the wall, and as I passed he didn't even look up. But from my superior height I could get a good look at his face. And there wasn't the shadow of a doubt. It was my pugilistic friend!

As I passed him, my heart beginning to beat a bit quickly, I heard him remark to the flower-girl that Something-or-Other had won the one-thirty. I slightly quickened my step, wondering if my height had given me away, but when I'd got as far as Massey's book-shop I ventured to look back, and there he was, still apparently engrossed in his paper.

Inside another five minutes I was telephoning to the Yard and asking for Wharton. I didn't expect to find him there, but there he was.

'Just been ringing your place,' he said reproachfully.

That's just like George, expecting me to sit at the end of a line, awaiting his good pleasure.

'Listen, George,' I said. 'I'm ringing from Victoria station. The pugilistic friend of mine, as you call him, is parked outside Rhoda Yarnell's shop. Could you meet me at the Army and Navy Stores as quick as you can make it?'

'You're sure?'

'Dead sure.'

'Right,' he said, and the line was dead before I could say another word.

I took a bus and got off just beyond the Army and Navy, and I'd hardly got there when a taxi drew up and George got out.

'Still there, is he?' he wanted to know.

'By that flower-girl,' I said. 'You can see for yourself. She's a bit of a screen for him. Probably keeps her eyes skinned while he goes for a meal.'

A quick pow-wow and then we crossed the street, and as we moved towards our man we were in what is known as animated conversation. Then when we were right abreast of him, George caught sight of the flowers.

'Nice chrysanthemums. Lovely chrysanthemums,' chanted the girl, but George had gone back, and he was one side of our friend and I the other. The man looked up, eyebrows lifted. My height still apparently conveyed nothing to him.

'Pardon me,' George said, 'but do you think you could spare me a couple of minutes?'

'Me!'

'That's it,' said George, and suddenly produced his credentials. 'Superintendent Wharton of New Scotland Yard.'

Our friend had a look.

'Some mistake, isn't there, sir? I can't see what you want with me.'

'You'll learn,' said George amiably. 'There might be a little matter of assault on the person of this gentleman who saw you at Rainsford in highly suspicious circumstances in the garden of a house called "Homestead". That convey anything to you?'

Our friend gave me a look of such comical dismay that I almost laughed.

'What about it?' George went on. 'There's a tea-shop further along. What about a nice friendly chat? And don't try to bolt. There's a couple of my men nice and handy.'

'I don't want to bolt, sir,' he said, but as he folded his paper and put it away in his pocket, his eyes were everywhere nevertheless. 'I haven't the faintest idea what you're getting at, but a cup of tea'll suit me all right.'

There was no bravado. It was the tone of a man who knows he's nothing to fear. His was a Midland accent, but not aggressively so, and he spoke like a man of some education. As we strolled towards the Daffodil Tea-rooms I thought I'd make things more cheerful, for Wharton wasn't saying a word. 'You know how to use your fists pretty well!' I remarked. 'Me?' he said, and then at the smile on my face he gave a bit of a smile himself. 'I was runner-up for the cruiser-weight amateur championship in 1913. Tommy Lark beat me.'

'Good going,' I said. 'He turned pro., didn't he?'

'That's right,' he said. 'Killed on the Somme, he was. Not a mile from where I got a packet myself.'

'You're a pretty good runner too, they tell me,' I said slyly. He gave me another quick look at that.

'I used to be,' he said. 'Reckoned the fastest outside right in the Birmingham League in the old days. Might have turned pro. if it hadn't been for the war.'

We crossed the street again and there was the Daffodil. Up the stairs we went and from the way my man looked about him, I gathered that he was seeing it for the first time. The place wasn't too full and we found a table just back from the window where I'd sat on a certain morning. Wharton ordered a pot of tea for three and cakes – he always had a sweet tooth – and not till he'd poured out the tea did he open his mouth. 'What's your name, by the way?'

A card was produced and he read it aloud.

MR H. TIPTON

representing the

MIDLAND INQUIRY AGENCY

Headquarters, 115 Waverley Street,

BIRMINGHAM

Wharton put the card unblushingly in his pocket.

'Have one of these cakes,' he said, and: 'So you're an inquiry agent, Mr Tipton.' He sighed. 'Well, we've all got to live. But what exactly are you inquiring into these days?'

'It'll take a fairish time to say,' Tipton told him.

Wharton waved an inviting hand.

'Our time's our own. Yours can go on the expense account. So let's hear it. And tell it your own way.'

And there began, as they say in the classics, the story of Herbert Tipton.

There was a Mrs Emily Stanbury of Edgbaston, who was the widow of a chemist who'd had a shop in the city. She was comfortably off and with her lived her widowed daughter, and that daughter's small son, James Hanley. His father had been killed in the last war, and then his mother died when he was twelve years old. The grandmother had him educated at the grammar school nearby and later he took an engineering course at the University of Birmingham. In 1940, much against his grandmother's wishes, he joined up, and after serving some time in the tanks he went to an O.C.T.U. and on passing out was given a commission in the Hampshire Regiment. As Tipton pointed out there was no guarantee in those days that a man was sent to his own county regiment.

James Hanley went abroad and he corresponded fairly regularly with his grandmother. Then word came that he was missing. That was followed some months later by the news that he was a prisoner of war. The Red Cross furnished an address and the grandmother wrote. But she received no answers. That, by the way, was towards the end of 1944. So she made urgent inquiries of the Red Cross who said they'd take the matter up. Maybe the grandson, they said, was suffering from loss of memory, due to a head wound, but in any case they'd do what they could.

Then came the spring of 1945 and the chaos among prisoner-of-war camps in Germany. But whatever it was due to, Mrs Stanbury got no news of her grandson. And then in July she received word from the War Office that her grandson was back in

England. He'd been held in one of the last German pockets and had only then managed to escape.

A week or two passed with Mrs Stanbury expecting every day to hear from the grandson, and, when nothing happened, she applied to the War Office again. There was a longish delay before she was informed that Lt J. Hanley had been demobilized. He had been paid his gratuity and the War Office was now unaware of his whereabouts. So Mrs Stanbury consulted a firm of solicitors and they discovered that Hanley had cleared his banking account and had disappeared. At least his whereabouts were quite unknown, even at the headquarters of his old regiment, and there seemed no means of getting on his tracks. But the solicitor did advise a placing of the matter in the hands of the Midland Inquiry Agency.

'Tm beginning to get you,' Wharton said. 'Did you see the old lady yourself, by the way?'

Tipton said he had seen her twice. He added with something of a grimace that she was a tough one. Asked by Wharton to enlarge on that, he said she had struck him and his principals as bigoted and straitlaced. Their opinion was, though naturally they hadn't mentioned it to their client, that James Hanley, now just about thirty, had chosen an opportune moment to cut adrift from what must have been a highly restrictive influence on his earlier life. But they'd undertaken the task of finding the grandson and that was where Tipton himself came in.

After the usual routine enquiries had produced nothing new, except perhaps the fact that what with his gratuity and accrued pay Lt Hanley had a nice sum of money in his possession, the firm drew a bow at a venture. A newly demobilized man would have to have a ration book, and unless he moved almost daily from hotel to hotel he would have to use that ration book. So a notice was inserted in a couple of trade journals, and in such Sunday papers as the *News of the World* and the *People*, offering a reward for information about a James Hanley, aged thirty, late a lieutenant of infantry. A week or so later they heard from a grocer at Rainsford asking about the reward and saying he might have information. Tipton was at once sent down with power to act.

'It was the late afternoon of the same night when you and I first ran across each other, sir,' he told me, and I thought that was diplomatically put. 'This grocer told me that about a month previously he'd had registered with him a young gentleman of the name of James Hanley. The description tallied as well as descriptions do, so that satisfied me so far. He said this Mr Hanley was living at that "Homestead" house, and it also appeared that whoever else was living in that house was registered elsewhere, and that struck me as interesting. Still, we left it like that and then the most extraordinary thing happened. Blow me if that Mr Hanley didn't go by the very shop where I was!

'The grocer said, "There *is* Mr Hanley. Reckon he's just come off the train". I said I'd follow him to his house and try to get a word with him, which I did. It was about five o'clock or so then. I let him keep well ahead and when he was safe indoors I gave a knock. Nobody answered, so I knocked again. Believe it or not, nothing happened. "That's funny," I said to myself. "Perhaps he's gone out again by the back way." So I let it rest for an hour or so while I got myself some tea and then I tried again. Nothing doing.

'Well, I wasn't going to be beaten when I'd got so far, so I kept an eye on the house. Then about a quarter past six or so, along comes a smart young woman and she goes into the house too. Then just as I thought I'd try making inquiries of her, along comes a man who looks to me as if he's been tailing her. You can't mistake 'em when you're in the game, same as I am. And sure enough this fellow digs himself in to watch the house and I'm watching the house and him. What it all adds up to I don't know, but there we are. I stuck it out till it was pretty near dusk and then this other chap moved off". I followed him as far as a telephone box and when he was safe inside I nipped back and knocked at the door. The smart young lady opened it.

'"Pardon me," I said and raised my hat, "but could I have a word with Mr Hanley?"

'"Who?" she said, and I repeated the name.

'"Never heard of him," she said. "It must be some other house."

'I said I thought I'd seen him go into the house at about six o'clock. Would you believe it but she brazened me out that I was wrong. She didn't know Mr Hanley and the house had been locked up all day and she was the only one who had a key. And she was alone in the house then. Then she had the nerve to say I'd better get off or she'd send for the police. Reckoned she'd been reading about people like me who found out when women were alone in the house.'

He was certainly a man with a grievance as he looked round at Wharton and me for sympathy. George nodded sagely and asked him to go on.

'That was why I came back that night,' he said, 'just to hear if she was talking to anyone in the house. Then I ran up against this gentleman here.'

'You certainly did,' I said, and he was looking so abject about it that I had to smile. Wharton told him impatiently to get on with it.

'Well, that's all, sir,' he said. 'I did a guy and I didn't think it'd be too healthy to hang round that house any more. What I did was pick the lady up and follow her as far as here. Then I followed her home again at night and when I'd got that far I thought I might as well have another look round after dark. Then I got disturbed again – not this gentleman; somebody else – and that put the wind up me properly. Things seemed to be happening that I hadn't been told about, so I got in touch with my firm on the phone and they told me to stick to the Victoria Street end and watch the lady in case she was still in touch with Hanley. And that's about the lot, sir.'

'You don't think Hanley's still at her house?'

'Not him,' he said. 'You bet your life, sir, that he was expecting that grandmother of his to get on his tracks. Then I blew the gaff by asking the lady if I might speak to Mr Hanley.'

'Maybe you're right,' Wharton told him. 'But right or not we're grateful to you for being so frank.'

Then he was giving a reproachful look at the empty cake plate, and pouring himself out the last of the tea. Tipton was watching him just the least bit nervously.

'Just one or two questions, Mr Tipton, but nothing for you to get worried about. What are your personal ideas about the whole set-up? You've had plenty of time to do some thinking.'

'To tell you the honest truth, sir, I don't know where I am,' Tipton told him. 'All I can think of is that she met this Hanley somewhere. He had plenty of money in his pocket and he gave her a good time. He told her the truth about his grandmother, and perhaps in due course they were intending to get spliced.

'And meanwhile they were living in sin,' Wharton added, and the comment had an unctuous regret. 'But to get back to Hanley himself. You could give us a description?'

'I can do more than that, sir,' Tipton told him, and produced a photograph. It showed Hanley in uniform and had been taken in 1943. He looked tallish, serious to the point of stolidity and he was wearing glasses.

'You had a good look at him,' Wharton said. 'Has he changed at all?'

'Not a lot,' Tipton said. 'A bit thin, though. I reckon he'd been through a pretty bad time with the Nazis. That's what I thought. He looked a bit older than thirty or so, if you know what I mean. Then again that may have been due to his beard.'

'Wearing a beard, was he?'

'That's a regular fashion nowadays,' Tipton told him. 'A lot of these demobilized officers have beards. Makes them look like toughs who fought in the desert and Burma. Or sailors.'

'A black beard, was it?' I said, and tried to make the tone casual. 'Most of the beards one sees are black.'

'I wasn't close enough to him to see if it was actually black, but it looked black,' he told me. 'But mind you, sir, he may be wearing that beard as a disguise. If the old lady were on his tracks, she'd never recognize him.'

As I saw it, that was pretty startling information and I didn't quite know what to do about it. But George was putting another question.

'And there's no other information you can give us, Mr Tipton?'

There was none, he said, and then I was scribbling a note for George.

'Where are you hanging out?' George was asking him.

'With an old friend of mine at Finsbury Park,' Tipton said. 'Nice and convenient for everywhere.'

'This might interest you,' I told George and passed him the note. George had a look. His eyebrows lifted inquiringly and I nodded.

'And you're sure there's nothing else you can tell us?' he asked Tipton again.

'Nothing at all, sir.'

'Well, that's that then,' George said heavily. 'What train do you think of catching? Tonight or in the morning? You can give me the tip and I'll know what to say to your firm.'

'You mean, I'm to go back to Birmingham?'

'That's it,' George said. 'Othello's occupation's gone. In other words, you're out of a job – this job. But I hope to give you a pat on the back when I ring your employers.'

We got to our feet. I signalled to the waitress and by the time the bill was paid the two were down the stairs. George was holding out his hand.

'Goodbye, Mr Tipton, and thank you very much. If ever you're in need of bail, send for me and I'll get you out.'

'No hard feelings,' I said, and held out my hand too. Tipton had to grin.

'It's been a pleasure meeting you two gentlemen,' he said. 'Just shows the rum things that happen.'

A final nod and off he moved across the road. George watched him benevolently till the traffic came by and concealed him. Then he whipped round on me.

'What was the idea of getting rid of him?'

'Because unless I'm wrong we've got to handle this ourselves,' I said. 'But let's slip in somewhere where we can talk.'

'What's wrong with going back in there?' he asked me, and nodded at the Daffodil.

'Dammit, George, you can't eat another tea,' I told him. 'Think of the decencies. If you're still hungry, let's go somewhere else.'

Five minutes later we were in another and much more crowded tea-shop near the station. It was run on cafeteria lines, and so I took only a cup of tea. George had a cup too, and a monstrosity that belonged apparently to the family of currant buns. But he didn't chew regularly and methodically. What I had to tell him made mastication a highly irregular process.

'There we are then,' I ended. 'In the Daffodil that morning was a man of Hanley's description, with beard and glasses. And he came in after Bill Ellice arrived with Violet Lancing. If that doesn't show that he'd tailed her till she met Bill and then followed him and her into the tea-shop then I'm badly wrong. That business of going across the road too, and pretending to ask Rhoda the way to somewhere – that was only a blind. It had been previously arranged. Bill doesn't look unlike a copper, and I'll bet Hanley reported to her that Violet was with the police, and she'd fainted; which meant there was nothing else to do except clear out. Hanley took a bus and Rhoda went to the shop, if that's any verification.'

'Sounds reasonable to me,' George said. 'But why wasn't I told of it before?'

'Have a heart George,' I said. 'What significance had the bearded man to me? Was I to take an inventory of everybody I saw in the Daffodil, just on the hundred to one chance I'd have something to report to you?'

'You're taking me too seriously,' he told me speciously. 'But how did this Hanley get himself mixed up with it?'

'Take Tipton's theory,' I pointed out. 'Rhoda and Hanley were living together till they'd made up their minds about the future. She had a shop on her hands, remember. He told her about his grandmother and why he wanted to lie doggo for a bit. He didn't want the old lady busting that, or any other, ménage. She told him about Violet – and don't ask me what she told him. Then they concocted the blackmail scheme together. It was he who rang Violet originally, even if Rhoda put the words into his mouth.'

'Maybe you're right,' said George. 'But there's one other thing. Was it bluff when Hanley rang Violet and said she needn't be afraid of any more payments after the one five hundred? According to what you told me, he added that as soon as she saw him she'd have a guarantee that she wasn't going to be bled any more. How do you explain that? Violet didn't know Hanley.'

'I know she didn't. That was all bluff. It was Rhoda whom Violet was going to see. Rhoda would tell her to go to the shop as if she was going to have her hair done, and then she'd have told Violet just what she knew. It was something inherent in that, that would be the guarantee.'

'Don't like it,' George said, and frowned. 'You and your theories! It doesn't hang together. According to you again, Violet saw Rhoda clearly and wasn't frightened or scared.'

Perhaps I hadn't been any too clear. In any case George wasn't as deep inside things as I had been.

'Let's leave it,' I said. 'You're in charge from now on. What I'm interested in is what you're going to do.'

'Damned if I know what I *am* going to do,' George told me gloomily. 'I might put a couple of men on that hair-dressing place –'

'Why two?'

'There'll be a back way out, won't there? What about the premises on top? They'll have a fire escape besides the side door.' The glare subsided and he went on. 'I'll make a few inquiries about the Yarnell woman. What else I don't know. It's that James Hanley that's worrying me.'

I didn't dare ask why. Happily he told me.

'Suppose we get him, what can we do? We can't bring a charge. There's no law against two people living together. If he'd deserted a wife and family, that might be different.' He looked so regretful that I told him what was the point of view of Bill Ellice; that his pledge of secrecy had been given to a Mrs Upson, not to a Violet Lancing. And it was implicit in any unwritten contract that the two parties should be acting frankly and in good faith.

'That's an idea,' he said. 'I might put that up to the Big Bugs. All the same I don't think they'll take direct action till we know a hell of a lot more. We'll have to go steady. Pick up a bit here and a bit there.' He shook his head. 'If only we could show a definite tie-up with the Manfrey Case, then they'd give us our heads.'

On that note we parted. I was to see him at the Yard in the morning, and meanwhile he'd get me co-opted on the Case. But even that didn't cheer me up. Routine inquiry, and even that heard at second hand through George, was the devil of a way from excitement or even action. What I didn't know was that I needn't have worried. Before very few hours had gone by, I was to get far more action than I'd dared to hope.

CHAPTER XII
Action

IT WAS ABOUT ten o'clock when I entered Wharton's room that morning, and he was just concluding a telephone conversation. The few words I heard were more than interesting.

'Thank you, Mr Nevall. Then if it's no trouble Mr Travers will be along . . . Right, goodbye.'

He gave me a nod or two, and I was wondering just what I'd done wrong. But it was nothing of that. George was merely in a bit of a jam. Too many things to do at once.

'What do you think has happened? Violet Lancing's missing. Didn't turn up for the show last night. Didn't sleep at her flat.'

For once I could suggest nothing; I just stood and gaped.

'I've had a report from the theatre,' George went on, 'and they haven't any idea where she can be. The people at the flat say she went out just before lunch yesterday morning and they haven't seen her since. The bed wasn't slept in.'

'Where does Nevall come in?' I asked. 'I heard you telephoning.'

'He's sort of head cook and bottle washer of that show she was in. I've got to go to the flat. Good chance to have a look round. You see if you can get anything from Nevall. He just told me he hadn't any idea why she hadn't turned up last night. The last woman to miss a show, according to him. But you slip along and get what you can. Here's a set of new credentials for you. I've fixed up about a car.'

So George had intended me to see Nevall whether Nevall was agreeable or not. That seemed quite interesting.

'And where do I report?' I wanted to know.

'Come round by her flat,' George said. 'I might still be there. Got a thing or two to do before I can leave here.'

In another quarter of an hour I was in Gower Street again. A smart looking youngish man opened the door.

'Mr Ludovic Travers,' I said. 'Mr Nevall is expecting me.'

He took my hat and stick in the anteroom.

'You Mr Nevall's man?' I asked him.

He said he was. Then he tapped his leg and told me it was an artificial one. He'd got that packet at Walcheren, he told me, and we'd have had quite a chat if he hadn't suddenly remembered that Nevall was probably waiting.

The flat looked much about the same: spacious and exceedingly comfortable, but Nevall had grown older in the three years or so since we had met. His temples were greyer and he looked like the Brutus who'd spent a sleepless night before Philippi. The eyes were heavy and the skin sagged a bit beneath eyes and chin. He spoke more slowly too, but that I put down to several weeks of sustaining the part of the bishop. Maybe I was wrong and an actor can shed the slough of the stage more easily than the layman thinks. In any case I didn't ask him.

We got to business almost at once. It was a mystery to him, he said, why Violet Lancing had not put in an appearance the previous night. He too had rung her flat and had received no answer.

'She's not the sort to miss a performance,' he said. 'She had a career to make and she was always very keen. She must have had some extraordinary reason.'

'I suppose I'd be wrong to call her career meteoric,' I said, 'but hasn't she moved up a bit quickly? It seems only the other day that she'd been on the stage at all.'

'She'd done cinema work,' he reminded me.

'That shows where we laymen are wrong then,' I said. 'We're always given to understand that the two careers are very different. It's only a finished stage actor who can learn the other technique at all quickly, and vice versa.'

'I wouldn't go so far as that,' he said. 'But don't make any mistake about Violet Lancing. She got where she is by merit. She had it in her. It only needed bringing out. Have you seen the play?'

I said I hadn't.

'Have a look at her some time,' he told me. 'Then tell me if I'm not right.'

'You think she'll be back then?'

He stared.

'What I mean is, this absence is nothing serious?'

'My dear fellow, why should it be serious? She probably has her own reason for her absence. I shall be surprised personally if she doesn't turn up some time today.'

'Let's hope so,' I said. 'Will her absence affect the receipts? Or is the understudy capable?'

'Quite capable,' he said firmly. 'Please don't misunderstand me. Miss Lancing isn't a finished actress. One part doesn't make a career. In her case it only begins it.'

He was becoming a bit pontifical so I thought I'd be on my way.

'May I get you a sherry?' he asked me. 'I generally have one at this time.'

It struck me as a queer time to have a sherry. It must have been well on to the way to midnight when he went to bed, and if he rose as early as nine o'clock, he couldn't very well want a sherry on top of breakfast. In any case I said I was on duty and one had to abide by rules.

'By the way, did you ever come to any conclusions about poor Manfrey?' he asked me, and then I knew that the offer of sherry had been a kind of ingratiation.

'Afraid not,' I said. 'It's one of those unsolved mysteries that may go down to history – the history of crime.'

He didn't notice that I was talking clap-trap. In fact he nodded as if I'd uttered the profoundest wisdom.

'I'll tell you why I asked,' he said. 'If the matter is as you say, perhaps I'm permitted to ask a question. That visit you and Superintendent – er –'

'Wharton?'

'Yes. Wharton. That visit of yours when it was hinted that I'd been heard in his room, quarrelling. Did you really have information to that effect, or was it bluff after all?'

I adopted an attitude both grieved and dignified, or I think so.

'But surely we assured you at the time that it wasn't a bluff, as you call it? Whatever you may read in books, Mr Nevall, those are not the methods of Scotland Yard.'

'Unpardonable of me,' he said frankly. 'But it always worried me. It was so utterly untrue. Sure you won't change your mind about that sherry?'

I refused again, and then at the door I thought of something.

'One thing you might tell me, in confidence.' It was curious how warily he watched me when I said that. 'Miss Lancing's salary. What was it?'

'Fifteen pounds.'

'Quite useful,' I said. 'Any extras from film or other work?'

'No,' he said slowly. 'She had a pension, I believe. Her husband – Yarnell was his name – was killed a year or two ago.'

I held out my hand and uttered the conventional thanks. His man saw me out and I asked my driver to step on it. I too wanted to see Violet Lancing's flat, and as it chanced, I was in plenty of time. George was still pottering around when I walked in.

But even before I got as far as the actual door I had a good deal to think about. The foyer of that block of flats was a palatial affair, with a carpet into which I appeared to sink up to the hocks. Two superb staircases led upwards with more deeply piled carpet, and the walls were decorated with what looked like murals by a first-class man. The lift openings – I'd preferred the stairs – were all metal scrolls and arabesques, and altogether it was like a honeymoon hotel for millionaires. In any case Violet Lancing had had reasonably good value for her three hundred a year, if only in publicity and prestige. An actress of her ambitions could not have invested in a finer *milieu* or have announced more clearly her intention of reaching the top of the tree.

I told George what I'd learned from Nevall, which was practically nothing at all. But he was interested to hear what her salary had been.

'Take income tax off it and it's a different tale,' he said. 'Make her income as much as five hundred a year nett and then you begin asking questions. Three hundred a year for this place. It isn't so big a flat as I'd thought but it's select, not that that's the point. The point is that three hundred from five hundred leaves two. And they tell me here that she used to lunch out and have supper out as often as not. And she wouldn't have gone to cheap places. Best part of ten bob for lunch and the same for supper. A night club or two now and then. And take a look in here.'

He opened the door of the wardrobe in the charming little bedroom.

'See that fur coat? It mayn't be mink, but it cost a packet. Look at the name on this label. That firm doesn't sell rubbish. And this coatee thing. Ermine, isn't it? A hundred guineas at the least or my name's Robinson.'

He slammed the door with a gesture of exasperation.

'You and your fifteen pounds a week!'

He went off fuming to the lounge room again.

'Where'd she get her money from – that's what I've got to find out.' His lip curled. 'Unless she earned some of her daily bread by night.'

'Anything in that bureau?' I asked him.

'It's locked,' he said. 'We mustn't try any monkey tricks like that. For all we know she might be back at any minute. You know as well as I do that we've got no real excuse for being here at all.'

'You don't believe she's coming back!' I told him quietly.

'Oh?' he said. 'And why not?'

'You just told me why,' I said. 'If we made a personal call at the homes of every missing person, we shouldn't want another job. And she's been missing only twenty-four hours.'

'Fancying yourself as a thought-reader?'

'I wouldn't go so far as that, George,' I said. 'What I do know is that you're thinking much the same as I am – that this ties up with the Manfrey Case. And there's that nasty little bit of black-mail business in the background. How it ties up is quite another thing. And how the blackmail business ties up too.'

'Well we'd better be getting out of here,' he told me. 'Don't want to give the management ideas.'

But that brief argument had given me an idea, and as soon as we stepped out of that block of flats I was asking him what was next. And that he didn't know, at least as far as I was concerned. He himself was going back to the Yard to see if anything had come in. I said I'd be at the flat till one o'clock and after that I'd ring him up or call round.

What I had in mind was a visit to Hampstead, and the last thing in my mind was any nostalgic wish of a detective to return to the scene of a crime. What was sending me back to The Cote was that call I'd paid on Henry Nevall. Something had been wrong with the man and his attitude. Three years had gone by since Manfrey's death, and since Nevall had then been given a clean bill of health, the matter should have been no more than a casual recollection in his mind. And it wasn't as if Manfrey had been his friend.

As for that call we had paid three years before, Wharton had given the most explicit assurances that there was no bluff in his mention of a witness who claimed to have heard Nevall's voice. Then why did Nevall revert to that question of a bluff? Surely because there was something troubling his conscience. A fear perhaps, that after three years something might still come out. And he had seen fit to preface his question with that very doubt-ful statement about taking a sherry at half past ten in the morning. Something was wrong and I knew it, and it was up to me to find exactly what.

I had a service lunch at my flat and just after one o'clock I walked to Tottenham Court Road and took the Hampstead Tube. We had been talking about The Cote a few days before, and Wharton had told me May Clarke was still there, and it seemed to me that immediately after lunch would be a good time to catch her in. Then when I got to Hampstead I thought I'd test the time it would take me to reach The Cote; not at my usual pace but at the pace at which Violet Lancing might have walked on that Saturday morning. She had virtually run back, she had said, as she had an engagement, but I proposed to go at what might have been her usual walking pace. And starting from the hat shop I took just under five minutes to get to the front door.

May Clarke opened the door. For a moment she looked inquiringly at me, then her face showed recognition.

'Why it's Mr – er –'

'Travers,' I said. 'Three years since I saw you, May. How are you?'

She was very well indeed, she said, and she didn't seem to me to have changed at all. I said I was passing and had wondered how she was, and by that time I was in the house.

'What about a nice cup of tea, sir?' she asked me. 'I'm just making one for myself, so it won't be any trouble.'

I said that'd be fine, and it'd be fine to see her kitchen again. And what about her sister. Was she still living with her?

While the kettle was coming to the boil and the tea was drawing, we had a great gossip. The sister had gone to Bromley for the day to see some friends and wouldn't be back till evening. The new owner of the house had called twice when he was on leave, and he wasn't expected to take up residence for quite a time, but when he did, he was hoping May and her sister would stay on.

'A bachelor he is, sir, and ever so nice. He sort of hinted, though, that he might be getting married before long. Sugar, sir, or don't you take it?'

I said I took it when nobody was looking, and for some reason or other that made her laugh. Then she produced some home-made cake, and maybe it was that that reminded her of Wharton. I said he was very well.

'What I call a real nice man,' she said. 'And him being so homely and all.'

'Well, we're all getting older,' I said heavily. 'All except you. You're even looking younger.'

I asked for that and I got it. Five good minutes went by before I'd heard about her bad knee and the things she'd tried for it. Then as she poured me out my second cup, I remembered something.

'That secretary who was here. Let me see, what was her name?'

'Miss Lancing?'

'That's it,' I said. 'Didn't someone tell me she was on the stage?'

'Oh, she is,' she told me. 'I saw her name in the paper the other day.'

'Do you see anything of her?'

'What me, sir?' She smiled, and wholly without malice. 'She's got on too well in the world for me.'

I'd been hoping there'd have been a jealousy, but there wasn't. But perhaps I could do something about it.

'But surely she sends you theatre tickets occasionally?'

She shook her head.

'It wasn't as if we were really friendly. She was very nice, though, in the house.'

No openings there, so I tried another approach.

'Time flies you know, May. Seems only a week ago since Mr Manfrey died, and yet it's three whole years.'

'That's just what I was saying to Minnie only this morning. Two years, I said, since you last went to Bromley, and it only seems last week.' She paused. There was a question she was wanting to ask me, and I wondered what it was.

'Was anything really found out, sir, about poor Mr Manfrey?'

'That's all settled long ago,' I told her. 'If I tell you something, you won't repeat it?'

'As if I would!'

'Well, we came to the conclusion he'd had a fit or something and had struck his head against the edge of the desk, and that was what killed him.'

I hoped she'd be disappointed, and she was.

'Fancy that now! Just shows how you gentlemen can make mistakes.' Then again she thought of something. 'Wonder who that was, sir, he was having a fine old row with just before he died.'

'That's all over and done with now,' I said, and then I frowned. 'Don't ever breathe a word of this to a soul, but would you be surprised to hear it was Mr Nevall after all?'

'No!'

I shrugged my shoulders.

'So I *was* right,' she said. 'I didn't dare say anything at the time. It doesn't do to make trouble, not when you're dependent on people for a living.'

Then a curious expression came over her face as if she'd thought of something really startling.

'That just reminds me. Talking about Miss Lancing did it. She thought the same as I did.'

'No!'

'But she did. I'll tell you how it was. Let me see now. When was it she came to see me? Oh yes; just before that Christmas it was. I remember now because she brought me a little present. Nice pair of gloves it was, and I thought how handy they'd come in. Then we got to talking about poor Mr Manfrey, and then she asked me if I'd ever wondered who it was that was having that row with him that morning, and I told her. I didn't give myself away too much. I had to be careful, like I was telling you. And then, do you know, she actually told me that she'd heard them two quarrelling, though she said she hadn't. She was like me, you see. Didn't want any trouble. And she was positive it was Mr Nevall who was in there having that row.'

'Well, it just shows you how things come out,' I said. 'Still, it's all over and done with now. Not that I wouldn't keep everything to myself if I were you. I oughtn't to have told you what I did, and if anything got round to Mr Nevall's ears, he might make trouble.'

'Don't worry about me, sir,' she told me. 'I never was one to talk. Live and let live, that's me.'

Five minutes later we were out in the hall again. I slipped her a tip which she didn't want to take, but I insisted fatuously that she should buy herself some little present as a souvenir – though heaven knew of what.

'Mr Manfrey's room been altered much?' I asked.

'Have a look for yourself, sir,' she told me, and opened the door. 'Everything just as it was, except tidied up a bit. Mr Hugh said he didn't want any of his uncle's things touched till he came here for good. Then perhaps there might be some alterations.'

'Everything certainly looks spotless,' I said, and with that final encomium I made my exit. But I didn't hurry back to the Tube; there was far too much to think about for that.

I got to Tottenham Court Road and managed to grab a taxi that took me to the Yard. George was in his room, and a tray on his desk still held the ruins of a late lunch.

'Anything been happening?' I asked him.

Nothing much, he said, except the results of some inquiries he'd set in motion the previous evening. Rhoda Yarnell's house was not actually her own, since it was being paid for through a building society. As for the shop in Victoria Street, she had been connected with that when Yarnell married her, which was two years before the out-break of war. The shop had been called 'Monica Braye', which was the name of the principal owner.

He explained more fully. Three girls who had been school friends originally acquired the business and had equal shares. Then the Monica Braye had been killed in the blitz and her heirs had been rather obstructionist, fearing perhaps that some future bombing would wipe out both shop and goodwill. The second partner, however, had managed to buy the Monica share, and so what Rhoda Yarnell owned was a third. And as the other partner was in the A.T.S. there had been a new arrangement. The name of the business had been changed, and Rhoda was paid a salary in addition to her share of the profits.

'I think the salary's five pounds a week,' George said. 'What the third share of the profits amounts to I can't say. Pretty big overheads in a place like that, however well they're doing.'

'You think a nice little five hundred pounds would come in handy?'

'It looks like it,' George said. 'Payments on the house, travelling and living expenses, odd man for the garden, and income tax. She can't have a lot left.'

There was no point in going any further into that. Had the inquiries disclosed that the firm was tottery, or that Rhoda herself was heavily in debt, that might have made a difference. And even then there'd have been nothing on which to take immediate and direct action, as George told me sadly. Then I told him about the hunch I'd had to call at The Cote. In fact, I gave him almost a verbatim report.

'Do you know, I think we've got something there,' he told me.

I should explain that when things are going badly, George says *you*. When they're going reasonably well or show promise, then it's *we*. When they're going uncommonly well, there are illusions to the *Old Gent*.

'So Violet called on her, did she?' he went on. 'Brought her a nice little present to make everything friendly, and ever since has treated her like a small bit of dirt.'

'She told us she thought it was May herself that Manfrey was quarrelling with,' I reminded him.

'I know, I know,' he told me. Then his eyes bulged a bit and he was wagging a finger at me.

'Wait a bit. There's more in this than meets the eye. How the devil did Violet know that Nevall might have been in the room? She didn't know we'd taken May to the theatre?'

'I don't get you,' I said. 'As I see it, it's simple. Violet deliberately told us lies. She did recognize Nevall's voice. She called on May with one object and with one object only – to try to impress on May that the voice May heard was Nevall's. But she had a tremendous bit of luck, because May was of the very same opinion.'

'Maybe you're right,' George said. 'And if so, tell me this. Why did Violet wait all that time before calling on May? Put it another way. What had happened to make it urgent that May should think it was Nevall who had been quarrelling with Manfrey?'

'There we come to conjectures,' I said. 'But Violet was a thruster and a gold-digger. Look how she threw herself at Yarnell. Got him away from his wife and married him, and all for the sake of a career. That was what I'd call long-term planning, when you think back to that morning when Manfrey was killed. And if she was a long-term planner, why shouldn't she have decided to have Nevall up her sleeve as a possible future second string.'

George clicked his tongue.

'Everything goes back to Manfrey and yet we can't get to grips with it.'

'Wait a minute,' I said. 'We can move on a little bit further –'

But there wasn't any moving on, for at that moment the buzzer went.

'Put him through,' George said, and picked up the receiver.

'Yes,' he said. 'Wharton speaking. What's your trouble, Broad?'

I pricked my ears at that, and then in another second I was straining them.

'My God, you don't say so! . . . Where? . . . I see. Past the pond and then to the right and the wood . . . Yes . . . Yes . . . Yes . . . I'll be there rightaway . . . Oh yes, you'd better keep them there. Keep 'em calm . . . I'm sure you will . . . Right . . . Goodbye.'

He let out a breath and leaned back in the chair. Then he was suddenly getting to his feet.

'They've just found Violet Lancing. Been dead about a day. Somebody strangled her.'

CHAPTER XIII
Murder by Whom?

We left the car at a side road and went through an opening to the Heath. It's folly to speculate beforehand about a case and Wharton had said hardly a word during that twenty-minute drive, but as soon as we set foot on the Heath, he couldn't help remarking on the coincidence.

'If it *is* a coincidence,' he went on. 'That wood isn't a quarter of a mile from Manfrey's house.'

There were few children on the Heath that afternoon, for the schools had reopened, but there were couples sitting on the grass and mothers with perambulators. We made a wide detour round the pond and as we came near the wood we could see a man on duty. I had sat with my wife in the shade of the outer trees on a lovely autumn day the year before when she was on leave from her hospital in the north, but now that wood had undergone a change. Then the fence had been in reasonable repair and there were no defined paths that led through it. Now the wire had been cut to leave numerous gaps through which the earth had been trodden flat by innumerable feet.

We took a path that soon petered out among the undergrowth. Everywhere was dense shade and we might have been at a loss which way to go had it not been for a moving something to the left. It was Broad who'd been on the look-out for Wharton, and I remember we shook hands solemnly like distant relatives who had not met for years but now assemble for a funeral.

A man whom I recognized as the old doctor who'd been at Manfrey's house that far-off Saturday morning was stand-by the body, and a short distance away were some of Broad's men and a young soldier with a girl. Again there were solemn handshakes. Then Wharton went briskly to work.

'Who found her?'

'That soldier and his girl over there,' Broad told him.

'They didn't touch her?'

'They swear they didn't, sir. The girl was too scared if you ask me.'

'So this is how she fell,' Wharton said, and squatted down by the body. It was lying face downwards in a patch of short, scrubby undergrowth, arms thrown out and legs sprawling. Then he edged an arm beneath and with his fingers gently twisted the head. I knew that face in spite of the horribly protruding eyes, and I knew the very hat that clung to the head by the merest wisp of hair.

'No doubt about the strangling,' said Wharton. 'And how long do you think she's been dead?'

'Twenty-four hours or just over,' the doctor told him.

Wharton felt the tweed of the smart skirt and coat.

'Still a bit damp. A heavy dew last night, wasn't there?'

Broad said there was, and Wharton got to his feet.

'Who identified her?'

'I did, sir,' Broad said. 'If I hadn't known her, we might have been hung up for a bit.'

'Why?' said Wharton. 'Hadn't she any cards or letters or anything in her bag?'

'There wasn't a bag,' Broad told him.

'No bag!' He looked round at me to share his surprise. 'Damnation, Broad, you're a married man. Did you ever know a woman go out without a bag? What was she going to do if she wanted money?'

'That's what I thought, sir,' Broad said. 'Nothing in the pockets of that coat but a handkerchief.'

Wharton bent down and began looking at the hands.

'No rings either. I'll bet she was wearing some. You can't imagine a woman like her going out and not slipping on a ring or two. Look at the marks on this finger. The knuckle looks chafed to me. Make a note of that, Cave, will you?'

He stood looking down at the body, frowning away and pursing his lips. Then he said he'd see the soldier and his girl, and Broad motioned to one of his men to bring them over. Wharton met them half way, but still in sight of the body. The girl was still looking scared stiff.

'I shan't keep either of you a minute,' Wharton assured them. 'Nothing to be worried about. Just a simple question or two.'

The soldier, a gunner on the second day of leave, was engaged to the girl, and she was that rarity – a domestic servant – having an afternoon off from a house nearby. The two had come through the wood from Barton Road along a rough path that had been made in the course of the last few months, and they'd caught sight of a grey squirrel. The soldier had left the path and chased it, and it had run up a tree. He had called his girl to see it, and it was as he was manoeuvring his way round for a better view that he'd stumbled across the body.

He owned up frankly that they'd been scared, not of the corpse so much as of being vaguely embroiled with the law, so they'd got out of the wood intending to go on as arranged to the cinema. Then they'd talked it over and had finally made up their minds when they caught sight of a policeman.

The girl hadn't been nearer the body than a good ten yards, and the soldier had been under her eyes all the time, so Wharton elicited. He was quite a smart looking young fellow, by the way, who spoke frankly and freely, and she was a pleasant girl of about twenty with nothing of guile about her. There didn't seem any doubt that neither could have taken a bag or stolen a ring.

Broad had their names and addresses and had warned them about an inquest. Wharton gave a word or two of thanks and praise and off they went.

'Well, there we are,' he said to Broad. 'We're faced with two problems. Either the man who killed her took the bag or else somebody found her before those two did. Any sign of feet?'

There was devil a sign, Broad said. The odd paths were like concrete and off them the ground was too yielding.

'She certainly wasn't carried here,' Wharton said. 'And there's no sign of a struggle. Looks to me as if she was collared from behind, and when she ceased to kick she was sort of thrown here. Look how she's sprawled out.'

'That's what I thought, sir,' Broad said. 'And if it's a case of unpremeditated assault for the sake of robbery, then we've got the devil of a case on our hands.'

'You finished with her?' Wharton asked him.

Broad said he had. The flashlights had been taken and the ambulance was waiting in Barton Road.

'Right,' said Wharton. 'Get her away. Have the whole area cordoned off. Go through it, right from Barton Road, with a small toothed comb. You might find the empty bag.' Broad's men took her away on a stretcher and the three of us stood watching till they'd disappeared. I expect we were all thinking the same thing – of a Saturday morning a long time ago. But Broad wouldn't have been thinking as far as Wharton and I. He wasn't looking along that tricky primrose path that had led Violet Lancing from the cubbyhole at The Cote to a Westminster flat and photographs outside the foyer of a theatre. And Broad hadn't seen a frightened woman lying like hell to Bill Ellice, and the same woman in a faint on that tea-shop floor.

Wharton let out a deep breath.

'Well, her good looks didn't do her much good in the end.'

A valedictory grunt and he was pulling out his notebook.

'That theory of yours, Broad, about an unpremeditated as-sault. You really believe that?'

'Well, it's got holes in it, sir,' said Broad uneasily.

'You're right,' said Wharton grimly. 'It's got more holes than a ruddy colander. I want to know one thing and one thing only – what she was doing in this wood at all. Look at her. Look at the clothes she was wearing. Was she the sort who'd want to go through a place like this, where there isn't a proper path?'

'You mean, sir, that she was lured in here?'

Wharton opened his mouth, then the lips clamped tight.

'No point in arguing, or theorizing. The answers aren't this end. They're some other end. You get on with that search. If you don't find the bag, notify the pawnshops. We'll try to get a de-scription of the bag, and maybe her rings.'

But as we walked back to the car, George began to open up.

'That theory of Broad's,' he said, and pursed his lips in dis-gust. 'Not that you can blame him. He hasn't moved on much since three years ago. Yet I don't know what to do about telling him. Maybe there'll be nothing for him to do but routine.'

'If you mean letting him in on the blackmail business, I agree,' I said. 'If he does ultimately have to be told – well, that'll be that.'

'Got any ideas yourself?' he asked me.

'I have,' I said, and I thought ironically that Hampstead Heath, the land of roundabouts and coconut shies, was the very place for an Aunt Sally. 'That bag of hers. Suppose she had the five hundred pounds in it.'

'Just what I've been thinking myself,' he said. 'A rendezvous here with the blackmailer. She waits by the pond, shall we say. He – or she – goes by and whispers, "Follow me," and follow she does. Inside that wood he strangles her, collars the bag, takes the ring or rings to make it look like Broad's unpremeditated assault, and then circles round and out of the wood where he likes.'

'Wait a moment, George,' I said, and was suddenly polishing my glasses and blinking away in the sun. 'I've thought of something pretty ghastly. Remember how the supposed man who rang her up told her that as soon as she saw him she'd know she'd have only the one payment to make?'

'My God, yes!' George said, and was staring at me as I re-placed my glasses. 'That was a hellish joke if you like. No sooner did he meet her in that wood than he had his fingers round her throat. No more payments. No more nothing.'

We moved on again, and he was telling me that now we knew where we stood.

'No more kid gloves. Blackmail's one thing and murder's an-other. We'll just have a little look round and then that Yarnell woman's going through the hoop. And we've got to get the hooks on that man Hanley.'

But when we got into the car he was telling the driver to go to the Euston Road end of Gower Street.

'We've got to get Nevall to lend a hand,' he told me. 'Any-thing for a short cut.'

I could never be immediately aware of the precise workings of George's mind, but I asked no questions. Up the familiar stairs we went together, and Nevall's man opened the door. He raised the politest of eyebrows and told us Mr Nevall was in.

'Then we'll see him,' George said brusquely. 'You go ahead and tell him we're here.'

When we entered the room, Nevall was sitting in an easy chair by the far window. A book was in his hand, and he didn't at once get to his feet. The book dropped and his fingers came together. His look was uncannily intent.

'Yes, gentlemen?'

'Don't get up,' Wharton said, and grabbed a chair for himself. I grabbed one too, though more in the background.

'We've some bad news for you, Mr Nevall. Violet Lancing is dead. She's just been found strangled in a wood on Hampstead Heath.'

Nevall stared. His hands fluttered.

'No. No.'

'No doubt about it,' Wharton told him. 'Don't ask me questions because nothing will be released till after your show tonight. We thought that would be convenient for all.'

'But it's incredible!' Nevall said. 'Who should wish to murder a woman like her?' Then something struck him. 'It couldn't have been murder. What you're telling me is that she was attacked.'

'It comes to the same thing in the end,' Wharton said bluntly. 'But about what I was saying about nothing being released till after the end of your show tonight. That's for your convenience and I want a *quid pro quo*.'

'My dear sir, anything I can do I'll be only too glad to do.'

'That's the sort of cooperation we want,' Wharton told him. 'What I'm telling you is in the strictest confidence,' and he wagged an admonitory finger. 'If a word of this gets out, there'll be trouble. What I'm asking you is this. There was no bag found with her. And it looked as if somebody had yanked a ring or rings off her finger. Do you know any bags she had?'

Nevall frowned, finger-tips together.

'Offhand – no. There was a kind of alligator skin bag. But let me see. When did I see her with it last?'

'Leave it,' Wharton said. 'What about rings?'

'There I can help you – perhaps,' Nevall said. 'She had a very nice little diamond ring. She wore it in the play. It calls for it, you know.'

'Valuable?'

'Three or four nice stones. Three, I think it was. Worth a hundred pounds perhaps. But I'm no authority.'

'Then we come to the point,' Wharton said. 'Women know all these things better than men. Your play's been on a goodish time now. Immediately after the show tonight, get them all together and tell them the news. Ask them about a bag or bags, and her jewellery. Take down all details and give me a ring at the yard. Simply ask to be put through to Superintendent Wharton.'

'Most certainly I'll do it,' Nevall said. 'Anything else?'

George had got to his feet. Now he sat down again.

'Yes,' he said. 'Something in even stricter confidence. I must ask you to give me your word.'

'Certainly.'

'It's this. We have information that Miss Lancing was being blackmailed.'

Nevall's start of surprise could only have been genuine. Wharton smiled ruefully.

'I rather fancy that you're not going to be able to help us, but I'll ask you all the same. Miss Lancing had to find the sum of five hundred pounds. We know that from an inquiry agency whom she approached under a false name. And we have an idea that she didn't have anything resembling five hundred pounds. To come straight to the point, did she make any excuse to try to borrow money from you?'

Nevall spread his hands in bewilderment.

'Never. Mind you, I did let her have an advance from time to time.' He shook his head with a certain ruefulness. 'As a matter of fact she owes me a few pounds at this moment. But to borrow money in the way you mean – never.'

Then he was getting to his feet with a 'Pardon me' and going to his desk. He found a sheet of paper and wrote something on it, then blotted it and handed it to Wharton.

To the Manager, Barclays Bank, Hodges Street.

DEAR SIR,

Please place the whole of my account and any financial transactions of the past year at the disposal of Superintendent Wharton. Confidential.

Yours truly,

HENRY NEVALL

That was what George read.

'Very handsome of you,' he said, 'but it's unnecessary. We take your word.'

'But please.'

Wharton shrugged his shoulders.

'Well if you insist.'

He got to his feet and Nevall followed us through to the hall. There were thanks and apologies, with Nevall still metaphorically blinking his eyes in bewilderment, and then down the stairs we went. The driver was told to take us to Violet Lancing's flat. Then George pulled him up at a post-office and went in to do some telephoning. In ten minutes he was out again, and all I knew was that when we got to the flats, a plainclothes sergeant was waiting for us. George ripped a page from his notebook and scribbled something on it, and pinned it to Nevall's note.

'Take this to Hodges Street,' he told the sergeant. 'The bank will be closed but someone'll be there. Hand it personally to the manager and bring a written reply. If I'm not here, report to the Yard.'

The car went off with the sergeant.

'Might as well check up on Nevall since he volunteered it himself,' he told me. 'Nothing like clearing lumber out of the way.'

We went through to the foyer. I was making for the stairs thinking that we were about to go through Violet Lancing's flat. George went across to the office and I waited for him to come with the key. But he didn't come, so I went back to inquire.

It was another half-hour before we left that office. Wharton saw the girl on the telephone exchange, the manageress, the chambermaid, and Tom Bruce's pal, the commissionaire. It was the latter who swore that Violet Lancing had been carrying that alligator skin bag when she had left before lunch on the previous day. Asked whether the bag looked full, he couldn't say. He did say that Violet had been quite cheerful. She had given him a smile and had said, 'Isn't it,' when he had said it was a grand morning.

The manageress remembered the three-stone diamond ring and so did the telephone operator. The chambermaid said there was also an amethyst and pearl ring which Violet had often left on the dressing table. A wrist-watch – gold, with a gold flexible bracelet – appeared also to be missing. The commissionaire remembered she had been wearing it.

Wharton took the key and we made our way up the stairs. The flat seemed just as we had left it, though Wharton stood for a moment or two inside the door having a look round.

'You never know,' he said. 'Someone might have taken that bag because her keys were in it. There might be something in here that he was anxious to get.'

We then had a peep in the bathroom, the main and the little spare bedroom, and the tiny kitchen which was used apparently for such meals as the service restaurant didn't provide for it was hardly more than a box with a microscopic pantry and a small electric stove. In a locked drawer of the dressing-table Wharton found some jewellery – the amethyst ring, two brooches, a string of cultured pearls, a wedding ring, four sets of earrings, and some oddments.

Back in the living-room he made for the bureau. The lock was manipulated and he drew the flap down. Inside were the usual small drawers and central cupboard, none of them fitted with locks. There were various letters and bills but those could come later. What he was interested in was the almost new cheque book and the bank passbook.

But there everything seemed normal. Checking up with the counterfoils and the pass-book, we found that a week previously – and that was before she'd called on Bill Ellice – she had had a balance of fifty-three pounds, and since then only one cheque had been drawn, and that to a London store whose receipt we found.

'If she raised that five hundred,' Wharton said, 'she didn't contribute a penny towards it herself as far as I can see. Then where the devil did she raise it? Could she have gone to a money lender?'

'What security could she have offered?' I said. 'Whatever their clap-trap about loans on note of hand only, you know as well as I do that there has to be good security. All she had was her career. Whatever Nevall says, I don't think she'd have raised five hundred on that.'

'Did she raise it?'

'Ask me another,' I said. 'All I know is that she told Bill Ellice in my hearing that she *could* raise it. She even implied that she could raise it within twenty-four hours.'

'Well, we mustn't get out of our depth,' George said. 'No use rushing to conclusions. Perhaps she had relatives. We don't know. There might have been one of them she could have touched.'

'If you'll give me permission to break the news to May Clarke, she might know something,' I said. 'I'll bet those two women told each other all the family history. I know there was an aunt who's been dead for some years.'

Wharton thought there'd be no harm in breaking the news to May and so I used the telephone that stood on the side table just inside the door. May was in, but she seemed very scared of the telephone.

'Yes?' she said in a frightened sort of voice.

'How are you, May?' I said. 'This is Mr Travers speaking. You remember –'

'Of course,' she said, and she shouted into the telephone as if we were both stone deaf. 'Doesn't seem so long since we were having a cup of tea.'

When I told her the news she didn't burst into tears, maybe because I merely said Miss Lancing had died very suddenly.

'You never say so!' she said. 'And her as young as she was. And doing so well for herself too.'

'Well, there we are,' I told her in my best funereal tone. 'Here today and gone tomorrow.' And before she could cut in again: 'What we're worried about is relatives. They ought to be told you know.'

'She hadn't any relatives,' she told me emphatically. 'The poor girl was absolutely alone in the world after that aunt of hers died.'

'You're sure?'

'Of course I'm sure,' she said. 'I remember once we were talking about somebody in the papers who'd left somebody a lot of money and she said to me, "No such luck for us, Ma. We're both orphans." Which I am, except for my sister.'

That seemed pretty certain as Wharton admitted. He had been going through letters, bills, and receipts, and had run across nothing of interest. There were sixteen letters, and thirteen of them were fan-mail of various dates that had been addressed to the theatre. Then we went through all the drawers and again drew a blank. He even tried the pockets of the coats in the wardrobe and turned out every hat box, though he admitted he was looking for nothing in particular.

Then a man arrived for duty. No one was to be admitted on any pretext whatever, Wharton told him, though in an hour or two there'd be someone coming to make an official inventory of personal belongings. After that we made our way down the stairs again.

'No will and no solicitors,' Wharton said. 'Wonder who'll get her money. Those things of hers ought to make a tidy sum.'

I said there'd be no argument about that since it looked as if she'd died intestate.

'Pity she didn't leave a few millions,' George said. 'Then we might get a bob or two off the income tax.'

We went back to the Yard where there was no news. Then the sergeant arrived with a written message from the bank. The manager said that an unofficial summary would reach Wharton early the following morning.

'Nevall will be pretty sick that you took the matter up after all,' I said to George.

'That's his headache,' he said. 'It was he who made the suggestion, wasn't it?'

I hung on till about six o'clock and then George kicked me out, though I didn't need a great deal of propulsion. I told him in any case that I shouldn't be leaving my flat and if he wanted me he could get me there. I also said that unless anything turned up I'd be along at about nine the next morning. He didn't seem too enthusiastic.

'I doubt if we'll be able to get very far for a day or two,' he told me. 'All we want is just something to pin on that Yarnell woman. Maybe I'll have a word later tonight with You-Know-Who. I don't like bringing Ellice in till I'm forced.'

I could have told him that he'd soon lost his bellicosity, but I didn't. A few hours before he'd been talking about taking the gloves off, and now he was going all subtle again. But I could see his point. But for the evidence of Bill Ellice and myself he had nothing on Rhoda Yarnell. Even with that evidence he hadn't much, and so all he could do was to hope for some sort of lucky break.

For my own part I had little doubt that I knew who had killed Violet Lancing. Rhoda Yarnell and Hanley had been behind the blackmail, and it was he who had done the killing, and off his own bat. If so, when Rhoda saw the morning paper she'd have the shock of her life, and things ought to begin happening.

How right I was I could never have dreamed. I was also to learn, and before a day had passed, that I had never been more wrong.

CHAPTER XIV
End of a Chase

BEFORE BREAKFAST next morning I went along to the newsstand by St Martin's to have a look at the front page. My two papers had only brief inside notices but the more popular dailies had the murder on the front and one illustrated had splash headlines and a photograph of Violet Lancing.

MURDER OF ACTRESS
STRANGLED IN HAMPSTEAD WOOD

I wondered what newspaper Rhoda Yarnell read, though that didn't matter. She'd be bound to read the news some time and those girls of hers at the hairdressing establishment would be discussing that spicy murder.

Wharton had evidently been thinking along the same lines.

'See the papers?' he asked me, and without waiting for an answer, 'Wonder what the Yarnell woman thinks about it.'

He had two good men on the job – Wilson and Groom – he told me, and it was Groom's turn to pick her up that morning. At the shop Wilson would take over in Victoria Street and Groom would be on duty at the back.

When I asked if there was any news, he passed me the chit that had come in that morning from the bank manager. Nevall's current account showed no payments or receipts beyond the normal, and he had realized on none of his investments which the bank administered.

'I've just rung him up and thanked him,' Wharton said. 'I don't think he liked being got out of bed but he cheered up when I told him we shouldn't have to worry him any more. He sent me the information I asked for, by the way. Only that diamond ring and the wrist-watch missing as far as we can make out. No handbags except that alligator one and those two evening ones we found in the flat.'

There was nothing to do but wait. George pushed his chair back from the desk and began filling his pipe. Then the buzzer went.

'Right. Send him straight up,' George said.

It was Broad, and what should he be bringing with him but that alligator bag. It had been found only a half-hour before and in some undergrowth in the far corner of the wood on the Heath side.

'That's where he came out then,' Wharton said. 'Circled right round and off the beaten track. Any prints on the bag?'

'Only hers.'

'Nothing of the unpremeditated attack about it then,' Wharton told him. 'A casual attacker wouldn't have had gloves on, and if he wiped his own prints off the bag he'd have wiped hers off too.'

'But the murderer must have had gloves on,' I said.

'I know that,' he said. 'That's why he didn't mind handling the bag and why he didn't have to wipe it. Let's have a look at it, Broad.'

Inside it the make-up apparatus was complete, even to a nail file. Her keys were there and a patent pencil, a tiny flat cigarette case and a utility lighter, and one folded wisp of a handkerchief.

'Never a print on anything, except her own,' Broad said.

'No papers, no letters, no money,' Wharton said. 'There never was a woman's bag yet that wasn't crammed with the devil knows what. And she'd have to have money unless she was walking home.'

The buzzer went again. From the way George shifted excitedly in his chair, I guessed something was coming.

'Put him through,' he said, and then turned to me. 'Wilson on the line.'

I won't bother you with the scraps of conversation I heard, for Wilson's voice, was coming through distinctly. Wharton's report gives the picture much more clearly.

Groom had picked Rhoda Yarnell up at Rainsford and had got into the same carriage, and within a few feet of her on the opposite side. She had evidently not read her paper – a picture one – for it was folded and held by the strap of her bag. When the train moved off she lighted a cigarette and took out the paper. And at once she was in a state of tremendous agitation. Groom hadn't quoted the symptoms but what followed was to reinforce his judgement.

For when she got out at Piccadilly, Rhoda Yarnell didn't take a bus. What she took was a taxi! Groom looked like being left high and dry for there was no other taxi about, but luckily he saw a private car being driven by a chauffeur only. It was held up, like Rhoda's taxi, in the traffic queue, so he showed his credentials and found the chauffeur amenable. But there wasn't much of a chase. The taxi stopped outside the Victoria Street shop. Rhoda scrambled out and the driver evidently had been told to wait.

Groom then picked up Wilson and, while he held the fort, looked about for a taxi of his own. He found one, showed his credentials again, and made it wait. Meanwhile Rhoda had opened the shop and as soon as the first of her assistants arrived, she was giving her orders and then getting in the taxi again. Wilson had tried unavailingly to overhear her instructions to the driver, so there was nothing for Groom to do but follow. That was the position. Wilson was returning to the Yard and Groom would doubtless ring as soon as he had anything to communicate. Wharton said a car would be waiting for him so that he could push on to Groom as soon as word came of his whereabouts.

George rang down for a car to be ready for us as well, and once more there was nothing for it but to wait. Broad had gone before George told me Wilson's story, and that story would have conveyed nothing to him in any case. And he would have his hands pretty full what with pawnshops and trying to obtain information about a suspicious character who might have been seen at a certain time emerging from the wood. But George couldn't leave him wholly in the dark. He had to hint mysteriously that we had a suspect in mind, and there followed a description of the bearded, bespectacled Hanley.

A quarter of an hour went by. George was just saying, 'Damn that fellow Groom. What the devil's he doing all this time?' and then the buzzer went again. Groom was on the line.

He was speaking from the Brentford Hotel in Pitt Street. Mrs Yarnell had paid off her taxi well short of it, and when he got to the hotel on her heels, he saw her going up the stairs. Then he had a private word with the manager. James Hanley was staying there, and had been for some days, and his name was in the register. Then Rhoda Yarnell came down again and went straight out of the hotel. Groom told the manager that if Hanley attempted to check out, he was to be detained, and then he rang from the manager's room while the manager stood by at the desk. Wharton, now in a fluster, told him to keep his eyes skinned for Wilson and to post him at the back where there would be a fire escape. He himself would be along as fast as he could make it.

Inside five minutes we were away. Wilson had already gone, and we never caught sight of his car. At every holdup George was fuming, and when we drew up at last just beyond Bloomsbury Square he fairly bolted out of the door. In a doorway just short of the Brentford, Groom was waiting for us.

'Room 37, sir,' he said. 'He's still there.'

'You come behind us,' Wharton told him. 'When we're inside, stand by the door.'

The manager was in the vestibule and he gave us a nod towards the stairs. At the first landing we turned right as directed by the number board. A turn left and we were outside Room 37, and our feet had made never a sound on the carpet.

Wharton stooped, ear at the door. He nodded to himself, then gave a knock. There was silence. He knocked again.

'Who is it?' came a voice.

'Telegram for you, sir,' George told him.

'Push it under the door.'

'Sorry, sir. Manager's instructions. There has to be a receipt.'

Another silence, then feet were heard. The door opened to the merest crack, but Wharton's foot was in it, and his shoulder at the door, and we were inside.

'What the devil are you doing?'

'Just paying a call,' Wharton told him, and showed his credentials. 'Superintendent Wharton of New Scotland Yard.'

Hanley looked bewildered.

'New Scotland Yard? . . . I don't understand.'

'You will do,' Wharton said. 'We just want your help that's all.'

'Help?'

Wharton recited the old soothing paragraph about the right of the police to question anyone whatever if they had reason to believe that that person could supply information.

I had been casting an eye round the room. Everything, including Hanley himself, was highly significant. We had disturbed him while he was packing his second bag, for the first was already packed and stood by the door. On the bed were still some unpacked garments including pyjamas.

As for the man himself, I doubt if we'd have recognized him. He had shaved off his beard, but had left one of those new guardee moustaches that sweep outwards parallel to the mouth. His hair was short cropped, and what little there was was parted neatly at the side. His face was very much fatter than I had imagined from the description of my friend Tipton who'd described him as almost haggard. As for the horn-rims he wore, I think they were even larger than my own.

'I see we were just in time,' Wharton said, and drew back the chair from the dressing-table and sat on it. 'Going anywhere particular, Mr Hanley? You are James Hanley, I take it?'

'Of course I'm James Hanley.'

'Well, we shan't detain you long,' Wharton told him, and quite pleasantly. 'But you haven't been behaving too well, you know. It's taken the devil of a time to run you to earth.'

Hanley was staring.

'That grandmother of yours is worried about you,' Wharton went on. 'She's started inquiries and, well, here you are. The only thing is, what are you going to do about it?'

'About my grandmother?'

He had a curiously thick kind of voice that reminded me of my pet aversion among announcers: the gent who can be unctuous without ceasing to sound asthmatical, and who always has a small but hot potato in his mouth.

'That's the idea,' Wharton told him cheerfully.

'But if I don't want to have anything to do with my grandmother, you can't force me?'

'I know we can't,' admitted Wharton. 'All we'd like to know are your intentions. As regards your grandmother, I mean.'

Hanley told us a few home truths about her. He spoke dispassionately and there was no abuse, but his mind was quite made up.

'Don't you think it would be more manly to write and tell her so yourself?' Wharton asked him. 'If you'd done so originally it'd have saved all this bother.'

Hanley said perhaps he would, but added that we didn't know all the ins and outs. I was wondering when George was going to come to some sort of point, but the camouflage of talk was to end more quickly than I was beginning to hope.

'Well, we'll leave it like that,' he said. 'From now on it's a private matter between you and your grandmother. But between ourselves, I suppose there's some money she might leave you?'

'Money isn't everything,' Hanley told him.

'True enough,' said Wharton heartily. 'Not compared with the love of a good woman.'

The remark startled me. It startled Hanley more. He opened his mouth, but the words wouldn't come.

'We of the police know more than we're credited with,' Wharton went on roguishly. 'Your friend – or should I say fiancée – Mrs Yarnell for instance.'

'Mrs Yarnell!'

'Look,' said Wharton patiently. 'Don't be foolish. If you're thinking of telling us lies – don't. Mrs Yarnell was what I said. The Mrs Yarnell with whom you were living at Rainsford till you moved in here. The Mrs Yarnell who was in this room talking to you not an hour ago.'

Hanley licked his lips. Then he looked up.

'Well, what of it?'

'Nothing,' said Wharton, and shrugged his shoulders. 'Morals don't come within my jurisdiction. But would you like me to tell you why Mrs Yarnell came here this morning? Oh no. I'm not a thought reader. I just happen to know. What she came here for was to tell you that a woman named Violet Lancing was dead.'

Hanley couldn't say a word. He tried, but once more the words wouldn't come.

'I'm glad you're seeing sense,' Wharton went on. 'You haven't even asked me why she should come here to tell you about this murdered woman. So I'll tell you myself. Violet Lancing married the man that Mrs Yarnell divorced. Am I right?'

Hanley admitted that Mrs Yarnell had told him that, but he persisted that that wasn't the reason why she had come to the hotel that morning. Why she had come was because he had been none too comfortable in the Brentford and it was expensive. She had come to say he ought to come back to her own house till they could be married, which would be almost at once. If the grandmother made herself a nuisance, they might call on the police to put a stop to it.

'Well, there we are then,' said Wharton. 'But Mrs Yarnell is connected in a way with the dead woman. And you're connected with Mrs Yarnell. Both of you will have to be questioned. Nothing official. And you've nothing to fear. It's a routine questioning and no more. All we want to know is just where you were the day before yesterday from – say – one o'clock till three.'

It was curious how eager Hanley suddenly became in the matter of cooperation. He had lunched at the hotel, he said, and then before he could state any exact times, Wharton was getting to his feet.

'Leave your things here and we'll just go down and confirm. You'd better put on your hat if you think we'll have to go elsewhere.'

So down we went and everything began swimmingly for Hanley. Two waiters – one male and one female – said that he had lunched at the hotel every day. Lunch was at one o'clock and it was about a quarter to two that day when Hanley finished his coffee and went out. The desk clerk saw him go, and she recommended a certain picture. He told her he was probably only going for a walk.

That seemed to clinch matters, for Violet Lancing had left the block of flats at half past twelve and by no conceivable chance could she have reached that wood till close on one o'clock. But the doctor's time had been vague. Maybe Violet had not been killed till much later in the afternoon. In any case Wharton wasn't satisfied.

Hanley told us that after lunch he had walked slowly through to Tottenham Court Road and then to Oxford Circus.

'Why slowly?' asked Wharton.

'Well, when you've been out of England as long as I have, you take an interest in things,' he said. 'I wanted to see the shops and flying-bomb damage.'

'Did you meet anybody you knew?'

'That's just what I didn't want to do,' Hanley told him with a faint smile. 'But I'll tell you what I did do. I went into a tobacconist's at this end of Oxford Street.'

'Right,' said Wharton, and into the car the three of us got. Hanley directed us by the way he had gone and Wharton wanted to know what he'd bought. Then when we got to the shop – it was only a tiny inset – Hanley said that the girl there was the very one who had served him. Wharton said he'd do the talking.

'My friend and I have been having an argument,' he told the girl. 'He says he bought two packets of Old Gold cigarettes here the day before yesterday at about two o'clock. I say he didn't because he was with me.'

She had a look at Hanley and then shook her head.

'I believe I have seen him but I couldn't say when.'

'I had a beard then,' Hanley broke in. 'I only shaved it off this morning.'

'That's right,' she said, and her face lighted. 'I asked you if you was in the Navy and you said you was. It *was* the day before yesterday. I know because I'd just taken over for the afternoon. Two o'clock it was or just after. Two of Old Gold – two twenties – was what you bought.'

'That's good enough for me,' Wharton said, 'though I still claim it was yesterday.'

'It couldn't have been yesterday,' she said. 'I wasn't on yesterday. I was at our other branch where someone was away.'

'I'll pay,' Wharton told her smilingly, and bought a couple of ounces of his brand of tobacco for the good of the firm.

'And where now?' he asked Hanley when we were back in the car again.

Hanley said he had gone strolling on towards Oxford Circus. Then he had gone into a news cinema – Studio Two – for an hour, after which he had gone up to the restaurant at Dickens and Jones for tea. That was a quarter to four, and he was sure he could identify the waitress. He also said he'd told the girl he'd been in the Navy to put her off.

'What about the cinema?' Wharton asked him. 'Could anyone identify you there?'

Hanley thought for a bit and then remembered something, and into the theatre we went to verify it. This time it was an attendant on the lower floor. Hanley had been going down the stairs and, his eyes not used to the dark, had barged into her at the bottom. After his apologies she had shown him to a seat.

This time Hanley and I waited in the narrow vestibule while Wharton went to investigate, and it was a good ten minutes before he came back and then he owned frankly that Hanley's story was correct. But he wanted to know about the programme. Hanley's answers seemed to satisfy him, and back to the pavement we went.

'Well, that's about all,' Wharton said. 'We're much obliged to you, Mr Hanley, and now we'll run you back in the car.'

'There's no need to give you all that trouble,' Hanley said. 'I'd much rather walk.'

I was standing close to George with pedestrians crowding past us, and I gave him a nudge with my knee.

'No, we ought to take you back,' George said. 'It's up to us to replace you as found, so to speak.'

He was already moving Hanley towards the car and down Regent Street we went to save a turn. Another ten minutes and we were back at the Brentford.

'Now I'm here I might as well take a look at your civilian identity card,' George said, and motioned Hanley towards the stairs. Wilson was there and George gave him the tip to follow us. When we got in the room I saw that Wilson and Groom had made a job of searching the two bags. Nothing whatever looked disturbed.

Wharton had a look at the identity card.

'Well, that seems to be the lot,' he said. 'Anything you'd like to ask before you go, Mr Travers?'

'Yes,' I said. 'One thing's been puzzling me, Mr Hanley – or two things. I seem to think vaguely that we've met before somewhere, though there's no time to go into that. The other thing is that you speak without a trace of a Midland accent.'

'Should I?' he said, and it was strange how warily he was watching me.

'Well, you were born, bred, and educated in Birmingham. I'm an East Anglian myself, and when I'm not thinking I often use a dialect word or intonation. The Superintendent here is an Oxfordshire man, and even though he's spent most of his life in London, I'd know he was Oxfordshire before I'd been in his company half an hour.'

Hanley shrugged his shoulders, and as he did so he slightly turned. The light from the window fell across his face, and suddenly I saw something that made me stare. It was incredible and yet it had to be true. And then I knew it *was* true.

And then again as I stepped between Hanley and the window, with George between Hanley and the door, he knew perhaps what I'd seen.

'Your name isn't Hanley,' I told him. 'You're masquerading as Hanley. *You're Yarnell.* Victor Yarnell.'

'You're talking nonsense,' he was saying, and backing towards the inner door.

'Oh no,' I said, and George took a couple of steps forward. 'You can crop your hair to get rid of those nice wavy curls. You can put plumpers in your cheeks and sport that moustache, and wear those glasses, but there's one thing you forgot – that nick in your ear.'

'My God, he's right!' said Wharton. 'Victor Yarnell. Large as life and I didn't spot him.'

With an eye on the room he stepped back and opened the door.

'Fetch Groom and get back at the double,' he told Wilson.

He closed the door behind him.

'Sit on that bed,' he told Yarnell, 'and don't try any tricks. And tell us, just between ourselves, how you worked the oracle.'

Yarnell kept his poise. He sat on the bed and he took his time about it. But his mouth was shut and he kept it so. When Wharton spoke to him again, it was as if he hadn't heard a word.

There was a tap at the door and Wilson and Groom came in.

'Put the cuffs on him and take him away,' Wharton said. 'I'll charge him later.'

They put the handcuffs on him and Wharton recited the usual warning about evidence. Then Yarnell refused to move.

'You can't do this,' he said. 'What charge are you bringing against me?'

'Well,' said Wharton slowly. 'I might give you quite a few. I can arrest you without a warrant under the False Personation Act of 1847, since you've impersonated in order to draw a gratuity to which you're not properly entitled. You've also committed an offence under two different Army Acts in respect of military pay and rewards. And in so far as you may have signed for a gratuity in the name of another man, you've committed the further felony of forgery.' He turned to me. 'Anything I've missed?'

I shook my head. I never liked Wharton so little as when he baited a witness or an accused, though God knows I had little reason to feel sympathy for Yarnell.

Wharton waited for Yarnell to speak.

'Right then. Take him away. And these two bags. I'll look round myself to see if there's anything else.'

There was nothing else. Wharton locked the door behind us and we went downstairs. He had a few words with the manager and then we moved on to our car. Yarnell and the two detectives had gone.

He told the driver to take it easy and then he leaned back in his corner.

'Had some luck there, didn't we,' he said, as if he could still hardly believe it. 'And what a hold-on! No bail for Mr Yarnell. A few hours more and we'll have that murder pinned on him, or my name's Robinson.'

'What about his alibi?' I ventured to ask.

'We've broken better alibis than his,' he told me. 'We've got to break it. We can't help breaking it.'

'Why?'

'Why? Because it has to be a fake. I tell you he's had this scheme in his mind for months. Maybe that Hanley was a pal of his who died in hospital or somewhere and Yarnell swopped identities. And why? So that he could get home and get his own back on that woman. I'll bet she refused to divorce him and that's why he did her in. Stabbed her for that five hundred first. Or if he didn't it doesn't matter. What he did was kill her so he could marry his first wife again.'

There was something a bit wrong about that, though George wasn't in the mood to be told so.

'One thing I do know,' I said, 'and that's why Violet fainted in the Daffodil. It was Yarnell she saw. She thought he was a ghost. And that's the answer to why she threw over Bill Ellice.'

'Just what I was saying,' said George. 'He saw her afterwards and told her to have that money ready. Then he killed her. And there's something else. It explains what he meant over the telephone when he told her that as soon as she saw him she'd know there was only to be the one payment.'

Once more, as I saw it, there was the devil of a lot wrong about George's facile deductions, but once more I wasn't prepared to point the fact out.

'Well, we've got a line of approach at last,' I said heartily.

'And what'll the first move be? Get officers from his own and Hanley's regiments to prove the fraud?'

'That's it,' George said. 'Get everything signed and sealed. War Office and everything. Then we can hold him till the cows come home.'

Then he was giving a confident nod of the head and saying it wouldn't have to be as long as that. And then the traffic lights changed and we slipped across the Strand and along Northumberland Avenue.

CHAPTER XV

Not According to Cocker

JUST BEFORE I left the Yard, Wharton succeeded in getting hold of Cave, the police surgeon. The report on Violet Lancing had long been in, but Wharton wasn't satisfied.

'You're prepared to stand by your statement that death occurred not later than half past one?' Wharton asked him.

'It depends on the information you supplied yourself,' Cave said. 'If you can guarantee that she didn't have breakfast till eleven o'clock, then I'll stand by the report. You can't argue with a stomach content.'

'She ate what she ate and when I said she ate it,' Wharton told him. 'The evidence is absolutely reliable. There couldn't have been any digestive or other peculiarities that might have affected things?'

'Not a hope,' Cave said. 'It's not only my opinion, remember. Time of death was half past one, within a very few minutes either way.'

'There we are then,' Wharton told me. 'If she died at half past one, then Yarnell's alibi's faked. After we've seen Mrs Yarnell, you might get to work on it.' His nod had warmth and a nice touch of congratulation. 'As I've said many a time before, if anyone can bust an alibi, it's you.'

'Very handsomely spoken, George,' I said. 'If I believed you I'd be almost overcome. But about Rhoda Yarnell. You're not seeing her till the morning?'

'That's the idea,' he said. 'If Yarnell was telling the truth about leaving the Brentford, she'll get nothing out of the manager except that Yarnell left for somewhere unknown. What sort of a state is she going to be in by tomorrow morning?'

George was certainly right about that. Then I left him with the usual understanding that I'd be on call at the flat and if nothing happened I'd be along before nine in the morning. So that evening I had a service meal and then got into slacks and slippers and turned on the electric fire. But I couldn't settle to a book, and soon there was nothing for it but to get out pencil and paper and try to make some kind of logic out of the day's happenings.

Wharton, it had seemed to me at the time, had been rushing to extremes. A series of unexpected facts had emerged, and those facts had seemed to bolster up a previous and hasty theory. But since the facts were definitely facts he was now assuming that the theory too was fact; and, worse than that, he was proceeding to deduce even more so-called facts from the theory. A bit involved, you say, so let's get down to facts ourselves.

It was a fact that Yarnell had changed his name and that he had returned to and been taken back by his first wife. That was certain, and then as what I might call almost a fact was the certainty that he and the first wife had been mixed up in that blackmailing of Violet Lancing. And on the strength of those facts, Wharton was taking it for granted that Yarnell had killed his second wife, and that in defiance of what seemed as water-tight an alibi as I had ever known.

Take that alibi, which it was to be my job to tackle the following morning. How *could* Yarnell have faked it? How could there have been collusion with the girl in the tobacconist's or the cinema attendant, and, above all, with the waiters at the Brentford? And *why* should he have faked an alibi? The facts showed nothing but that he had suspected either that Hanley's grandmother was on his tracks or the police were wise to the blackmail, and that therefore he had hidden himself in the Brentford. And if by an enormous stretch of imagination one could think seriously that he had faked that alibi in advance, and knowing that he was about to kill his wife, then all I could say was that he'd shown an organization and a prescience – and his collaborators had shown an amenability and veniality – beyond all reasonable experience.

Take the change of name. Wharton had said casually that the change had taken place probably in a hospital. But that was out of the question. In a hospital, even as a prisoner of war, Yarnell would have his own identity, and if Hanley, supposedly in the same hospital, had died, then he had died and that was that. The change, then, as I saw it, must have been made long before, and probably on some battlefield where the two men had been left behind for dead upon some counter-attack.

But that was a small point compared with the implications of that change of name. Wharton was working on the assumption that Yarnell had had a tremendous hatred for his wife and had hit on the change of identity as a means for getting his revenge on his ultimate return to England. Well, as a theory there was nothing outrageous about that. What it did, as I saw it, was to forget one thing.

When he changed his identity, Yarnell lost the work of a life-time. He was an actor; not in the first flight, maybe, but with an established career and with prospects. Benny, for instance, had spoken highly of him. But in taking the name of Hanley he could not take up the career of Hanley. He was an actor, and nothing else, and an actor, it seemed to me, would renounce a career for only the most vital of reasons.

Very well then, you may say. He did have a vital reason – to get his revenge on his wife. Wharton, in other words, was right. But was he right? Isn't there an unconsidered factor? Have you asked yourself why Yarnell voluntarily joined up at all? He was deferred and might have continued his career. He was doing well in pictures and making money, and the war would give him even more chances. And yet he threw everything up. And why? And there I could only shrug my shoulders. It was a question I couldn't answer myself. All I knew, and with something beyond intuition, was that the solution of all our problems lay in the answer to that one question.

And then there was the question of the blackmail. Wharton was ready to assume that there was no blackmail. His theory, as far as I could judge, was that Yarnell had rung his wife and said he was back from the grave. She simply didn't believe it. She daren't believe it, for if it was right, then the only one who knew a vital secret would soon be proclaiming it to the world. So she went to Ellice with that cock-and-bull story of blackmail, and Ellice was to find out if Yarnell was really alive. Then Violet fainted in the tea-shop when she saw for herself that disaster was imminent and her husband was really living. And since the services of Ellice could be of no more use, she naturally paid him off.

But I knew that there *had* been an attempt at blackmail. The five hundred pounds were only too real. In Bill Ellice's office Violet Lancing had said she could raise the money and she would bring it if necessary the following morning. Suppose Bill had told her to bring it, what would she have said? That she had been bluffing? I say most certainly not. I'd swear, not on a stack of Bibles but on the whole premises of the British and Foreign Bible Society, that she didn't have the money on call, that she knew where she could raise it, and that she would have raised it and produced it by that following morning.

And so back to the most vital question of all – *why was she prepared to pay?* What hold had Yarnell over her? Could she have killed Manfrey? Might she not have faked the times and been back long before May Clarke that morning? Could it have been she who was quarrelling with Manfrey, with the muffled voices seeming to May Clarke like the voices of Manfrey and Nevall? Was that why Violet Lancing had called on May Clarke just before Christmas of that same year to impress on her that it had really been Nevall's voice that she had heard? And how had Yarnell become aware of the dreadful fact that his new wife had killed Manfrey? From something he had found in her possession? From a confession he had forced out of her? And, if so, had he joined up so that he should never be forced to give evidence against her?

But by that time my brain was almost reeling. In some ways it had been a tiring day, and mental chess can exhaust like nothing else. And, to tell the truth, the more I delved into those dark obscured possibilities of the past, the more I began to feel something of horror. Each hidden furtiveness had twisted and distorted the even trend of lives as then unknown – the dead Hanley and that grandmother who had clung to him as the last tenuous immortality of herself. There had been the ruin of Yarnell, and Violet Lancing with her face in the sodden undergrowth of the Hampstead wood. And in the background, like figures dimly discerned in a mist, would be Henry Nevall with his watchful eyes and shaking hands, and there would be May Clarke who had been afraid to tell the truth: credulous, warm-hearted, and in the hands of Violet Lancing as easy to knead and shape as soft clay in the hands of a potter.

And that was where I left things. My brain might be tired but I was still active, and I knew the danger signals that warned me of restless hours before sleep.

So I took a sleeping tablet and went to bed, and I don't think I have ever slept more soundly. And when I woke I had left behind me the introspections of the previous night. In an hour or two, as I knew, I should be listening to Rhoda Yarnell, and maybe it would be from her that we should get the answers.

It was half past nine when we entered the shop. It was to me that the assistant turned, perhaps because she was wondering vaguely if she had seen me before. I asked if Mrs Yarnell was in.

'Give her this,' Wharton said, and handed her an envelope. 'We'll wait here.'

We had to wait for a good five minutes, with that assistant pottering round among the cosmetics and pretending we were not there. Then suddenly Rhoda Yarnell appeared. She was wearing a white overall, and against it her face had a curious pallor. But she gave us a slow, careful look before she spoke.

'Will you come this way, please?'

She turned back the flap of the side counter and we went through to what looked like her office. The door was closed behind her. There was never a tremor in her voice as she asked us to sit down. She sat with her back to the desk and facing us.

'You know who we are, Mrs Yarnell,' began Wharton. 'Perhaps you would like to inspect our credentials. Or ring up New Scotland Yard.'

'It's quite unnecessary,' she said, and once more I was thinking what an attractive voice she had. 'Perhaps you will tell me why you're here.'

'Your husband – your former husband, Victor Yarnell. Have you any idea of his present whereabouts?'

'Whereabouts?' she said, forehead wrinkling in a frown. 'But he's dead.'

'But he wasn't dead when you saw him yesterday at the Brentford Hotel?'

She was suddenly motionless. The fingers moved nervously on her lap, but her eyes never moved from Wharton's. A long minute went by.

'You've nothing to say?'

Another few moments and she was shaking her head.

'Then I'll give you the latest news about him,' Wharton said patiently. 'Yesterday morning he was arrested. He's being held on various charges, among them conspiracy to defraud and forgery. What I have to ask you is if you'd care to make any statement.'

Another slow look and she shook her head again. And all the time she was sitting there motionless, and only the fingers just faintly moving where the hands lay almost idly in her lap.

'You prefer not to talk?'

'There's nothing I can say,' she told him calmly.

'Let me put a point of view to you,' Wharton said, and still very patiently. 'And believe me that I'm not exaggerating for the purpose of extorting information. Victor Yarnell is under charges for which the maximum penalty is penal servitude for life. He may soon be under another charge for which the penalty is something far worse.'

'You mean. . . . Violet Lancing?'

Wharton shrugged his shoulders.

'The interpretation's your own. All I'll say is that I don't deny it.'

'He didn't do it!' she said, and passionately. 'He'd never have done a thing like that.'

'You wish to make a statement after all? If so it will be my duty to warn you.'

In a moment she was motionless again, and shaking her head.

'Then why did you say that Yarnell couldn't have done it? What were your grounds? Could you prove he didn't do it? If so, isn't it your duty to do so?'

'There's nothing to say,' she told him. 'I know him better than you do. That's all.'

'Let me talk entirely without prejudice,' Wharton said. 'How old are you, by the way, Mrs Yarnell?'

'Does it matter?'

'Perhaps not,' he told her. 'But I have a daughter who's just about your own age, or so I thought. I'm human, not a machine. The job of the police is to protect, not to condemn. I'm here to help both you and Yarnell.'

'But what have *I* done?'

'You understand that we're talking without prejudice?' Wharton asked her. 'You know what that means?'

'I don't,' she said, 'unless it means that it's not officially.'

'That's just what it does mean. At the moment it's just a friendly chat. All I'm suggesting is that you allow me to help both Yarnell and yourself. Yarnell by telling me the facts as you know them, and yourself because you're in some ways an accessory after the fact. I see you don't quite follow that. In blunt language it means that you were fully aware of Yarnell's masquerading as another man, and you were aiding and abetting as the law has it.'

'But I've nothing to say.'

'Nothing to say,' echoed Wharton. 'Do you mean that you refuse to give any information?'

'I've nothing to say.'

Wharton looked round at me, shook his head slowly and solemnly and then got to his feet.

'Well, Mrs Yarnell, I've done my best. But let me tell you something. There's little about Victor Yarnell since his arrival in England that we don't know. We know, for instance, that he was living with you. We know why he left your house. Before many hours go by we'll know just why he was in the Daffodil Tea-shop on a certain morning while you were across the pavement at Massey's bookshop. Does that surprise you?'

A look of something like misery came into her eyes. For a moment I thought she was going to cry. The lip actually quivered, and then once more she was shaking her head.

'Think it over, Mrs Yarnell,' Wharton told her quietly. 'And if you happen to think that you'd like to talk after all, just give me a ring. Ask for me personally.'

She didn't even shake her head.

'Very well then,' said Wharton after a minute. 'I have to warn you that from now on you'll be under observation. You may not notice it, but we shall know where you are. Don't try to run away or do anything foolish.'

Another long look and he was saying his last words.

'Whether you'll be arrested yourself I can't say. It may depend on several things. Whether or not you decide to speak, for instance. Good-day, Mrs Yarnell.'

Then as we were at the very door, she did speak.

'Do you think I should be allowed to see him?'

'At the moment, no,' said Wharton bluntly. 'The next time I see you it may be yes. It depends on yourself.'

'Let's slip along to the Daffodil,' George said. 'I'd like to think this over.'

We turned back and as we strolled towards the teashop, he was asking me what I thought of Rhoda Yarnell. In his voice was more awe than curiosity. Rhoda Yarnell had been something out of his experience.

'She didn't look a guilty woman to me,' I said. 'Somehow I felt sorry for her. I don't know why. I had no reason to. Perhaps it was that look in her eyes when you mentioned Massey's bookshop.'

'Yes,' George said. 'And never a word to be got out of her. Except in defence of him.'

We went up the stairs to the old familiar room and ordered coffee. George couldn't get those last few minutes out of his mind.

'She's still in love with that chap, you know. Took him back as if they'd never been parted. And why?'

'Don't ask me to explain women,' I said. 'Or love.'

'You think she'll weaken?'

'Don't know,' I said. 'She might do if she thought anything was going to happen to him. One thing we do know. She couldn't give him an alibi for the murder or she'd have done it like a shot.'

We went on talking about Rhoda Yarnell: the way she'd sat with her eyes on George, making no sign and giving nothing away. Never a loss of poise even in that short, passionate defence of Yarnell. And though she had almost broken down when that look of despair had come to her eyes and her lip had quivered, there had been no tremor in her voice when she had asked if she might see Yarnell.

'The more I think things out,' I said, 'I'm convinced that she thinks there's no real danger to him or herself. That's why she wouldn't talk.'

'Well, we can put the pressure on him,' Wharton said. 'Up to now his name hasn't been published. If it is, then he's absolutely finished for on the stage. That ought to make him talk.'

He glanced at his watch and said we'd better be going. At eleven o'clock there was a conference to decide on future action, and a couple of army officers were coming along to identify Yarnell or prove that he wasn't Hanley.

'You and I know he's Yarnell all right,' he said, 'but it's got to be official. Perhaps the one from Hanley's regiment might give us some news about him.'

I paid the small bill while George fumbled absent-mindedly, and when we were out on the pavement again he supposed I was going to tackle Yarnell's alibi. And that is what I did do for the rest of that morning and most of the early afternoon. At the news cinema the alibi was confirmed even more strongly than ever it could have been to Wharton himself. The girl at the tobacconist's didn't come on duty till two o'clock, so I got myself a scratch meal and waited for her. Again there was never a shadow of doubt in my mind but that she and Yarnell had both told the truth.

And so back to the Brentford, and I walked all the way in case the time taken would have given Yarnell a chance to get to Hampstead and back before appearing at the tobacconist's. But his times tallied, and an aeroplane could scarcely have landed him there and taken off again in the twenty minutes or so that it took me to stroll along at his pace. And so to the hotel. Every word was confirmed, and a great deal of tact was required to keep the two witnesses from thinking their evidence had been called in question. After a long hour of that, I walked at my own pace back to the tobacconist's and found it had taken me twelve minutes.

My feet ached like blazes and I treated myself to a cup of tea before going on to the Yard. George looked surprised to see me.

'Been a bit quick, haven't you?'

'Call it insubordination or what you damn-please,' I said, 'but as far as I'm concerned, that alibi stands. I wash my hands of it.'

I told him what I'd done and he'd nothing new to suggest, but somehow he was still loath to part entirely with the idea that Yarnell must have killed Violet Lancing. I could feel it in his mind while he was telling me the news.

At the conference it had been agreed that the original case against Yarnell should be proceeded with and all evidence collected. Meanwhile it was hoped that Rhoda Yarnell would come forward and tell anything she knew.

As for the identification parade, the officer from Yarnell's regiment had identified him, and the one from Hanley's regiment had said he was definitely not Hanley. But it was significant that Hanley had been attached to Yarnell's regiment in Italy for some weeks before he became a casualty. Comparing seniorities, it was found that in taking Hanley's gratuity instead of his own, Yarnell had actually lost a few pounds. How the bank accounts would work out would have to be seen, and there was the complicated matter of setting off Yarnell's pay as a prisoner against the allowance that Violet Lancing had received as a widow.

'If he's made nothing out of it, it may be some extenuation,' George said. 'But there's more in it than that. Tonight, all being well, I'm going to get into my chair at home and either I'll see daylight or else I won't go to bed at all.'

'What about Yarnell during the identifications?' I asked him.

'Just like a dummy,' he said. 'Never opened his mouth. Never said a word. Didn't take a damn of interest.'

'Just like her this morning,' I said. 'Something about those two is beginning to get me, George. Is he shielding her? Or she him? Or each trying to shield the other?'

'Don't ask me,' he told me. 'You get along home and do some quiet thinking like me.'

An evening and night of thought terrified me, so I went on to my club, had a bath and then an early dinner, and rang George from there. He had gone home so I didn't ring him at his private address. What I did was to walk to my flat.

Then I settled down to do some quiet thinking. Not the promiscuous thinking of the previous night but the steady following out of one idea. When a skein of wool is tangled, the last thing to do is to go at it with all your fingers with the hope of disentangling the lot. That is what I had done the previous night. Now I was proposing to find one loose end and work along it methodically and carefully till I had at least a goodish length of the Case in my hands. With luck I might unravel most of the skein.

I don't quite know why but I began with Violet Lancing. I accepted her original story of how she had broken into crowd work at the film studio, and after that I used my own judgement. Then she had gone back to secretarial work, but only as a stepping-stone. I still thought she had been Manfrey's mistress and that he had promised to get her at least a stage trial. Then, opportunist that she was, she had set her cap at Yarnell who seemed more likely to produce quick results. Then had come Yarnell's divorce and re-marriage and his discovery that she had no use for him except as another stepping-stone to a stage or screen career.

You may say that most of that was fact already known, and I agree. But what I now began to see was a continuation. Violet Lancing's life had been a groove. It had a uniformity. What she had schemed for had always been a someone who would further the career she had planned for herself. And as soon as I recognized that continuity I began to see things. As early as the Christmas of the year of Manfrey's death, she had looked around for a second string. Maybe Yarnell hadn't been in a coming-on disposition at that time, and an alternative had seemed to her essential.

Very well then. She had heard – or not heard – Nevall's voice in Manfrey's room. If she had not heard it, it was enough to know that May Clarke had heard it, and then to be in a position to confirm that she had heard it herself. Maybe she acted at once. Maybe she waited to see what Yarnell would do after she had married him. But in time it became necessary to approach Nevall. Pressure was applied. Nevall had to yield, and Violet Lancing was given her chance to make good on the stage. And she did so in Nevall's own play! And that was why Nevall had been so careful to insist to me that Violet Lancing was a born actress. Born actress, my foot!

Now the camel was in the tent. Nevall had admitted to Wharton and me that he had advanced sums of money against salary, and that money was still owing to him. And why? Because he knew that Wharton might somehow trace the payments. What he had been forced to do was to submit to a kind of silken blackmail. There was the origin of the fur coat and the ermine wrap, and maybe that diamond ring. And so to the moment when Violet Lancing had been faced with the prospect of finding five hundred pounds. And Nevall was the only hope. And he didn't know if that five hundred would or would not be the prelude to further demands. And so he had decided to end things. He was nothing but a man with a cancer that gnawed at his ribs, and there was nothing for it but the knife. *It was he who had murdered Violet Lancing.*

Somehow it didn't surprise me when I reached that conclusion. To me it seemed inevitable, so logical had the sequences been. All I do know is that I glanced at my watch and saw that it was about a quarter past nine. Unhurriedly I made my way to the street and began looking for a taxi.

CHAPTER XVI
Half the Story

WHEN I REACHED the theatre Nevall was still in his dressing-room. I tapped at the door and, at what sounded like an invitation, I entered. Nevall was sitting at the dressing-table, adjusting his tie. At the sight of me his fingers were suddenly motionless as if the whole man had been paralysed. Then he got to his feet.

'My dear Travers, what brings you here?'

I didn't answer. Wharton has his technique and I have mine, and mine is what I might call the direct method. I try to be quiet and even urbane and still keep a witness guessing. That was why I got myself a chair and sat down before I spoke.

'I'm here purely on business,' I told him. 'You've never inspected my credentials, by the way.'

He waved aside the warrant card a bit impatiently. 'Business, you say? What sort of business?'

I took my time as if I had to choose my words. He was looking even older, by the way, and in that artificial light his skin had an unhealthy pallor.

'We consider it necessary,' I said, 'to inquire into your whereabouts from noon onwards, the day before yesterday.'

'Into *my* whereabouts! My dear fellow –'

'So perhaps you'd be so good as to tell me,' I cut in. 'You can refuse to do so if you like. But you can't refuse to make a statement in a coroner's court if it should be thought desirable to make you a witness.'

'Look, Travers,' he said. 'This is all very mysterious. Why a coroner's court? And why the day before yesterday?'

'Because that was when Violet Lancing was murdered!'

'Ah!' he said. His eyes refused for a moment or two to meet mine and then he made a gesture which I took for annoyance. 'Do you come here seriously to suggest that I had anything to do with that woman's – with Violet Lancing's death?'

'Let's leave all that,' I said. 'Are you or are you not prepared to give me the information?'

He shrugged his shoulders.

'Why not? From noon onwards, you say. Well, I lunched in my flat, that was at about one o'clock. At about two o'clock I took a stroll in the Park, and then went on to my club where I stayed for tea.'

'Right,' I said. 'That ought to be ample. But to begin with lunch. Your man would verify the time?'

His eyes opened in a pretence of dismay. Then he was clicking his tongue.

'Damnation, no! Most unfortunate.' He waved a hand at me as he leaned forward. 'Let me explain. It was his day out and he left at midday. A cold lunch was laid and all I had to do was eat it.'

My eyebrows lifted regretfully.

'Unfortunate, as you say. And there were no telephone calls or callers of any kind?'

'Afraid not,' he said, and moistened his lips.

'The Park then. Did you meet anybody on your way there?'

'No,' he said. 'I can't say that I did. I took a bus, you see.'

'You don't remember what bus? Or the conductor or conductress? Well enough to give a description?'

'It would be difficult,' he said, and shook his head. 'Naturally I wasn't anticipating an inquiry into my movements. One doesn't notice such things.'

I got to my feet and he rose too.

'That is all you want?'

'Yes,' I said. 'What I wanted from you was an alibi. I'm being perfectly frank. But you have no alibi. Your whereabouts depend on your statements alone.'

'But my reputation!'

'The law takes no account of reputations,' I said. 'Reputations are very minor things compared with facts.'

He was turning away and I opened the door. Then I closed it, hand still on the knob.

'Listen to me a moment, Nevall,' I said quietly. 'I'm like you and most of the rest of the world. I'm two men. One has a job of work to do and does it. The other's an ordinary citizen, and that's what I am now. Wharton would put it another way. He would say he was speaking without prejudice. Take it how you like.'

His eyes were on me but he said nothing.

'We have information which you never dreamed we'd have,' I went on. 'Beyond that I can't go. All I will say is that I know what you've been through.'

I pulled myself together as if I'd said too much. I moved the knob of the door.

'Tomorrow morning Superintendent Wharton will ask to see you. That's as certain as there'll be a tomorrow's sun. Think it over, Nevall.'

I had taken a chance and what the outcome would be I still could not tell. But he did turn away and it seemed to me that he was in the grip of some extraordinary emotion.

'Good night,' Nevall,' I said, and gently closed the door.

I slipped along to my club and rang Wharton's private address from there. It was Jane Wharton who answered me.

'Hallo, Jane,' I said. 'Is the great man still up?'

'There's no hope of your seeing him,' she said. 'He's literally locked himself in. I've just taken him a cup of strong coffee.'

'You slip a note under his door and say I'm coming,' I told her. 'If he gets rough leave him to me.'

She laughed at that, and no wonder. Not only did Jane Wharton know me for a man of peace, but in my bachelor days it used to be hard work to keep her from mothering me. At any rate when I got to George's house she gave me a shake of the head and a smile, and then waved towards George's den.

'A nice time of night to pay calls,' he told me belligerently. Then he weakened and asked if I'd like some coffee.

'No more brain-work for me tonight,' I said, and then I told him what thinking I'd done.

'Nevall!' he said, and gave himself a nod or two. 'Just what I'd begun to think myself.' Then he couldn't keep back a glare. 'Done anything about it?'

I told him of my informal call and what I thought of Nevall's alibi.

'And what about his reactions?'

'He's a beaten man,' I said. 'The strain's been too much for him. Tonight he'll have the worst night he ever had. Tomorrow morning he's ours.'

'I wonder.' He shook his head and tapped away at his palm with a clenched fist. 'It'll be a hell of a risk.'

'Oh, no,' I said. 'Suppose he doesn't crack absolutely. We shall have taken a statement about his own movements and we can do a considerable deal of hinting. That'll weaken him still more. Then we can give him a day or so's rest and be at him again.'

'Well, we'll see him in any case,' he said. 'I'd like to see what he looks like.'

'You wouldn't care to take a big risk? You could always say you weren't serious.'

'What risk?'

'This,' I said, 'though far be it from me to tell you how to handle Nevall. But why not say never a word till he asks why we're there. Then in your own time you tell him. You say, "We've come to ask you precisely why you killed Violet Lancing!".'

I could see him visualizing the scene. Himself asking that dramatic question. The startled look of Nevall. The assessing of reactions. A confession maybe, or a breakdown. Or of indignation, then the bland smile and the mention of just a little joke.

He let out a breath.

'Don't know,' he said. 'I'll have to think it over.'

It was on the stroke of eleven o'clock the following morning when we made our way up the familiar stairs. Nevall's man let us in.

'Mr Nevall's expecting us,' Wharton told him quietly. 'What's your name, by the by?'

'Miller, sir. Walter Miller.'

But he didn't make a move to announce us, and he was looking worried about something.

'I don't know if you ought to see the master, sir,' he told Wharton in little more than a whisper. 'He's looking very ill, sir. I told him he ought to see a doctor, but he wouldn't let me.'

'He's in bed?'

'No, sir. As a matter of fact he didn't go to bed at all last night. I think he just slept *on* the bed, sir.'

'I see,' said Wharton and nodded heavily. 'All the more reason perhaps why I should see him. We might cheer him up. Just announce us and hear what he says.'

'Very good, sir.'

He moved across to the far door and we heard his quiet voice.

'Superintendent Wharton and Mr Travers to see you, sir.'

There was a pause and then Nevall spoke. He spoke so low that we couldn't make out a word, but we did hear Miller's 'Very good, sir.'

And then as he motioned to us there was a sudden, dramatic sound. George beat me to the door, but Miller was in that room first.

'Oh, my God!'

'Stand back,' Wharton told him, and was getting to his knees. I craned over him to look.

Nevall was lying there, the gun by his hand, and his body gave a last convulsive quiver. As Wharton let the head fall I turned my eyes away. That head was not a pretty sight, but it was of something else that I was thinking. Cassius had long since gone, and now Brutus too had met his Philippi.

Wharton got to his feet.

'Not much point in sending for a doctor.' He glanced at his watch and made a quick entry in his book. Then he glanced at Miller and his hand fell on his shoulder. 'A sad business, Miller. You've been with him long?'

Miller couldn't speak. Wharton gave a nod or two.

'You just go to your room and sit by yourself. If we want you later, we'll send for you.'

'No matter who we are there's always someone to love us,' George told me sententiously. And then his eyes fell on the opened desk at which Nevall had been sitting. He reached across the dead man and picked up the envelope.

TO SUPERINTENDENT WHARTON
IN THE EVENT OF MY DEATH

He gave me a look, and then a nod. Across at the window he slit the envelope with his knife. A moment or two and he was beginning to read.

On that morning when Manfrey was killed, I was at his house. Let me explain. I had rung him and insisted on seeing him, and he knew that the interview would be unpleasant. Eleven-thirty was the time agreed on, and he told me to come in from Grove Lane and straight to his room where he'd be waiting. He said his secretary would have gone and we could talk undisturbed.

I knew his mania for punctuality and it was just short of half past when I arrived. But there is something else to explain. The previous day I had had a caller, a young squadron-leader on leave. His name doesn't matter. He has since been killed in any case. But he told me he was going to see his sister at Highgate on his way back to his aerodrome and, as the times fitted in, he was only too glad to make a slight detour. I met him at Merridew's garage in the Euston Road and he dropped me near Grove Lane. I was a little early and so it may have been at about three minutes to the half-hour when I made my way up the path.

Then through the opened french window I saw Manfrey lying dead. I ask you to believe me when I say that everything happened so quickly that I cannot recall the exact sequences. He was lying on his back, mouth agape, and all I know is that I had the feeling of being caught in some extraordinary trap. Why I should have thought he had been killed I do not know, unless it was some connexion with the poker that I could see lying across his body. All I did was panic. I realized that he might have told his secretary of my visit, and have said unpleasant things about me, for he was an unprincipled and violent man. At any rate I made my way hastily from the house and through an opening to the Heath, and so to Haverstock Hill. I repeat that I did not set foot in the house. The french window was open and I could see everything as plainly as if I had indeed been inside.

At your visit I told a perfectly true story as far as it went, but for many weeks I lived in a state of fear. I know that at any time I could have come forward with a true account of events, but perhaps you will appreciate the position in which I stood. One lie had led to another and whereas at the beginning my statement might have been believed, now I had gone so far that it was impossible to turn back. Also I had a ray of hope. Since someone had been, according to yourself, in Manfrey's room and had been heard quarrelling with him, I hoped you would find that man, for he would be Manfrey's murderer.

Slowly I regained normality and then something happened. I received a visit from Manfrey's former secretary, Violet Lancing. She told me about her aspirations and asked if I could help her. She also mentioned her husband, with whom I was slightly acquainted. When I told her as politely as I could that there was nothing I could do, and that there were many possible channels by which she might perhaps enter the profession, she came to the point. All my fears returned for I saw that I was dealing with a dangerous and utterly unscrupulous woman. And though the charges she threatened were nothing but lies, I was not in a position to prove them so. Everything, on the other hand, would now point to my guilt.

Her statement was that she herself had seen me enter the room and then had heard me quarrelling with Manfrey that morning in his room. Also she had another witness – the one perhaps at whom you yourself had hinted. Neither she nor that witness wished to speak, she said, but only on the condition that I proved amenable. Naturally I denied everything but nevertheless there was a tacit understanding. When she later approached me with the story of how her husband had left her, and a consequent need of money, I gave her fifty pounds.

From time to time I gave her small sums and then I was forced to give her a small part in a play of mine that unfortunately had a very short run. Then in my next play she insisted on a much bigger part. I had to train her from the beginning. In a way it was like Svengali and Trilby. When at last she played the part each intonation, gesture, and movement were mine. What she did she did by rote.

Her mentions were more than favourable and went to her head. Now she considered herself at least half-way up the ladder and her private life expanded accordingly. More demands were made on me from time to time, and then came the culminating demand. That other witness, she said, was in great need of money. So desperate was her need, in fact, that unless she was paid five hundred pounds at once, she would go to the police. And if she went, then she would call Violet Lancing as a witness. But I had got to the end of my tether. My life had ceased to be a life.

I put her off by saying that I had not that amount of money in the bank. If however she could wait a day or two I would realize on certain securities. I managed to put her off, in fact, till I had made my plans. Then I told her in her dressing-room that night that I should have the money the following day. I stressed the need for secrecy, and said that my man had become suspicious. She agreed to meet me and receive the money.

I went past her to the wood and waited till she had come. It was about twenty minutes past one and at that time the Heath is practically deserted. When I turned to meet her with a dummy packet in my hand, I said I should not pay her unless she told me the truth.

'I don't mind who has the money,' I said, 'but I'd like to know, if only as a matter of curiosity, whether this story of yours is true.'

She owned up at least to my satisfaction, that it was she herself who wanted the money. Brazen as she was, I was sufficiently convinced to take the final step. The rest I prefer not to mention. But I took her bag and ring and watch to give the impression of robbery with assault. Then I assumed a rough and ready disguise and made my way to Haverstock Hill and from there by bus to St James's Park.

Since then I have barely slept a moment. Last night when Travers saw me in my dressing-room I realized that the end was not far off. I shall take that end in my own way. The reputation for which I risked everything now seems as nothing.

The writing changed slightly, as if the next words were a later addition.

Standing as I am on the threshold of the Unknown, I ask you to believe that in whatever light it shows me, every word I have here written is implicitly true. I thought last night that I saw on Travers's face an understanding and a sympathy. Perhaps you will thank him.

HENRY NEVALL.

Wharton took off his antiquated spectacles and let out a breath.

'Well, we weren't far wrong,' he said. 'A bad business for him. But, my God, what a fool! One lie and look where it landed him.'

I didn't feel like casting stones. If I felt anything it was a dull fury.

'He rid us of that woman,' I said. 'He ought to be forgiven a good deal for that.'

'You think that everything he says is true?' demanded George, wagging that confession at me.

'It has to be true,' I told him. 'A man doesn't lie under the circumstances in which he wrote that confession. And if he admitted the major crime of murder, then he must have told the truth about everything else. The whole includes the part.'

'Then if he didn't kill Manfrey, somebody else did. The Lancing woman for a fiver. Isn't that right?'

'Don't ask me, George,' I said. 'I'm not in a thinking mood.'

I spent most of the morning at that flat supervising routine. George had gone back to the Yard to report developments, and when my job was over I went back there too but he was out. I had a tray lunch sent up to his room and when I had finished it and a pipe, he had still not returned, so I left word where I should be and then walked through to the Embankment seats and sat for a time in the afternoon sun. But for the life of me I couldn't concentrate. Though it was the last thing I should ever have admitted to Wharton, that face of Nevall kept coming between me and my thoughts, and not only the face as I had seen it that morning – the blood and the shattered temple – but the tortured face of the man who in that dressing-room was already envisaging the inevitable end.

I didn't realize how late it was till I looked at my watch and then I found it was half past three. And then George suddenly appeared and sat down heavily beside me. He'd been seeing Nevall's solicitors. Nothing much had happened, he said, except that he had lost his lunch, and what about getting a cup of tea. So we strolled along towards Fuller's in the Strand. The upstairs room was open and we found a corner seat. When we'd got going on tea and cakes, he was asking if I'd any ideas.

'I don't know that I have,' I said, 'except the obvious ones. Yarnell didn't kill Violet Lancing, for example.'

'If only we could get him to talk,' he said, and then was wagging a finger at me. 'What about this? I have him brought to my room and I let that ex-wife of his see him there. Then we can talk to the pair of them together. Tell them we know who killed the Lancing woman, and then see what happens. Throw in a hint or two that we mightn't press the other charges so far if he can only convince us his reasons weren't what we thought they were.'

'You've already said that,' I pointed out. 'We thought his reasons for changing his name were to create a sort of alibi that would enable him to kill his wife and get away with it. That falls to the ground. Therefore the question remains – why did he change his identity? Was it because he had anything to fear?'

'If he did, then it was something to do with his Army career,' was George's opinion. 'Maybe he'd failed in his duty or something. But one thing we do know. He didn't change his identity because the Lancing woman had anything on him. It was he who had something on her. Hence the blackmail attempt.'

'Look, George,' I said. 'We did very well by taking one strand of the skein and unravelling it. We haven't quite unravelled it yet, so let's try to finish the job. Let's stick to Violet Lancing.'

'Not a bad idea,' he said. 'We might begin on those times at Manfrey's house that morning, and do a re-check.'

I had to shake my head.

'Those times largely depended on Violet's evidence, so they aren't worth a damn. May Clarke's aren't worth a deal more. Not because she was a liar too, but because Violet may have tampered with the kitchen clock or put ideas into her head.'

'Take Yarnell's own evidence then. He swore at the time that he'd arrived at eleven o'clock and had left at ten past. A rough check satisfied us that it was true –'

'Not necessarily,' I said. 'It was the Lancing woman who bolstered up that evidence. She walked with him as far as the shops that morning and why shouldn't she have put ideas into his head too.'

'But, dammit all, we've got to begin somewhere!'

'Then why not begin at what we think is incontrovertible fact?' I said. 'Nevall saw Manfrey lying dead at just before eleven-thirty that morning.'

'But Lancing saw Nevall!'

'Admitted,' I said. 'I think that's true or else she couldn't have blackmailed him. And therefore the times she gave us were wrong. She was back in the house well before half past eleven.'

'Then what about the quarrel? Who was the man quarrelling with Manfrey? The man whose voice sounded like Nevall's? All that must have taken place before Nevall arrived. Therefore both Lancing and Clarke must have been back at twenty past eleven at the latest. And that's balderdash. How could Lancing have walked to the shops, bought that hat, gone on to the tea-shop and walked back in ten minutes. It's impossible, I tell you. Absolutely impossible.'

'Let's leave the whole thing, George,' I said. 'I'm not in good form at the moment. I'll go to a cinema show, or something, and clear my brain, and then get down to things tonight. You'll be doing some thinking, and in the morning we'll compare notes.'

'Not a bad idea,' George said surprisingly. He wiped that monstrosity of a moustache of his with vast sweeps of a voluminous handkerchief, and then got to his feet. With what had become almost instinct, I collected the bill.

I hate a cold bath but when I got home from the cinema I took one, and it certainly freshened me up. Then after a late and frugal meal I treated myself to two inches of whisky, filled the glass with soda, got my pipe going and settled down to a bit of quiet, unhurried thinking. And I kept myself to Violet Lancing. And I didn't move to any new position till I was sure that the ground was firm.

My first fact was that the Yarnells had blackmailed her, and had had such effect in their threats that Violet had had to raise the five hundred pounds. What could that something have been?

Not the fact that as a supposed widow Violet had been drawing a pension. The onus for that lay on Yarnell. There-fore it seemed a certainty that Violet had killed Manfrey and the Yarnells knew it, and could prove it. Mrs Yarnell had not known it till her ex-husband had returned, and then it had been she – hating Violet like hell – who had suggested the blackmail. Yarnell would need money. His occupation had gone and somewhere he would have to make a new start under Hanley's name.

So far everything seemed logical. But the question arose as to *why* Violet had killed Manfrey. There I had an idea. She had admitted that she had hoped to use Manfrey as a stepping-stone to a stage career. But he had done nothing about it – the facts proved that beyond question. So she had been furious at having to be merely a mistress. She had returned earlier that morning than she had stated – certainly before May Clarke – and he had suggested some amorous arrangement for the weekend. There had been a violent quarrel – the faint words that reached May Clarke had for some strange reason made May think one voice was Nevall's – and Manfrey had made an attack on her. She had struck him with a poker. Then she had locked the doors and made her way through the french window to Grove Lane and so to the front door where her entry had seemed normal. She had seen May in the kitchen and had heard about the quarrel. The she had said she must fly and she had fetched her belongings and left.

That seemed reasonably clear to me. One thing only remained – how Yarnell had been aware of what had happened. And there I thought I had a solution. Yarnell found he couldn't live with her. There had doubtless been scenes and quarrels. In one of them he had taunted her with being Manfrey's mistress. She would have denied it vehemently. To prove it she had confessed that the only time he had attempted an attack on her honour, she had struck him.

But there seemed a slight snag in that. She would have made that confession to Yarnell since he was her husband and could give no evidence against her. Then how could he have blackmailed her on his return? And then I saw the answer to that question. He didn't blackmail her as Yarnell. No one was more staggered than she to find that he was alive. So it was Rhoda who had really done the blackmailing at first, and Violet must have been aghast and terrified, not knowing how she had acquired the information. Then when Violet knew how Rhoda had learned the truth about Manfrey, she was aware that there was no longer the evidence only of her husband. There was also the merciless evidence of Rhoda Yarnell. And she knew what exposure would do to her in her new career. No wonder she had been prepared to pay up – if with Nevall's money.

By the time I'd arrived at all that, it was best part of eleven o'clock, and I was satisfied to call it a day. In the morning, I told myself, I would propose to George that he should hint broadly to the two Yarnells the facts as I had just assembled them, and use them as a lever to force the two to speak.

If only I'd known how wrong I was to be!

CHAPTER XVII
The Truth

THE MORNING PAPERS had their notices of what was called the tragic death of Henry Nevall, though none had as yet been given the facts. I had no time to read the appreciations, even if I had felt like it, for I had got up rather late and I had to hurry to be at the Yard by nine o'clock.

George had arrived at much the same conclusions as myself, though from a different route. We talked things over and then he was asking to be put through to the Victoria Street establishment.

'That you, Mrs Yarnell? . . . This is Superintendent Wharton speaking from New Scotland Yard. We can't be overheard? . . . That's fine. Well, it's like this, Mrs Yarnell. We've discovered that Victor Yarnell didn't commit that murder. . . . Yes, his wife. And we know the one who did it, and so there's that anxiety off everybody's minds – Oh yes, I know what you told me but even the police can make mistakes. But that's not the point. Under the circumstances there's now no reason why you shouldn't see Mr Yarnell. If you wish to. . . . You would? Then I'll send a car for you in half an hour's time. That'll be at ten o'clock sharp. . . . Oh yes, a perfectly plain van. And here in my room, by the way. . . . You what? . . . My dear Mrs Yarnell, I give you my word. We don't do that sort of thing. There's no catch in it at all. All you're coming here for is to see Mr Yarnell. After that the car will take you back to your business again. . . . That's all right then. Car at ten o'clock. Goodbye.'

'Thought we were up to some monkey tricks,' George told me and then was ringing down for arrangements to be made to have Yarnell in his room at ten o'clock sharp.

'See the cuffs are off him when he gets here,' he said, 'and have him brought up here to my room.'

After that there was nothing to do but to wait, and a long half-hour it seemed. Rhoda Yarnell appeared first. There was still that air of *chic* and quality about her, but some of the poise had gone. There was almost a timidity as she thanked me when I offered her the chair.

'Lovely weather we're having,' Wharton said. 'Is it good for your business or not?'

The weather made no difference, she told him, and all the time you could see her wondering and feel the thoughts that went through the door to the stairs on which a foot might sound. And then there were steps. Wharton went out and closed the door after him. Rhoda Yarnell bit her lip. Wharton reappeared almost at once, and Yarnell was with him. Now the plumpers had gone from his cheeks he was looking almost haggard, but as soon as he spoke I recognized the voice I had last heard three years before.

'Sit down, Yarnell,' Wharton said quietly. 'One reason why I brought you here was to tell you that we've found the murderer of your wife –'

'She was no wife of mine,' Yarnell broke in fiercely.

'But you married her?'

'Yes, I married her,' he said, and his lip curled.

'All we have against you now,' went on Wharton, 'are the possible charges I've already mentioned. Given extenuating circumstances – known only at the moment to yourself – we might decide not to press those either. It'll depend. What I advise you, and I'm almost old enough to be your father, is to get off your mind whatever there happens to be on it. The law isn't always harsh. It can even turn a blind eye. This time yesterday I saw a man who'd just shot himself because he'd been afraid years ago to tell the simple truth. I don't say let that be a lesson to you. I just leave it in your mind.'

He got to his feet.

'I ought to refer to a matter of attempted blackmail, but I won't. There may be a blind eye turned to that too. It all depends.'

He gave a look at me.

'Now you two people will be left alone for ten minutes. You have my word that your conversation will not be over-heard. Everything is open and above-board.'

George and I went out. I went to the lavatory and then smoked a cigarette, and where he went I don't know, but when I reckoned that the ten minutes had gone, I found him waiting for me outside his door. Rhoda Yarnell had been crying, and I rather think that Yarnell had too.

'Time's up,' announced Wharton, and waited.

The two exchanged glances. It was Yarnell who spoke.

'You were telling us about that man who'd been afraid to tell the truth. That's why I . . . I mean we . . . I mean I'd like to tell you what happened.'

'Take your time,' Wharton told him. 'Tell whatever you have to tell in your own way. You'd like a cigarette?'

'Thanks, I would,' he said, and his hand was shaking as he took one.

'And one other thing,' Wharton said. 'Sooner or later you'll be asked to make an official statement. Why not make it now and get it all over?'

The two exchanged glances. Rhoda Yarnell gave a quick nod.

'All right,' he said, and Wharton pressed the buzzer. Another five minutes and we were all set.

I shall give you the story of Victor Yarnell, not as he told it, but in chronological order and free of interruptions. It was to take a long time in the telling, and that is something else you will be spared.

Yarnell had met Violet Lancing well before that Saturday morning. She had begun to set her cap at him when they had both been in pictures, and after that he had taken her out to tea and dinner and was already becoming infatuated with her. They had actually met on the Friday night when he had told her of the shabby trick Manfrey had played on him. She suggested that he should see Manfrey personally. Manfrey should imagine he was alone in the house but she would let him in and then go to her room to overhear what Manfrey might say.

Yarnell wasn't sure of the time when he arrived. He thought it was about five minutes to eleven, and when Violet Lancing quietly let him in, she whispered that May Clarke had gone.

Then when Yarnell walked into Manfrey's room, Manfrey looked staggered.

'How the devil did you get in here?'

'That's my business,' Yarnell told him.

'Then get out!' Manfrey told him.

Yarnell told him that he wouldn't put him out till there'd been a show-down. Manfrey snatched up that paper-knife and Yarnell backed away. Then he caught sight of the poker. Manfrey came on and Yarnell struck. That was the simple story, and everything was over as quickly as that. Another moment or two and Manfrey was dead.

Violet Lancing rushed into the room.

'What have you done?'

Yarnell stood there, panting, and he could only point to Manfrey's dead body.

'What can we do?' she said. 'What can we do?'

It was she who took control and steadied Yarnell in his panic. The essential thing was for Yarnell to have an alibi. They discussed that quickly. What they would do would be to leave the body there and let May Clarke find it. Violet Lancing would swear that she had let Yarnell in, and out, and that they had left Manfrey alive.

Then Yarnell thought of something. May wouldn't be back till half past eleven and the police would know that Manfrey had died long before that. Violet remembered that Nevall was coming, too, at half past eleven, and so she made an entry in the engagement book to the effect that Nevall was due at eleven-twenty. He would inform the police and as she had gathered from Manfrey that his business wasn't going to be pleasant, maybe the police would think he had killed Manfrey. The poker would be left near the body. Nevall would pick it up and his prints would be on it. So she wiped all prints off and then Yarnell didn't like the idea. He thought the police would still know that Manfrey had been dead longer than it appeared.

It was he who thought of turning on all three switches of the electric stove so that the heat might delay *rigor mortis*. The body was placed close to the heat and Violet Lancing would have to be back early to turn off two of the switches. Manfrey, by the way, was wearing the tweed jacket of the suit.

All that took much quicker than might have been expected. Violet locked the door and that to her room, and they left by the french window which was left open. They hurried to the shops with her planning other details: how he must ask the time in the hat shop and she'd tell him what it was, and how she'd see him at twelve o'clock at the latest at a certain tea-shop in Tottenham Court Road to tell him what, if anything, had happened.

It was about twenty past eleven when she got back, and to her horror she found that the body had been too near the fire, and one sleeve of the jacket was scorched. So she took the jacket off and replaced it by the alpaca coat, and hid the tweed coat in her attaché case. As she had learned from Manfrey that Nevall would come in from Grove Lane, she slipped out for a look, and there he was almost at the gate.

Now she hid herself in her room and watched. Then as Nevall neared, she had her ear at the door. But Nevall stayed no more than a second or two and then hurried away. Violet locked her own door behind her and went out by the french window to see if May was coming. When she saw her she went round to the front door and secreted herself in the cloak-room till May was in.

Now comes the one interruption which I must mention. Wharton asked what about the sound of two people quarrel-ling in Manfrey's room. Tarnell looked most surprised and said he had never heard a word about a quarrel. Wharton told him to carry on.

Next Violet Lancing met Yarnell as arranged. Everything, she said, looked as if it would go swimmingly and she must get to her flat where the police would ring her. A further meeting was arranged for the same late afternoon and she then advised him to disclose to the police, in case they found it out, the real reason why he'd gone to see Manfrey. Yarnell had now got over his panic and thought he could carry everything off, though more than once he was tempted to go to the police and make a full confession. The only thing that really kept him back was the thought that he'd be letting Violet down, or incriminating her, too.

And that, as far as he was concerned, was the end of the affair. The police had accepted his statements and had no further use for him. He insisted that if the police had ever arrested Nevall, he'd have come forward but, of course, there was no arrest. He and Violet Lancing continued to meet, though in more obscure places, and intimacy ultimately took place. Then she began to put on the pressure. She was out of a job, thanks to him. And he, still infatuated with her and knowing a shamed indebtedness, finally asked his wife for a divorce. Then he married Violet Lancing.

Within a week of the marriage he was sick of her. Within a month he hated her. And he realized what the rest of his life would be with his personal safety at the mercy of her caprices. That was why he joined up, not caring whether he survived the war or not. And he'd begun to think of his first wife. He thought of her till life was nothing but a wretchedness.

In Italy he formed a friendship with Hanley who'd been temporarily posted to the regiment. The two men had a leave in Naples together, and while Yarnell couldn't tell much of himself, Hanley was more voluble. Yarnell knew all about the grandmother, Hanley's sole relative. And so to that enemy counter-attack when Hanley was severely wounded. Yarnell might have got away but he stayed with Hanley till he died, and it was during the dark of that night that he knew what he must do. He would cease to be Yarnell and become Hanley. If he ever got out of the prison camp and home, then he'd make for the colonies and begin a new life there.

The exchange of identities was made. Then in the prison camp Yarnell was again tortured by thoughts of his first wife. Finally he did a desperate thing. He wrote her a letter in Hanley's name, and in it he told her the guarded story of an experience he had just had – a story a brother officer had just told him: the tale of a man who'd become infatuated with another woman and had left his wife for her and had then discovered that it was his wife and his wife only whom he had always loved. He added that the recipient was not to believe any stories she might hear about his health. And as he didn't disguise his handwriting, he hoped Rhoda Yarnell would read between the lines.

And she did. She wrote to him, still naturally as Hanley, and two more letters passed between them. That was why when Yarnell was released, he made for 'Homestead'. There he told her unreservedly everything that had happened.

But what the two realized was that their lives had been ruined. Yarnell's career had gone, and somewhere or other they would have to make a fresh start. Rhoda was willing to sell her share in the business, but what infuriated her was that Violet Lancing should have gone on flourishing like the green bay tree, and that she should go on to the end of her days drawing a pension as Yarnell's widow.

That was how that naive blackmail scheme suggested itself. All they would ask of Violet Lancing was the rough amount of the pension she'd received. It was Yarnell who rang her in an assumed voice. No wonder she was mystified how an unknown man could have known the things he had to tell, though what he told her was that he had heard it from her dead husband, and he had in his possession a statement sworn to by that husband. If necessary, of course, such a statement could have been produced.

Then came the morning when Violet recognized him in the tea-shop. Later that day he called on her. Then he could threaten that unless she found the money, he was going to the police. What would happen to himself he didn't care, but his disclosures would most certainly ruin her stage career. She promised to get the money. But payment had to be deferred and at last she arranged for him to collect the money at a rendezvous near her flat that very afternoon when she was killed. That was where he went after leaving the cinema, and he had been furious because she hadn't turned up.

That was the true story, and he swore that every word of it was true. And that was the gist of the statement and what he afterwards signed.

*   *   *

'It isn't for me to talk about the pity of it,' Wharton told him. 'But about you, Mrs Yarnell. Much of this concerns you. Would you care to sign a statement too?'

She said she would, though it would only confirm what had already been said. It was best part of another hour before she had signed.

'What can I say to you?' Wharton said, and looked at them. 'A nice mess you've landed yourselves in. But there we are. I'll do what I can for you, but you mustn't rely too much on that. If you'd owned up to that manslaughter in the first place, you'd have got clear. You may now. I can only hope so. All I can say is that you'll know very soon. Meanwhile, keep your peckers up, both of you. That, by the way, isn't official. Forget that I said it.'

Then his tone became gruff as he opened the door.

'Right,' he told the sergeant. 'Take him back and don't forget the receipt.'

He nodded curtly to Yarnell as he moved out. Rhoda Yarnell was standing. Her lips quivered and I thought she was going to cry, but she was only smiling gently to herself.

'We won't keep you, Mrs Yarnell,' Wharton told her brusquely, terrified perhaps of his sentimental outburst.

'But one thing I'd like to ask you. You really think you could make something out of him, and yourself?'

'Yes,' she said simply.

Wharton grunted.

'You aren't afraid that one day there might be another . . . Violet Lancing?'

'I'm not afraid,' she told him. 'I know him. And he knows me. That's what we've both learnt.'

Wharton pressed the buzzer.

'Will you let me thank you?' she said.

Wharton shook his head.

'Not now. Nothing to thank me for, for one thing.' His hand moved to go out, then it drew back. 'Goodbye, Mrs Yarnell. I hope next time we meet it'll be in different circumstances.'

But suddenly she did an amazing thing. Before George could move an inch, she had moved quickly forward and had kissed him. As he drew back she was moving through the door. I watched her go down the stairs, and her handkerchief was at her eyes.

George was shaking his head.

'Damn all women,' he told me. 'Why the hell did she do a thing like that?'

'She's a grand woman all the same, George,' I said. 'Loyal as they make 'em. And the pluck of a lion.'

'She'll need plenty of both,' George told me surlily. Then he said he'd be busy for a bit, and maybe he'd see me later. Loose ends had still to be tied, so perhaps I'd drop in some time in the afternoon.

I went to my club, thinking I might lunch there for a change. The reading-room was practically deserted and I sat thinking of the morning's events, and principally of what a grand woman Rhoda Yarnell had shown herself. A nod of encouragement now and again to Yarnell when he had been telling his story, and even a little smile of encouragement as if to tell him he was doing fine. A naive sort of blackmail it had been, as Wharton had once said. Maybe Yarnell would swing practically clear after all. The War Office might cut up rough, but even the War House sometimes has something that functions almost like a heart.

Lunch time had come but I was thinking about Manfrey and Nevall. Then I remembered that I hadn't read a longish appreciation I had just glimpsed at breakfast in *The Times*. So I fetched the paper from the table and began reading it. It gave a résumé of Nevall's career, and then came something that suddenly made me lay that paper down.

> *If the late Charles Manfrey was by common consent the greatest Cassius of this, or as some say of any age, then Henry Nevall was the greatest Brutus. No one who was privileged to witness the superb exhibition of the ac-*

tor's act which the pair of them gave at the Coliseum concert in aid of the Red Cross in 1939 will ever forget it. . . .

It was a quarter past one but I sat on thinking. Then suddenly I sprang up. Another couple of minutes I was walking towards Regent Street. A quarter of an hour later I had made a purchase.

I was feeling hungry by then but all I had time for was a cup of tea and a bun at a cafeteria. Then I took the Hampstead tube and walked to The Cote. A strange woman opened the door.

'You're May's sister,' I said.

'Yes,' she said warily. 'But May's out. She'll be back soon, though.'

'Then I'll come in and wait,' I said jauntily, and just a bit suspiciously she let me in.

'My name's Travers,' I told her. 'Perhaps you've heard May mention me.'

That evidently satisfied her and she showed me into the drawing-room, a musty smelling room with the air of never being used. As I waited I heard her from time to time in the hall, as if she still wasn't sure of me. Then after a very long half-hour May returned.

She was full of the Nevall mystery and wanted to know why he had shot himself. I hinted mysteriously that that was why I was at The Cote. Something I wanted to look for in Mr Manfrey's old room. Finally she let me in and left me there.

About a quarter of an hour later I was ringing up Wharton. Could he come at once to Hampstead?

'What for?' he wanted to know.

'Never mind,' I told him. 'I guarantee it'll be worth it.'

'Why the hurry? I was just thinking about getting some lunch.'

'I've had no lunch either,' I said. 'You come along and we'll have lunch and tea together.'

It was curious that May should be asking me in a minute or two if I'd like a nice cup of tea. I thanked her and put her off with the excuse that I hadn't finished the job. I also added that Wharton was coming.

It actually took him twenty minutes to get there and I heard the brakes squeak as the car drew up. I let him in, making a gesture for silence. Then I locked the door of Manfrey's room behind us and took him into Violet Lancing's room.

'What's the wireless for?' he wanted to know.

'It isn't the wireless,' I told him. 'It's the old old story. A portable gramophone. In the cupboard, and I thought it was an old attaché case.'

I had whispered that, and he was pricking his ears.

'That's Manfrey's voice. . . . And that's Nevall's.'

I nodded and let him listen. When the first side of the record was nearing the end, I left him and stood by for the change. Then I came back again.

'What's the record?' he asked me.

'The quarrel scene from *Julius Caesar*,' I said. 'Sold on behalf of the Red Cross. Taken at a special performance by Manfrey and Nevall.'

'A damn fine record,' he said. 'I'll have to buy it.'

It must have been a fine record for he'd forgotten to glare at me and ask if that was why I'd brought him all the way to Hampstead. Then I was whispering to him to listen carefully. The crucial moment was approaching. Brutus's voice was trembling with rage and scorn, and Cassius was to answer him as fiercely.

> '. . . I did send
> To you for gold to pay my legions,
> Which you denied me: was that done like Cassius?
> Should I have answer'd Caius Cassius so?
> When Marcus Brutus grows so covetous
> To lock such rascal counters from his friends,
> Be ready, gods, with all your thunderbolts;
> Dash him to pieces!'
>   'I denied you not.'
> 'You did.'
> 'I did not: he was but a fool . . .'

Then I had suddenly cut the record off.

'Did you get it, George?'

'Not quite,' he said, so I put it on again at the spot I'd marked.

'Now I get you,' he said when I'd turned it off again. 'That *rascal counters* or whatever it was. It sounded like *rascally scoundrel*?'

'You've got it, George,' I said. 'Manfrey must have had that record in the house, and Violet Lancing knew it. I'll bet Manfrey played it to her. Then when Nevall had gone that morning, she turned it on for May to hear. Later she turned it off and took it with her in her case along with the coat. The old gramophone she shoved in the cupboard and put some old books and papers over it.'

'Would you believe it!' George said. Then he frowned. 'Better keep our mouths shut about that. Wouldn't do for anyone to think we'd been caught by a hoary old trick like that.'

I told him he could have the record as a souvenir, and then I put the gramophone back and out we went. May came fluttering up.

'You're not going already? And I'd made you both a nice cup of tea.'

George weakened and I gave him a nudge. Apologies and thanks and off we went to the car.

'Anywhere here where I can get a meal?' he wanted to know.

'What about trying the Yellow Tulip?' I said.

So to the Yellow Tulip we went, and George ordered what there was – scrambled reconstituted egg on toast, cakes, and tea. When he'd got well on the way through it and was pouring my second cup, he gave a satisfied nod.

'Well, the old firm's done it again. The Old Gent's a long way from dead yet.'

I might have added that judging by the way he was tackling that meal, he had hit one nail on the head.

'Nevall chucked that bag away,' he said. 'Wonder what happened to the ring and wrist-watch?'

'He might have hidden them somewhere,' I said. 'After all, she'd stung him for considerable sums of money. And she died intestate, now I come to think of it. Yarnell will get whatever she left, unless Rhoda Yarnell refuses to touch it.'

'That reminds me,' he said. 'That *rascal counters*. What's it mean exactly? I've got an idea, mind you.'

'Well, to talk like a ruddy schoolmaster, it means something like "filthy lucre",' I told him. '"To lock such rascal counters from his friends' means risking a friendship for the sake of a few miserable pieces of money.'

'Just my idea,' he said, and then asked if I'd have any more tea. There was no more in the pot, as it happened, so he wiped his moustache and began feeling for his pipe.

'Well, we'd better be making a move,' he told me resignedly, and the inevitable moment had come when the waitress had to be called.

'Yes,' I said reflectively. '*Rascal counters*. When you come to think of it, it's a damn fine phrase.'

I gave myself one of George's own sideways nods of appreciation and all the time I was hoping, though still without hope as you might say. And yet something must have given a twinge to George's conscience. For once in his life it was he who paid.

THE END